STRANGLER

Also by Parnell Hall

DETECTIVE
MURDER
FAVOR

STRANGLER

by

PARNELL HALL

DONALD I. FINE, INC.
NEW YORK

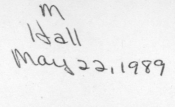

M
Hall
May 22, 1989

Library of Congress Cataloging in Publication Data

Hall, Parnell.
Strangler.

I. Title.
PS3558.A37327S77   1989   813'.54   88-45851
ISBN 1-55611-125-8

Manufactured in the United States of America

10   9   8   7   6   5   4   3   2   1

Designed by Irving Perkins Associates

This novel is a work of fiction. Names, characters, places and
incidents are either the product of the author's imagination or
are used fictitiously. Any resemblance to actual events, locales,
organizations or persons, living or dead, is entirely coincidental
and beyond the intent of either the author or publisher.

For Jim and Franny

1.

I don't look for it.

I know some people thrive on violence and action and mystery. I don't. You see, I'm not a real private detective. Not *really*. I'm an ambulance chaser. I work for the law firm of Rosenberg and Stone. I spend my time driving around New York City in my beat-up Toyota, signing up clients who have called in response to Richard Rosenberg's TV ads. Technically, that makes me a private detective, and that's where the trouble comes in.

You see, sometimes people want to hire me. And the thing is, I don't want to be hired. That's because the people who want to hire a private detective usually have a distorted view of what a private detective really is. The reason, of course, is television. The minute you say the words "private detective," people always think of some macho guy with a gun who has shoot-outs and car chases every week, and who always stays two steps ahead of the cops (who are always slightly dumb), and who always manages to solve murder cases that have the poor cops baffled.

In real life, of course, the reverse is true. In the few murder cases I've been involved in, I've always been a few steps *behind* the police, and they've always turned out to be smarter than I was.

Yeah, I've been involved in some murder cases. And, believe me, I didn't look for 'em. And solving them was not my idea of a good time. Hey, I'm not a movie hero—I'm just a fortyish old fart with a wife and kid to feed, trying to scratch out a living the best I can. The only reason I work this job for Rosenberg and Stone is I don't seem to have the brains or the gumption to find myself anything else. That, and the fact that in theory the job is supposed to be flexible to leave me time to write. Somehow it never does. Or, at least, I never manage to get anything written. The fault, dear Brutus, probably lies not in my stars but in myself, that I am an underling.

At any rate, I don't crave adventure. My idea of excitement is miraculously finding a babysitter and taking my wife, Alice, out to the movies, preferably (my preference, not hers) something fast-paced, funny, unsubtitled and with no redeeming social value whatsoever.

I could go on, but I think you get the picture. Hell, I'll go on anyway. The fact is, I don't carry a gun, I never punched anyone in my life and I don't even do surveillance.

And I'm not particularly brave. That is an understatement. In fact, in the murder cases in which I've been involved, my greatest act of heroism to date has been not pissing in my pants in tense situations. So if urine retention were the only requirement for bravery, I guess I could pass, but if there are any other criteria, count me out. See, if you wanted a recommendation from any of the policemen with whom I've been involved, I'm sure you could get one: "Stanley Hastings? Oh yeah, that's that chicken-shit asshole."

STRANGLER

So, as I say, I don't look for it. And I must tell you, as I drove up the Grand Concourse in the Bronx on that sunny September morning to interview Jesus Pagan, who had fallen on the stairs in his building and broken his leg, the last thing in the world I was expecting was murder.

2.

The most dangerous part of my job is calling on clients who are economically deprived. That's because the places they live are inherently dangerous.

If you're a white man in a suit and tie, you might be slightly wary walking through the South Bronx. You might keep your eyes open, saying, hey, I don't want to get mugged. But let me tell you, that's nothing. Suppose you had to go into the buildings?

All right, here's a huge, six-story apartment building. The glass in the front double doors has been smashed, the lock has been kicked in and the doors are standing open. Inside is a cavernous lobby, two stories high, fifty feet wide, a hundred feet deep, unlit. And no windows. No light at all in the cavern, except what filters in through the front door. Somewhere in the back, dimly perceived on either side of the back wall, narrow staircases leading up to floors where the hallways may or may not connect. And you, looking for 6D. And realizing that once you choose a stair, you won't know if it will get you there until you reach the second floor and find out if you're on the A,B,C,D line or the E,F,G,H line in the event the hallways don't connect. And then if you've chosen wrong, you'll have to go down and take the other stair. And you don't want to do that. Because in situations like this, you want to get in fast and get out fast, to minimize risk.

And to top it off, standing next to this front door are two unwashed, unshaven guys in tattered army coats, passing a bottle of cheap booze back and forth.

Would you want to go in there?

Well, that's where Jesus Pagan lived.

So that's what I did.

I chose the wrong stair, too. I always do. When I got to the second floor, I found, as I'd feared, four apartments clustered around the stairwell. Most of the apartment numbers had fallen off. Two of the doors still had 2s on them, somewhat less than helpful, since I knew I was on the second floor. One of them had a flimsy H.

Wrong line.

I went down the stairs and tried the other side. No 2s this time, but a dangling B told me I was getting warm. I figured by the time I reached the sixth floor I'd know the whole configuration.

I'd just reached the fourth floor when a door flew open. Standing in the doorway was a large black man in blue jeans and a short-sleeved undershirt. Billowing out around him from the apartment came clouds of marijuana smoke, and I could hear the sound of voices from within.

My heart leaped. It always does in situations like that. I walk in paranoid and tense as hell, and then when something happens they almost have to scrape me off the ceiling. So I'd have to say that it was a bit of a shock to me.

11

But it was also a bit of a shock to him. His eyes widened; he said, "Oh, shit!" He hopped inside and slammed the door in my face.

You see, he thought I was a cop. That's what most people think when I do signups like this. Because, assuming that I was a sane, rational person, why else would I be there?

At any rate, I was glad to see him go, and I hustled on up the stairs.

Jesus Pagan was a thirty-year-old Hispanic with a chip on his shoulder and a cast on his leg. The chip on his shoulder had to do with the City of New York. Jesus Pagan figured, as long as he was giving the City of New York $159 a month to live in his three-room apartment, they could damn well fix the fucking stairs.

The stair that drew Jesus Pagan's wrath was only slightly cracked, and it would be a bit of a stretch for Richard to make a case for negligence about it, but that wasn't my concern. I'd been assigned the job, and if I did it I'd get paid, so I damn well did it. I took down all the facts about Jesus Pagan's accident, got him to sign a retainer agreeing to give Richard Rosenberg one third of any settlement and shot two rolls of the stairs from the sixth to the fifth floors, where Pagan had fallen down. I usually only shoot one roll of film on an accident of this type, but I couldn't *really* see any defect in the step, and in a case where there is no discernible defect, Richard Rosenberg's theory was shoot more pictures, because maybe one of them will show *something*.

The other part of my assignment, in filling out the fact sheet, was to ask if there were any witnesses. Usually, in accidents like this, there aren't, but Pagan had one, one Gilbert Star. He took me down to meet him, and Gilbert Star turned out to be the black man I'd encountered on the stairs on my way up. He was a little shocked to see me again, but when Jesus Pagan explained the situation he got

12

real friendly. Then we all went in and sat down with him and some of his buddies, and they all passed joints around and tripped out on rapping about how Jesus Pagan had fallen down the stairs.

They offered me a joint, of course, seeing as how I wasn't a pig, but I courteously declined. It wasn't just that I am a straight, uptight family man (though I am); it was also that there was no way I wanted to be stoned out of my mind in that building. I mean, whatever gets you off, but at some point this party would have to end. I didn't really feel like standing around the South Bronx in my suit and tie going, "Wow, what's happening?"

The other thing was I got beeped. The beeper on my belt went off with its high-pitched *beep, beep, beep*. And by the time it went off, Jesus Pagan and the guys had gotten themselves thoroughly whacked. Their reactions were pretty incredible, ranging from "Oh shit!" (dropping joint), "Muthafucker!" (attempting to climb wall), to "What the fuck was that?!" (dropping out of chair).

The dropping out of chair was Pagan, and I sure hoped he hadn't reinjured his leg.

The fourth guy didn't say a word, but his reaction was the one that got me. Suddenly there was a knife in his hand. I didn't see him pull it, and I have no idea how it got there, but there it was. I mean, the man was quick, and the man was ready.

I was quick too, switching the damn thing off, calming them down and explaining what had happened.

And that turned out to be the end of the party, at least so far as I was concerned, because what the beeper meant, of course, was for me to call the office, and these guys had no phone. So it was either go back up to Pagan's or leave. Since I had what I came for and Pagan showed no signs of wanting to go anywhere, I opted to split.

13

I went on outside, encountering no one, which is always a blessing. You always wonder, when you go into a building like that with guys hanging out outside, whether they'll be waiting for you to come out. No one was. I hopped in my car, drove six blocks and found a pay phone. I got out and called Rosenberg and Stone.

Wendy/Janet answered the phone. Wendy/Janet used to be Wendy/Cheryl, Richard Rosenberg's two-headed monster, two secretaries that were like each other only in that they had identical voices and were both incompetent. Cheryl had moved on to greener pastures, but Richard, in his infinite wisdom, had managed to find *another* secretary whose voice was indistinguishable from Wendy's and who was equally incompetent. I don't know how Richard did it. It was as if he'd put an ad in the paper: "SECRETARY WANTED: young, incompetent, adenoidal voice, dumb." At any rate, he'd done it, and Wendy/Cheryl was now Wendy/Janet.

"Rosenberg and Stone," came the voice of Wendy/Janet.

"Agent double-O five," I told her.

"Hi, Stanley," said Wendy/Janet. "I have a new case for you."

"Oh? where is it?"

"In Harlem."

"Hell."

The thing was, I didn't want to go to Harlem. I was in the Bronx already, and I had three photo assignments that I was planning on knocking off that afternoon. But in my work a new case takes precedence over everything. That's because, when you get a new case, the client hasn't *signed* yet. And he doesn't become a client until he signs. And Richard Rosenberg's prime directive is Sign the clients. Sign them up as fast as they come in. Because there's a lot of accident

14

lawyers working New York City. And Richard Rosenberg figures if we don't grab off a client fast, the client will get pissed off and call Jacoby and Meyers or Davis and Lee. Richard's only number three in New York, and he figures he has to work harder. Or, to put it more accurately, he figures I do.

But, as I said, I had these three photo assignments I was planning on knocking off and putting in on my paysheet at a hour or two apiece, so I was damned if I wanted to drop everything and rush back to Harlem.

"I thought Sam was working Harlem," I said.

Sam Gravston was another one of Richard Rosenberg's investigators. Sam was new, but then most of Richard Rosenberg's investigators were. In the year and a half I'd been on the job, I'd seen a lot of 'em come and go. And most of 'em went pretty fast.

See, the idea is pretty appealing. You put an ad in the New York *Times* saying, "PRIVATE INVESTIGATOR WANTED: no experience necessary, will train," and you're gonna get a lot of young guys who think it's gonna be grand and glamorous like on TV. And they come in and train, and then they go out on their first assignment and walk into a building like the one I'd just come out of, and they come back to the office, turn in their kits and say they don't think they really want to be a private investigator after all. And I can't say I blame 'em.

Sam Gravston had lasted almost two months, which was pretty much of a record for Richard's investigators, with the exception of me. Sam Gravston was about twenty-four. He was a tall, thin, hulking guy, with longish blond hair and what a casting director would refer to as a ruggedly handsome face. And I'm sure one probably had, since Sam Gravston was an actor. He was only doing the P.I. shit be-

15

cause it was flexible enough to let him go to casting calls.

"Sam's off this afternoon," Wendy/Janet said. "He's got an audition."

I must say, I didn't feel kindly toward him. I never felt kindly toward actors who had auditions. After all, I'd been an actor, and *I* never seemed to get any auditions. Which was why I'd become a writer who couldn't get any work either, and wound up a private eye.

"Ah, hell," I said. "Let me have it."

She did. A Winston Bishop, in a project on Madison Avenue around 120th Street, had fallen on a subway steps and had a fractured arm. He was expecting an investigator between one and two P.M.

Ordinarily I'd have called and stalled the guy off until I had time to knock off those photo assignments, but, wouldn't you know it, the son-of-a-bitch had no phone.

Which also meant I couldn't call him and verify his address. And with Wendy/Janet on the job, cases like that made me incredibly nervous.

"You sure about that address?" I asked.

"Absolutely," Wendy/Janet said. "In cases where the client has no phone, Richard insists we make 'em give us the address three times."

I was glad to hear it, because that was at *my* suggestion.

"Then let me read it back to *you* one more time, just to be sure *we* got it right," I told her.

I did, and damned if she hadn't transposed two numbers in the address. I read it two more times just to be sure I had what she had, and figured that was the best I could do. I let it go at that.

I hung up, got in my car and got on the Major Deegan. I got off at the Willis/Third Avenue Bridge, had my windshield washed at a red light against my will for a quarter by a skinny ten-year-old kid, then went over the bridge and wound my way down into Harlem.

The address turned out to be a project of the kind you always dread. A steel outside door with the glass and lock smashed and no security of any kind, and grungy, foul-smelling elevators that you don't want to get trapped in but that you have to take unless you want to walk up to the twelfth floor.

Winston Bishop lived in 12C. I wasn't up to the walk, so I got in the elevator.

It stopped on the ninth floor.

And I hate that. I mean, I'm going to twelve, and someone on nine presumably wouldn't ring unless they were going *down*. That's not to say someone who stops the elevator on the way up is necessarily looking for an affluent-looking white man in a suit and tie to rip off. But people who ring both the up and the down buttons when they want to go down generally turn out to be young, aggressive, hostile types who are looking out for number one and don't give a shit who they're inconveniencing. Having a couple of them join me in the elevator never really makes my day.

This time, however, it was two young black girls. Teenagers. They looked at me as if I were from another planet, but the looks weren't hostile. And they engaged in some good natured whispering and giggling. I had a feeling it was about me.

It was.

"You a cop?" one of them ventured, and they both started laughing.

"No, ma'am," I said. "I'm a private detective."

I must say it was gratifying. It was as if I had told them I was James fucking Bond. On the other hand, I had a feeling that inside of ten minutes at least fifty other tenants were

17

going to know there was a private detective in the building, but there was nothing I could do about that.

I got off at twelve and left the girls on their way down. They seemed reluctant to see me go.

The hallway on the twelfth floor was empty, for which I am always grateful. I set out to look for *12C*. That's never as easy as it sounds. The numbers on the doors in the projects always seem to come from a box marked "flimsy." I strolled the long, narrow, shaftlike corridor, looking for a clue.

I got one. On one of the doors was penciled *12J*. All right, now all I gotta do is figure what direction they're running and count.

A little bit further I found *12H*. All right. Got it nailed. That's *G*. That's *F*. That's a stairwell. That's *E*. That's an alcove designed specifically for murderers and muggers to hide in. That's *D*. That's *C*. Jackpot.

The door once had a knocker, but it didn't now. I pounded on it with my fist. I waited. Nothing. No answer. I put my ear to the door. No sound of movement from within. I knocked again. Nothing.

I felt like strangling Wendy/Janet. I felt like strangling Sam Gravston. I felt like strangling Winston Bishop, if I could ever find him.

The thing was, it was a signup. If it had been a picture assignment, I could have just shot it, and if the address had been wrong, tough shit, it's not my fault and I'd get paid for it.

But a signup's different. You can't do it without the client. If I couldn't find Winston fucking Bishop, I wasn't going to get paid. That, on top of not getting paid for the three photo assignments I hadn't had time to shoot in the Bronx, was gonna make this a hell of a day. And, as usual, I was way behind on Tommie's tuition, Con Ed, Ma Bell and the rent.

Shit.

I jiggled the door handle and it opened. I pushed the door open. In front of me was a hallway and a turn. I called out, "Winston Bishop?" at the top of my lungs. I figured even if he was deaf he should have heard me. But then some of these large-family project apartments are really cavernous, so I figured I ought to make sure.

I went down the hall and around the corner. I immediately saw that this was not a large-family apartment. It was a small, two room, single-occupancy affair. I was in a dining room, living room, kitchen combination. In front of me was the door to the bedroom.

Winston Bishop was in the bedroom. I knew it was Winston Bishop the moment I saw him. I can always recognize my clients. They're the ones with the casts on. Winston Bishop had a broken left arm. It must have broken pretty bad, because he had a full-length plaster cast from his shoulder to his wrist.

But that wasn't his only problem.

It's hard to take when you wish for something, and your wish is granted right away, and it wasn't a good wish to begin with.

You see, Winston Bishop had been strangled.

3.

It was nice.

That is to say, if you can talk about a violent, cold-blooded murder being nice, this one was nice.

What was nice about it was the fact that I wasn't involved.

I'd found dead bodies before, and when I had, I'd always had something to cover up. Something to keep from the police. Something I had to withhold.

This time I wasn't involved at all. Any information that I had, the police were welcome to it. Aside from the fact that it robbed me of a client, the murder didn't concern me.

God, was that nice.

That's not to say I still didn't have problems. Cops can be very inquisitive, particularly when a murder is involved. The cops I drew were no exception. If I'd been lucky, the homicide cop would have been Sergeant MacAullif. Then I'd have had the advantage that he owed me a favor. More important, he knew me and would have known that I

20

wouldn't have done something like this. 'Course the sergeant I drew didn't know me from Adam.

His name was Sergeant Clark, and he was a sour man, to say the least. He was about my age, and of medium height and build, which I gathered he took as a personal failing and felt he had to make up for. I'm sure Sergeant Clark would have been much more secure had he been big and beefy, like MacAullif. But he wasn't, and he seemed to want to take it out on everyone in general, and me in particular. And he seemed to take the murder of Winston Bishop as a personal affront to his dignity.

"Now let me get this straight," he said, fixing me with a gaze that told me I was the biggest liar since the dawn of time and that any words out of my mouth could only be viewed with extreme skepticism. "Your office beeped you, you called in, they gave you this address and sent you over here?"

Déjà vu.

I suddenly realized what was happening to me had happened to me before. I'd been interrogated by the cops because I'd walked in on a client of Richard's and found him dead. Only that time it hadn't been true. I'd made it up. Not the part about his being dead, of course. The man, Darryl Jackson, had been quite dead. The part I made up was the part about his being Richard's client. But, had it been true, the situation would have been exactly the same. So the interrogation I was going through was somewhat familiar.

"That's right," I said. "When I got no answer, I tried the door, it was open, and I went in and found him dead. That's all I know, and you can interrogate me till doomsday."

"What did you do when you found the body?"

"I went in the bathroom and threw up."

21

Sergeant Clark regarded me with that superior disdain police officers have for civilians with weak stomachs.

"When was the last time you saw the victim alive?"

"I've never seen him alive."

"You sure of that?"

"I'm positive."

"I'd like you to take another look at the body."

"Why? So I'll throw up again?"

"I don't need any of your lip, either."

"Sorry, Sergeant. I know this is routine for you. But it's a little hard for me to take. I've never seen anyone strangled before."

Sergeant Clark looked at me as if he'd just cracked the case.

"How'd you know he'd been strangled?" he said.

I felt kind of gutsy, knowing I wasn't involved, and I almost came back with some jive rejoinder like, "Well, I didn't think someone kissed him." But I'm not that jive and I'm not that cocky, and I wasn't really feeling that great, what with having blown my lunch in the toilet before taking the elevator downstairs to call these cops.

"I don't know," I said. "That's just how it looked to me. But I have no experience with these things, and I could be wrong. *That* I have some experience with."

Sergeant Clark didn't quite follow that. "You have experience with what?"

"Being wrong."

Sergeant Clark gave me a look, then looked over his shoulder at the door to the bedroom. Inside, flashbulbs were going off. A pudgy, white-haired man in a rumpled suit and tie came out the door, carrying a black bag. I'm not the most astute observer in the world, but even I could have pegged him for the medical examiner, which he turned out to be.

"He was strangled all right," the guy said. "Probably within the last two hours."

Sergeant Clark looked at the medical examiner as if he'd just farted at the dinner table.

The medical examiner looked at me and then back at Clark, and I thought I saw a trace of a smile before he said, "Sorry. Would you like to talk privately?"

"I'll talk to you later," Clark said, brusquely. "Now, if you're finished in there I'd like to have this guy take another look."

"Be my guest."

Sergeant Clark grabbed my shoulder and pushed me toward the door. Always the gentleman.

It was crowded in the bedroom. Two plainclothes detectives were dusting all over the place for prints. Two medics were standing by with a stretcher, awaiting permission to move the body. One uniformed officer was standing by the door, looking very much like a traffic cop, which, in a way, he was. He stepped aside to let Sergeant Clark and me in.

I stepped in and got my second look at Winston Bishop. I hadn't gone back to look at the body after I'd called the cops. I'd gone back up to the apartment to wait for them, but I hadn't gone back in the bedroom. I had no reason to. Winston Bishop was nothing to me. I wasn't involved. The police could solve the crime, or not, as they saw fit—I really didn't care. Now, maybe that's a callous attitude, unworthy of a private detective, but then, as I said, I'm not really a private detective. I'm just a poor schmuck trying to get along. I have no sense of professional pride. Yeah, I was sorry for poor old Winston Bishop, but his demise was not of my making. And though I did feel a little sorry that I had flippantly wished him dead, I'm still sane enough to know that if wishes were horses, beggars would hang out at the track.

I looked down at the body.

Sergeant Clark was looking at me as if he expected me to throw up again. I was determined to disappoint him.

It took an effort. A person who's been strangled does not look pretty. I suppose I shouldn't generalize, seeing as how Winston Bishop was the first person I'd ever seen strangled. Suffice it to say, Winston Bishop did not look pretty. His eyes were bugging out of his head. His face was coal black, and against it, the white, bloodshot eyeballs seemed enormous. His pink tongue also protruded from his face. He looked like one of the Garbage Pail Kids, those incredibly ugly creatures depicted on the bubble gum trading cards my son, Tommie, insists on collecting. He'd have fit right in: Bug-eyed Bishop.

I looked at the body, didn't vomit, felt proud of myself and turned to Sergeant Clark.

"Well?" I said.

Apparently that was his line.

"Well?" he shot back at me.

"Well, what?" I asked him.

"Have you ever seen this man before?"

"As I told you before, no."

"Take a good look. And remember, this guy would have looked a lot different before."

"I realize that."

"Take your time. Think about it. Remember, a lot of these blacks all look alike, anyway."

I realized I didn't like Sergeant Clark very much. I shot a look at one of the detectives, who happened to be black. The guy never even blinked. I figured Sergeant Clark must be a known quantity among the detectives.

"I've taken a good look," I said. "I've made all the allowances I can. I've never seen this man before in my life."

"Uh huh," said Sergeant Clark. If he believed me, you

24

wouldn't have known it. He turned to the black detective. "Walker. Take this guy downtown, print him and get a signed statement."

Sergeant Clark was so preemptory, I half expected Walker to roll his eyes and say, "Yas, massah." He didn't. He just looked at me and said, "Let's go."

Walker turned out to be a nice guy. On the way downtown he talked to me conversationally about my job and life in general and my finding Winston Bishop in particular, so by the time we got there he had a pretty good idea what had happened, and taking my statement was really a snap.

Still, I'm sure being dragged downtown and interrogated and fingerprinted is no one's idea of a good time. At least, it's certainly not mine.

And while I couldn't really get angry at Walker, I must say I was angry as hell at Sergeant Clark. I won't say I wanted to strangle him—I think I've cured myself of using that expression—but I was good and angry.

I was also pretty angry with myself, for not having had the balls or the initiative to get out of this draggy job that had gotten me into this mess. And I was even a little angry with poor Winston Bishop for getting himself strangled on my time.

But I'm sure the person I was angriest with, bar none, had to be the fucking theatrical agent who had managed to get Sam Gravston that damn audition.

4.

Naturally, it was the talk of the office.

"I appreciate your fervor," Richard said, "but if they don't sign, they don't sign. You don't have to strangle them."

The demise of Winston Bishop had been a sufficiently unusual event to have disrupted normal office routine. Richard Rosenberg was holding forth in his outer office, something he rarely did. Usually he held himself aloof from his staff and received clients only behind closed doors. Today he was perched on the edge of one of Wendy and Janet's twin reception desks, desks that were largely taken up by the twin twenty-line switchboards Wendy and Janet manned.

Richard was a little guy, but he made up for it by burning up twice the calories of a big guy. His energy level was incredible. It has always been my opinion that Richard was a hyperactive kid who just never grew out of it.

Richard's audience consisted of the aforementioned

Wendy and Janet, Jack and Alan—two young college drop-outs Richard had hired as paralegals to do his filing—and Frank Burke, a young investigator on his second day of training.

I call it Richard's audience, rather than mine, because even though it was my story, and it had happened to me, Richard always seemed to make himself the center of attention wherever he was, and today was no exception.

"I didn't strangle Winston Bishop," I said.

"That's what they all say," Richard said.

The audience laughed. I guess you would expect the staff to laugh at the boss's jokes, but anyone would have laughed—Richard was quite a showman, and he had a real theatrical flair.

"I could get it reduced to manslaughter," Richard said. "In fact, knowing you, I bet I could get you off—not guilty by reason of insanity."

Richard was on a roll, and I wasn't about to try to stop him. I had to just sit there and take it.

"You see, Frank," Richard said to the trainee, "I want you to learn from this. This is an excellent example of how *not* to do a signup."

"Hey, give me a break," I said.

"No, Frank should learn," Richard said. "Frank, here's a quiz for you. You get beeped and sent out on a signup. Now which should you do—a) fill out the fact sheet and sign the client to a retainer or b) kill him?"

"That's a tough one," Frank said.

Frank was pleased to be having a good time at my expense. He had been out on his first signups that afternoon. And though the trainees are always given the easier sign-ups, and Frank's had been out in Queens and probably weren't that bad, I had a feeling they hadn't gone particularly well. I also had a feeling Frank wasn't going to last more than a couple more days. So he was getting his licks in now.

"Let me see," Frank said. "I gotta think about this. Does this mean the guy isn't a client, then?"

"Dead men sign no retainers," Richard said. "Which brings up a good point. Stanley, in the future, if you get this urge, remember, have them sign the retainer, *then* strangle them."

I suppose one shouldn't joke over another person's misfortunes, particularly over another person's death, but somehow people always do. Even when someone you know dies, eventually people get around to making jokes, and eventually you have to admit it's kind of funny. When someone you *don't* know dies, it's hilarious.

Jack and Alan, the two file clerks, laughed a lot, but neither had yet ventured a comment, and probably weren't about to. They were both new enough to be in awe of being in the presence, and new enough to still want to hold on to their jobs. Richard's file clerks never lasted much longer than his investigators. This was not surprising. For the pittance Richard was willing to pay, he could attract only the bottom of the barrel. Of them, those with any brains at all would soon quit, and those with no brains at all Richard would soon fire. Jack and Alan were too new to have sorted themselves out into one of those two categories, though I suspected they would both fall into the latter. Jack looked as if he would have been happier playing football somewhere, if only someone could have cheated for him on the English final. Alan was one of those little guys who looked as if he could have been a nerd if he'd only had a little initiative.

Wendy and Janet weren't saying anything either. Janet, the new arrival, was actually somewhat attractive, in a cheap, physical way. She was a skinny girl, with long, black hair hanging down to her ass. Her hair fell down her back in the shape of an arrow that always seemed to be pointing, "Look, boys, here it is." Her not unpleasant—looking face promised no intellectual complications whatsoever. Her voice, of course, was just as unpleasant as Wendy's, but put a gag in her mouth and you could have yourself a quite acceptable date.

Wendy, of course, was the iron maiden, the longest-standing employee of Rosenberg and Stone, with the exception of me. Unlike Janet, Wendy would not inspire men to carnal thought. At least not sane men. Wendy looked like every young college student's paranoid fantasy of his first blind date. Dumpy body, ugly face, hair supplied by electro-shock. She was the type of girl you always figured had to be the class genius, just because she had nothing else going for her. Unfortunately, in her case it wasn't so. When attributes were being handed out, Wendy had been passed over in every category.

Still, she was an old hand at the firm, and the one most likely to dare venturing a comment. Yet she hadn't, and in a sudden flash of understanding and horror I realized why. She liked her job. She didn't want to risk jeopardizing it. She was happy in her work, and she wanted to stay.

It was a sickening thought.

At any rate, that left the floor open for Richard, Frank and me. Or rather for Richard and Frank, as I was merely the butt of their humor. In fact, in the whole session, I think the only good line I got in was asking Richard if I was gonna get paid for the signup, and I don't think Richard really found that particularly funny. The answer, by the way, was no.

Still, as I said, it was a pretty hilarious time at Rosenberg and Stone, and a jolly good time was had by all.

PARNELL HALL

It was into this bizarre atmosphere that burst the irrepressible Sam Gravston, fresh from his audition, and ignorant of the events of the afternoon, and oblivious to everyone and everything in the world but his own self.

"It's terrific!" he screamed. "They like me! I got a callback! For a part. A real part. Not on a soap, either. For a TV show. Prime time. And not just a show. A sitcom. A series! I can't believe it. I got a shot at a series!"

5.

I hated him.

If you're not an actor, you wouldn't understand, but if you are, I don't even have to explain. You see, that's the thing about working in the arts. You can never be *really* happy about a friend's success, even a good friend. The thing is, life is such a crapshoot; there's such a huge distance between success and failure, with really nothing in between. For every actor who gets a part, there are a thousand who don't. And who never will. And not for lack of talent, either. That's the excruciating thing

And if you're an unsuccessful actor, what kills you is having to watch the successful ones on television. Not in their shows and movies. That's all right. At least there you have the opportunity to sit back and comment on how bad the show is, and what a ham the actor is and how poorly he's doing. No, the thing that kills you is watching them on talk shows. Particularly the early news shows, like "Live at Five," where an actor is treated as something slightly short of a deity. So you have to sit there and watch some snivel-

31

ing punk talk about this or that movie, and making the right career choice. And you want to scream out, "You fucking asshole! How dare you sit there talking about *career choices*, and what is right for your *image*. Don't you realize how lucky you are to be working *anywhere*?"

See, that's another thing about the business. For an actor to become successful, it is not necessary for him to be intelligent, likable or even particularly good. And if you're in the arts, and you've spent fifteen or twenty years banging your head against a stone wall, it's just impossible to relate to some twenty-four-year-old kid's success. You can't help feeling they don't deserve it. They haven't paid their dues yet. They're not old enough yet to have even developed a proper sense of futility. So it's hard to take.

It was particularly hard for me to take this time. Seeing as how I was the one who had to go to Harlem, lose a half a day's work, plus stare at a particularly disgusting dead body, and be hassled by an obnoxious cop, so twenty-four-year-old Sam Gravston could get a shot at a sitcom, a career and financial security. Yeah, it was a bit rough.

My wife, Alice, who is supersensitive to my moods, jumped on me the minute I got home.

"What's wrong?" she said.

"I've had a bit of a day," I said.

I told her about the demise of Winston Bishop and my ordeal with the cops.

"That's terrible," she said. "But it's over. And it doesn't involve you."

"I know," I said.

"Then why are you so depressed?"

"Sam Gravston."

"What about him?"

I sighed. "He may have gotten a series."

"A TV series?"

"Yeah."

Alice nodded sympathetically. "Oh."

Instant understanding. My wife has shared with me the frustrations of a career in the arts. The problem is, my wife is much more practical than I am, and always has alternative ideas, which, I must confess, I never truly appreciate. That's because they all involve work. Or, rather, the *finding* of it. I have no objection to work. But looking for it scares me to death. Getting up in the morning, pushing myself forward, facing the Void, competing with that rising tide of actors and writers. Yeah, when I think of it that way, I realize going into places like Jesus Pagan's building is not so brave at all. It's really just the coward's way out. A way of avoiding the greater fear of looking for work.

Alice, who is both sensitive and understanding, pointed none of this out to me.

She simply said, "Don't worry. Tomorrow will be better."

It wasn't.

6.

The day began on a sour note. I woke up at seven A.M. and realized my car was parked on the good side. Alternate-side parking in my neighborhood is from eight to eleven, which meant if I didn't hustle, someone parked on the bad side of the street would move their car and double-park in front of me and I wouldn't be able to get out. I tore on my clothes and stumbled out the door by seven-ten. Sure enough, on our block only one car was already double-parked, but that one car was right in front of mine. Seven-ten is too early to double-park and leave your car, so I was rightfully pissed.

There was a note in the window. If there hadn't been, I would have been angry enough to bite off the fender, but there was. Most people who double-park and know the system are thoughtful enough to leave a note in the window. Those who are not thoughtful enough find incredible notes in their windows when they get back.

This note gave a phone number and an address. I wasn't in my working gear, I'd just thrown on jeans and a shirt, so

34

I didn't have a pencil or anything to write the number down. So I kept repeating it over and over to myself as I staggered to the pay phone on the corner.

And discovered I didn't have a quarter. Which meant I could still make the call but I had to dial 0–212, and then the number, and then at the tone punch in my calling-card number for Rosenberg and Stone. The calling-card number was for business use only, but if I didn't get my car moved, I would be doing no business, so I figured its use was legit.

But the thing was that meant punching a total of twenty-five numbers into the phone. I'm foggy in the morning, particularly before I've had my coffee, and I misdialed the first time and had to start over. And, what with repeating the number over and over in my head, and then the digits of the calling-card number and all, by the time the phone was ringing I couldn't be at all certain the number I'd dialed was right.

And I got an answering machine.

Had I been certain the number I'd dialed was correct, I would have loved to have left a message telling how I felt about a person who double-parked his car, left a note in the window and then turned on his answering machine. But I wasn't sure, and the only way I could make sure was by going all the way back up the block to my car, memorizing the number again and coming all the way back and punching twenty-five numbers into the phone again and the whole bit.

I wasn't up to that. Instead, I memorized the address, which was an apartment building on West End Avenue, walked over there and rang the bell.

I rang five times before a sleepy voice on the intercom system said, "Yes."

"Your car's double-parked and your answering machine's on," I said, as politely as possible under the circumstances.

"I'll be right down."

He was, in about fifteen minutes, after which he moved his car and I moved mine. That left me just time to rush upstairs, shower and put on my suit and tie, and help Alice hustle Tommie downstairs so I could drive him to his school over on the east side.

By the time I got back from there it was eight-thirty, and since it was after Labor Day, and everyone was back from their summer vacations, and Columbia University had started and the college kids were all here, it was that insane time of year in my neighborhood when not a parking spot can be found. I cruised around for over half an hour before I was able to double-park.

Yes, I left a note in my window.

I walked to the newsstand on Broadway and bought the New York *Post*, then went for coffee and a muffin at Au Petit Buerre on the corner of 105th. Au Petit Buerre was doing a brisk business, as usual, which shows you what a French name will do. I doubt if the Little Butter restaurant would have done half as well.

I sat there, drinking my coffee and reading my *Post*, and suddenly, there it was, a kick in the face on page eight. Ordinarily, a routine, sordid strangling in Harlem would not have rated that much ink, but the reporter had found a handle for the story.

"INJURED MAN STRANGLED," ran the headline. A sub-headline, in smaller type, read: "CALLS LAWYER FOR HELP, WINDS UP DEAD." The story told how Winston Bishop, who had broken his arm, had called the law firm of Rosenberg and Stone (the reporter had quoted Richard's slogan from the TV ads: "No case too big, no case too small."), and the law firm had sent out an investigator, who had walked in and found him dead. The story concluded with the sentence, "The investigator, Stanley Hastings of

Manhattan, is not being held by the police at this time."

I was furious. That fucking reporter. What insinuation! What innuendo! *Not being held by the police at this time.* And yet there was nothing I could do about it. It wasn't slander. It wasn't libel. It was the truth. I was *not* being held by the police at this time. The reporter had made a simple statement of fact.

But the implications....

Damn!

I had just read that when a prim, prissy-looking business man in a three-piece suit stuck his head in the door and demanded, "Anyone here own a Toyota?"

I was pissed off as hell when I moved it. Those who play the alternate-side parking game are supposed to know the rules. If you're on the good side and you plan to leave for work at nine-thirty, you get up at seven like I did and dou-ble-park your car so you can get out. You don't show up at nine-thirty, acting indignant that you've been blocked in. Because the guys who double-park have rights too, and one of them is, except in emergency situations, they shouldn't be bugged to move their cars again between eight and ten-thirty, when everyone starts to move back.

I had just moved the car, and decided since I was in it I'd head out to the Bronx for those three picture assignments, when I got beeped, and when I called in Wendy/Janet sent me to Harlem again because a new case had come in and Sam Gravston couldn't take it because he had a meeting with his agent.

That was all I needed to hear. In the years I'd worked as an actor I'd never managed to get an agent, let alone have meetings with one. In fact, getting an agent had always seemed as hard to me as getting work. It had taken me two years to get an agent for my magazine articles, and even then I wouldn't have gotten one if Alice hadn't met someone who happened to know someone. But Sam Gravston hadn't had any trouble.

I was in a bad enough mood, what with having had my car blocked, having been bad-mouthed in the New York *Post*, and having had my coffee and muffin interrupted by a creep who didn't know the system, so having my photo assignments aborted for a second time for Sam Gravston did not endear him to me at all.

All in all, Sam Gravston was rapidly earning a place on my shitlist.

1.

I wasn't all that keen on going back to Harlem. I figured I'd
be sure to draw a bad building, and after yesterday my
nerves were not in great shape.

However, the building wasn't that bad. It was a fairly
new brick apartment building on Convent Avenue, and it
probably wouldn't have bothered me at all going in there,
except for the fact that when I did, once again I had a sense
of déjà vu. What do you call it when you get déjà vu again?
Déjà déjà vu? At any rate, it increased when I got out of the
elevator and looked for apartment 1B, where the client,
Shirley Woll, lived. The apartment door seemed familiar,
too.

But the guy who opened the door when I knocked sure
wasn't. I couldn't have forgotten him. He was a black man
of about thirty-five, with deep-set eyes and a protruding
jaw that made him look as if he were about to punch your
lights out. I must admit I took a half step backward when
he appeared in the door.

"Yeah?" he growled.

"Hello," I said. "I'm from the lawyer's office."

He stared at me for a moment.

Then he said, "Shit!"

Then he slammed the door in my face.

I stood there in the hallway. I must say, I was not in the best of moods.

Thanks, Sam.

From within the apartment came the sound of raised voices. I couldn't hear what they were saying, but I could tell that someone was not happy. The guy who'd opened the door for me seemed to be a good bet.

It had sometimes happened that a client would call Rosenberg and Stone and then their spouse, or mate, or whatever would turn out to be not particularly happy about it, and they would wind up canceling. I had had discussions of that sort take place in my presence. But I'd never had one of them take place with me standing in the hall.

Thanks, Sam.

The door was opened by a black woman of about the same age as the man. She was slightly plump and had a roundish face.

And she smiled at me, and said, "Mr. Hastings?"

I was not in a good mood to begin with. And meeting this woman's cheerful friend had not helped. But her seeming to recognize me blew my mind.

I should explain. I'm terrible with names, and I'm terrible with faces. I know these aren't great traits for a private detective, but then I'm not really a private detective. And working for Rosenberg and Stone I must have interviewed between five hundred and a thousand clients. So even if this woman was someone I'd interviewed before, there was no reason for me to remember her.

But she was black.

And ringing in my ears, like a death knell, was the

haunting, taunting voice of Sergeant Clark, saying, "Remember, a lot of these blacks all look alike, anyway."

The thing was, I didn't recognize her. Now, I happen to know that if she'd been one of Richard's white clients, I wouldn't have recognized her either. But that didn't help. Not after my encounter with Sergeant Clark.

I felt like shit.

I had her name in my notebook, Shirley Woll, but that didn't help me any, cause I'm as bad at names as I am at faces. So there I was with egg on my face and this woman grinning at me.

And I knew just what she was going to say.

"You don't remember me, do you?"

And those are the words I always dread to hear. 'Cause I'm always running into people who look vaguely familiar, and I can't place 'em. And sometimes they're people I really ought to know. Of course, I never know if they are or not, so every vaguely familiar face is a potential source of acute paranoia to me. Because, what if it's someone I'm supposed to know? I don't want to be rude. "So-and-so was very hurt that you didn't remember him." I'm sure he was, and I hope he gets over it. And I hope he also realizes the fault is not his, in not being memorable, but mine, in having no memory. At any rate, I'm always terrified that the person will turn out to be someone I should remember, like the principal of my son's school, or my mother-in-law, or someone else I can equally ill afford to offend.

In this case, my mind was reeling. At least I knew she wasn't my mother-in-law. She was obviously a former client, but which of the thousand broken limbs had been hers?

And that damn, familiar question, "You don't remember me, do you?"

Rather than a bold-face admission, I hemmed and hawed

with, "Well, now, let me see..." And as I had hoped, she jumped in with helpful hints.

"It was two years ago. I broke my ankle and you came to see me. I fell on the subway steps at 125th Street."

And immediately I placed her. And immediately I felt like a schmuck. Sure, I can't remember the people, just the places where they fell.

Shirley Woll had fallen on the stairs from the platform up to the token booth on the uptown side of the number six train. There was a crack in the stairs, and when I shot my pictures, school had just let out, so there were about a hundred kids crawling around all over the place. They all got real interested when they saw the flash going off, and by the time I finished shooting, I had a huge audience. And I could hear whispers in the crowd. "Private detective." I was new enough on the job to have gotten a kick out of it then. So it stuck in my memory.

"Of course I remember," I said.

But, having gotten over that hurdle, I was suddenly faced with another one. Why the hell was I here? I'd been told that it was a new case, but this was an old one. And the thing was, when I sign people up, and they ask me, I tell 'em, "Don't expect any money for a while. These things take twelve to eighteen months to sort out." But, of course, I don't really know. Once I sign the case and shoot the pictures, it's out of my hands. I never hear about it again. But seeing as how I'd told her eighteen months, and it had been eighteen months, I kind of hated to ask her. But I had to.

"So how'd the case go?" I said, rather hesitantly.

It was all right.

"Oh, it's all taken care of," she said. "I was in to see Mr. Rosenberg just last week, and we got a settlement. Thirty thousand dollars."

I blinked. Jesus Christ. I mean, I knew Richard Rosenberg had to be making money, or he wouldn't be doing what he was doing. But, really. Thirty thousand dollars. For a lousy broken ankle. His contingency fee is a third, so he made ten grand. I make ten bucks an hour plus thirty cents a mile. Seeing as how the case was in Harlem, with virtually no travel time, by signing the case and taking the pictures I'd have made thirty bucks plus mileage, tops. It occurred to me I was in the wrong line of work.

It also occurred to me that I was still at sea as to why I was there.

"Then why did you call us?" I asked.

She was wearing a full-length housecoat. She bent down, grabbed the fabric near the bottom and with a slightly sheepish or maybe even shit-eating grin, raised up the skirts.

On her right ankle was a fresh, white cast.

I looked at her. "Same ankle?"

"Yup."

"But not the same stair?"

"No. I fell on the front steps of a private house."

She was grinning and shaking her head, and I must admit I was grinning, too. It was a first for me. My first repeat customer.

In my mind, I immediately dubbed her Tessie the Tumbler, after a character in a detective story who made a living by pretending to be hit by cars, and turning in insurance claims based on X rays of a leg she'd managed to break somewhere.

I got out my fact sheet and began taking down the information, and Tessie the Tumbler and I were having a fine old time until my beeper went off, which precipitated the boyfriend out of the bedroom like a linebacker blitzing through to tear off the quarterback's head, and we had a tense moment or two before I got the damn thing shut off and explained.

"Charlie," she said. "It's just the man's beeper. He has to call his office. Everything's all right."

Charlie glared at me and retreated back into the bedroom, slamming the door. I was glad to see him go. It would not have surprised me too much if he turned out to be a crack addict. It occurred to me that if he was, it was a good thing Tessie the Tumbler had broken her ankle again, because her thirty thousand dollar payoff wasn't going to last very long.

I called Rosenberg and Stone. Wendy/Janet answered.

"I got a new case for you."

"Where is it?"

"In Queens."

"Oh?"

"Yes, I was going to give it to Sam, but the address is too far out, and he has an audition and says he'd never get back in time."

Great. A case way out in Queens. Time and mileage. I couldn't even begrudge Sam his audition. I was happy to have this one.

I was happier when I heard the details. A Gerald Finklestein, a door-to-door vacuum-cleaner salesman, had got his hand caught in the vacuum cleaner he was demonstrating, and lost a finger.

I've already admitted it's wrong to laugh at other people's misfortunes, but some cases I get strike me funny, and I must say, if I hadn't had a client standing right next to me, I'd have been on the floor. As it was, it was all I could do to keep a straight face.

I must say, I was getting in a much better mood. This day that had started out so poorly, was really looking up. First, Tessie the Tumbler, and now, Hard-sell Finklestein, the vacuum-cleaner man. Plus, I'm getting out of Harlem and driving way out to Queens on a nice, sunny day. And putting hours and mileage on the paysheet. Things could be worse.

They were.

I was just finishing up having Tessie the Tumbler sign the retainer when my beeper went off again.

At least Charlie didn't explode from the bedroom again, but when I called in it was worse.

Hard-sell Finklestein would have to wait a bit.

I had to keep an appointment with Sergeant Clark.

8.

"I have a problem."

My personal opinion was that Sergeant Clark had a lot of problems. I did not express this opinion, however. In fact, I did not express any opinion. I sat and waited.

I was seated in Sergeant Clark's office, which was not unlike Sergeant MacAullif's, with which I was well familiar. Sergeant Clark was seated at his desk. He was playing with a rubber band. I wondered if playing with things at their desks was something sergeants always did. MacAullif usually played with a cigar.

I must say I was in no way ill at ease at being called into Sergeant Clark's office. This marked the first time in my life that I'd ever been called into a policeman's office that this was true. But the thing was, I wasn't involved in Winston Bishop's death. Sergeant Clark was welcome to all the information I had. In fact, he had already had it. So anything he wanted had to be total bullshit. If anything I was annoyed. This officious prick was keeping me from my joy-ride out to Queens.

46

"Yes," Clark repeated. "I have a problem."

I wondered if we would sit there all afternoon unless I asked him what his problem was. I was willing to find out. The thing is, I was pissed as hell, and I was damned if I was saying a word.

"Yeah, big problem," Clark said.

Jesus Christ. I was tempted to say, "Is it bigger than a breadbox," but I'm not that jive, and I don't *really* like getting into adversary positions with people.

So I just sat quiet, which was as hostile as I could handle being. Good old passive-aggressive, that's me.

"It's the Winston Bishop case," Clark said.

I'd assumed it was. No new information there.

"That's what I have a problem with."

Good lord. A new police interrogation technique. Suspects crack through boredom.

I did.

"What is your problem?" I asked.

The question seemed to give Sergeant Clark great satisfaction. You would have thought he had cracked the case, rather than just my composure.

"Ah! Good question, Mr. Hastings. A very good question. Well, let me tell you something. It may surprise you, but we cops actually work toward solving crime. We take it seriously. We do our homework.

"Take this case, for instance. Do you know what M.O. stands for?"

"Modus operandi," I said.

He looked at me as if I'd just spoiled his lecture.

"How do you know that?" he said.

"Give me a break," I said. "I read murder mysteries just like anybody else."

"Of course," Sergeant Clark said, with a thin smile. "And that is why you think of the police as bumbling fools, and private detectives as the only ones with any sense."

I refrained from comment.

"All right," Clark said. "Modus operandi, method of operation. Because killers are not very imaginative. They often repeat themselves. So the first thing we look for is, is there a similarity to another crime."

"Have you had other stranglings in Harlem?" I asked.

The thin smile was even frostier now. "No."

Sergeant Clark reached into his file and pulled out a paper. "The similarity in this case is even more striking than that."

"Oh?" I said.

"Yes. The case of Darryl Jackson, murdered in Harlem last year."

"I couldn't believe it. My déjà vu. And Sergeant Clark had found it.

"Now," Sergeant Clark went on, "Darryl Jackson was stabbed with a knife, and Winston Bishop was strangled, but aside from that, the cases are identical. In each case, a black man, living in Harlem, called Rosenberg and Stone, asking for an appointment. The office beeped you, sent you over there and you walked in and found the client dead."

"Yes," I said. "It's quite a coincidence."

Sergeant Clark fixed me with a hard look. "I don't believe in coincidence," he said.

I resented that. That was MacAullif's line. Sergeant Clark had no right to it.

"All right," I said. "You don't believe in coincidence, but that's all it was."

"Maybe, maybe not," Clark said.

"There's no maybe about it."

"Don't be too sure," Clark said. "When crimes follow an identical pattern, we have to look for a common link."

"A common link?"

"Yes. To see if they are related. In two crimes so similar as this, we can't discount the theory that they were committed by the same person."

I stared at him. "What, are you nuts? The murderer of Darryl Jackson has been tried and convicted. He's in jail."

Sergeant Clark seemed unimpressed. "It wouldn't be the first time the courts have made a mistake."

"And he confessed to the crime."

"It wouldn't be the first time a man has made a false confession."

I couldn't believe what I was hearing. "Do you have any idea what you're saying?"

"Of course I do. What I'm saying is, in any case where we have two such similar crimes, we cannot discount the fact that they may be part of a pattern. We have to consider the possibility that we are dealing with a serial killer, as in the Son of Sam case, and that these two are part of a series of murders."

I stared at him. Good lord. The man was a total moron. A serial killer. A series of murders.

I knew who killed Darryl Jackson. I knew it very well. And that man was behind bars and had not killed Winston Bishop.

"May I ask you something?" I said.

"Certainly."

"Have you talked this over with Sergeant MacAullif? He handled the Darryl Jackson case."

"Yes, I have," Clark said.

"And what is his opinion?"

"Sergeant MacAullif feels, as you do, that the Darryl Jackson case has been solved."

"There you are," I told him.

"Of course, he could be mistaken," Clark said. "And, of course, it's only natural for an officer to want to feel he's arrested the right man." Sergeant Clark smiled at me. "We always have a horror of sending an innocent man to jail, in spite of how cold and uncaring the public might think us to be."

I hated him. Worse than that, I felt contempt for him. I flashed on what he'd said about private detectives always thinking they're smarter than policemen. As I've said, I'd always found the reverse to be true. In the cases I'd dealt with, I'd always found the police to be incredibly smart— or at least a lot smarter than I was. And I must say, I'd always had nothing but respect for their intelligence and abilities.

Until now.

Sergeant Clark kept me there for half an hour, asking me questions about the Darryl Jackson case. The best I can say is that I was not openly rude. I was not particularly cooperative, either. My answers were, to say the least, succinct. I volunteered nothing.

I left his office with a chip on my shoulder that must have weighed a ton.

9.

I strode down the hall to Sergeant MacAullif's office. He was in. Busy, but in. I waited for about ten minutes while he grappled on the phone with some subordinate who was having a problem with some fingerprint identification.

Finally, he hung up the phone.

"Hi," MacAullif said. "You look just like my detectives do when they spend six months working on a case and the judge throws it out of court. What's up?"

"As if you didn't know," I said. "Sergeant Clark."

MacAullif grinned. "Ah, yes," he said. "I thought he'd be getting around to you."

"I'm glad you find it so funny," I said. "I've just spent a half hour listening to that asshole."

"Now, now," MacAullif said. "Clark's a good man."

I stared at him. "What?"

"A good man. A little too straight-laced, a little too by-the-book, but still a good man."

"Give me a break," I said.

MacAullif laughed. "I'm sorry, but it is kind of funny.

Hoist by your own petard, aren't you? I mean, you mocked up that whole Darryl Jackson thing to get yourself out of a jam, and now it's come back to haunt you."

"I'm glad you think this is so funny," I told him. "Now that moron, Clark, thinks that those two murders are part of a series, that you arrested the wrong man and that there's a serial killer running around someplace. Now I've got to deal with him, and the man's a total idiot."

"Now, that's hardly fair," MacAullif said. "The supposition that Sergeant Clark is going on is the supposition that for two so similar crimes to be committed, it can't be merely coincidence. It couldn't just happen that way." MacAullif smiled. "And, he is absolutely right. It *didn't* just happen that way. The crimes are similar because you mocked up the evidence in the Darryl Jackson case. If you hadn't done that, there would be only one case of a Richard Rosenberg client who called in for an appointment and was discovered dead. And Sergeant Clark would not be bothering you because there would be nothing to go on.

"What he is reacting to is the fact that, because it happened twice, something must not be kosher, and as I say, he is absolutely right."

"But ... but ..."

"Not doing well, are you?" MacAullif said.

"Damn it," I said. "You know what the story is. Why don't you straighten Clark out?"

"Well, there we have a problem," MacAullif said. "In the first place, we are both sergeants. I am not his superior officer, he is not accountable to me, the Winston Bishop case is his and I got no business butting in."

"But the Darryl Jackson case was yours."

"True."

"And he's stirring it up again."

52

MacAullif shrugged. "Which he has every right to do."

"But as a result, he's making unfounded suppositions and reaching illogical conclusions."

"So what do you want me to do about it?"

"Straighten him out. Clue him in to what really happened."

"Well," MacAullif said, "that's the problem."

Jesus. Today everyone had a problem.

"Oh?"

"Yeah, see, the things you did in the Darryl Jackson case were not strictly legal. To put it another way, they were illegal. And, unfortunately, the statute of limitations has not yet run out on such crimes as suppressing evidence, compounding a felony and accessary after the fact to murder." MacAullif looked at me. "Now, as I've said, Sergeant Clark is very much by-the-book. And the book would tell Sergeant Clark to prosecute you on those charges."

I stared at MacAullif. "You're telling me there's nothing I can do?"

"That's one thing."

"And that I'm fucked."

"That's another. Now," MacAullif said, "I know I owe you a favor, but as you can see, straightening Sergeant Clark out on the Darryl Jackson case would not really be a big favor."

"I can see that," I said.

"So," MacAullif said, "there you are."

And there I was.

As I've said before, it was not a good day. But I was determined to make the most of it. When I finally got out of the police station, I drove out to Queens, feeling as carefree as I could under the circumstances, and ready to enjoy to the fullest, without actually laughing in his face, the plight of Hard-sell Finklestein, the door-to-door vacuum-cleaner salesman who had had his finger nipped off by his own machine.

Only when I got there, Hard-sell Finklestein had been strangled.

10.

It was hard to take. And not just finding another dead body. Sure, that was hard to take. I threw up again and the whole bit. No, what was hard to take was Sergeant Clark being right.

He was right, but for all the wrong reasons. All right, so maybe the Winston Bishop and the Hard-sell Finklestein murders were the work of the same party. Maybe we *were* dealing with a serial killer.

But Darryl Jackson was not part of the series. And the Darryl Jackson case was the case upon which Sergeant Clark had based his conclusion. An utterly false conclusion that absurdly, had turned out to be true.

And the dumb fuck didn't even know it.

"Three," he said, and I swear there was smug satisfaction in his voice. "Now we have three."

What an asshole. Yes, now he had three. And who, naturally, was his prime suspect? I didn't even need the New York *Post* to point it out to me. It was none other than yours truly.

And this time when he interrogated me, I had something to hide. Not about the Finklestein murder, of course. About the Darryl Jackson case. Which was enough to make me uneasy and keep me on my guard. What a mess.

The other thing was, I had information about the Finklestein murder. I'd spoken to him. Of course, that was Sergeant Clark's fault. Because of Sergeant Clark's insistence that I come in and talk to him, I'd had to call Finklestein and stall him along. So I, presumably, was the last person to talk to Finklestein while he was alive. Which, I realize, is a stupid way to put it. I'm pretty sure no one talked to Finklestein after he was dead. At any rate, I had that information.

If Sergeant Clark believed my story. Which he gave every indication that he didn't.

We were standing in Finklestein's foyer. The body was lying there on the living room floor. Having seen two, I can now go so far as to generalize that a strangled person is not a pretty sight.

Hard-sell Finklestein was about sixty years old. He was bald with a fringe of white hair. He had a protruding nose and appeared to at one time have had a protruding adam's apple, which was crammed backward into his throat. His eyes, like Winston Bishop's, bugged out of his head. In his death throws he'd apparently puked a stain of green slime down his shirt. Either that, or he was a terribly sloppy eater.

I'd managed to get to the toilet before I heaved my guts out, which so far seemed to be my only accomplishment in this case. Things were really not going well.

From where Sergeant Clark and I'd were standing in Finklestein's foyer we could see Finklestein's body lying on the floor in the living room. The living room was swarming with people, and the cast of characters was not that different than what it had been in the Winston Bishop case. This was somewhat remarkable, seeing as how we were in Queens. Indeed, the first detectives on the scene had been from Queens County. But someone must have tipped Clark off, for he had arrived not fifteen minutes on their heels, and citing a tie-in with a previous case, immediately preempted command, so the detectives now processing the crime scene were from his unit.

The medical examiner was different, however. Bad as my memory is for faces, the first one had been white and this one was black, and that much I could handle.

The medical examiner rose from the body and came into the foyer. He started to say something to Sergeant Clark, then looked at me, caught himself and looked inquiringly back at Clark.

"Outside," Clark said.

The medical examiner nodded and went out the door. Sergeant Clark looked at me briefly, then followed him out.

That left me alone in the foyer. I considered going over to the door and watching the activity going on in the living room, but the uniformed cop was eyeing me with extreme suspicion. On second thought, I didn't really feel like doing it anyway.

What I felt like doing, if the truth be known, was going home, lying down in bed, pulling a comforter up to my chin, having Alice make me a cup of hot tea with honey, turning on the TV and forgetting about life for a while.

I'd just had time to enjoy that daydream when Sergeant Clark burst in from the hallway. He jerked the door open and peered in suspiciously, as if suspecting I might have been listening at the keyhole. I doubt if the fact that I was standing in the middle of the foyer doing nothing convinced him that I hadn't been. He probably thought I was feigning a lack of interest. I figured later he'd interrogate the uniformed cop at the door on my movements.

"Do you know what the medical examiner just told me?" Clark demanded.

In my present state of mind, I assumed Clark had asked the question not because he intended to impart any information, but merely to see if I'd overheard the conversation, so I'm afraid my answer was flippant, to say the least.

"Sure," I said. "The murderer was left-handed."

Clark's head jerked around. "Why do you say that?"

I realized he'd taken it seriously. "I'm sorry," I said. "That was a joke. A facetious remark."

Sergeant Clark stared at me coldly. "Murder is no joke."

He was right, of course. And ordinarily I wouldn't have been joking. It was just that the man irritated me so much. With anyone else I wouldn't have done it.

And, with anyone else, had I done it, they would have recognized a joke as a joke, whether they appreciated it or not. But not Sergeant by-the-book Clark.

"You're right. I'm sorry," I said. "Were you about to tell me what the medical examiner said?"

"That's right," Clark said. "Seeing as how it involves you. He said it was just the same as in the Winston Bishop case. The man could have been strangled any time within the last two hours."

"I see."

"Which means you could have done it."

I said nothing.

"Just as you could have done the Winston Bishop and the Darryl Jackson killings."

Again I said nothing.

"Don't you have anything to say?"

"Do you really think I'm going to dignify that with a response?"

"You might at least deny it."

"Is that really necessary?"

He looked at me coldly. "Do you deny the allegation?"

"Well, let's put it this way," I said. "I don't admit it."

Sergeant Clark looked as if he wanted to strangle me. At least that was the impression that leapt to my mind. And since I had already made a conscious decision to stop using that particular expression, the phrase triggered a strange thought process in my mind. Sergeant Clark was the killer. A deranged homicide sergeant. A demagogue. Drunk with his own power. So infused with thoughts of his own superior skill that he must be right at any cost. Sergeant Clark had not killed Winston Bishop, but he had killed Hard-sell Finklestein. Sergeant Clark had predicted a serial killer, and by god there was going to be a serial killer. Sergeant Clark had killed Hard-sell Finklestein to make his prediction come true.

I looked at Sergeant Clark. I doubt if he realized I had just pegged him for the murderer. If he had, he couldn't have been so cool, so sure of himself. He just didn't know who he was dealing with. Try to pin this crime on me, bud? Well the same goes double for you.

"What are you smiling at?" Clark said.

I hadn't realized I was smiling. But I realized I'd better get a grip on myself. As I've said, I'm no hero, and my emotional stability is nothing to brag about. Finding my second dead body in two days was bound to unhinge me. I was sure to crack up sooner or later. It occurred to me that, with Sergeant Clark staring at me here in the apartment of a murdered man, it would be better to make it later. So I made an effort to push aside all ridiculous thoughts of Sergeant Clark's fancied involvement in the affair.

"I'm sorry," I said. "But as a rational man, I find your

suggestion ludicrous. I realize you don't. So, no, I did not kill Winston Bishop, and, no, I did not kill Mr. Finklestein."

"And Darryl Jackson?" Clark said.

I didn't roll my eyes. I did close them for a moment. I opened them, and with a conscious effort to keep the anger out of my voice, said evenly, "Or Darryl Jackson."

"Good," said Sergeant Clark. "Whether I choose to believe it or not, I like to have your denial in the records." Sergeant Clark turned toward the living room. "Walker," he bellowed.

Detective Walker appeared in the doorway. "Sir?"

"Wrap things up here, will you? This gentleman and I are taking a ride."

My jaw dropped open. I couldn't believe it. The son of a bitch was arresting me.

I gawked at him. "We going downtown?" I asked.

He looked at me and smiled that thin smile. "Not just yet."

That was nice. A reprieve and a threat, all in three words.

"Would it be expecting too much for you to tell me where we're going?"

"We're going to the source," Clark said.

"The source?"

"Yes. The source of all this trouble."

Jesus Christ. It wasn't enough that Sergeant Clark was a cold hostile prick. The son of a bitch had to speak in epigrams.

I tried to keep from clenching my teeth. "And where might that be?" I asked.

He looked at me as if I were a moron. "Rosenberg and Stone, of course."

11.

I must say, the gathering at Rosenberg and Stone was a lot different than it had been after the first murder.

For one thing, the personnel were different. Absent were Wendy and Janet, the two file clerks, Frank Burke and Sam Gravston. Present from the original gathering were Richard Rosenberg and me.

The added starter was, of course, Sergeant Clark.

The location was also different. Instead of being in the reception area, we were in Richard's office, behind closed doors.

Outside in the reception area, ready to be summoned at a moment's notice, were Wendy and Janet and the two file clerks. I must say, I sincerely hoped their presence wouldn't be needed.

Richard was seated at his desk. I was seated in a client's chair. Sergeant Clark walked back and forth, rubbing his forehead. Richard and I watched him. When the silence became prolonged, Richard raised his eyebrows in inquiry,

PARNELL HALL

and with a shake of my head, I told him to keep quiet and not volunteer anything. At any rate, that's the message I'd attempted to impart—whether Richard took it for that I couldn't know.

Sergeant Clark stopped pacing and turned to us.

"I have a problem," he said.

Jesus. Not again.

"A real problem."

Yes, again.

Fortunately, this time he went on.

"I have three killings involving the law firm of Rosenberg and Stone."

Richard's chair creaked as he shifted position in his seat. I knew he wanted to say something and was restraining himself with an effort. He glanced at me. I gave him another warning look. He took a breath, blew it out again. But he held his peace.

"Yeah, three killings," Clark said. "Which means we are dealing with a serial killer. I suspected as much yesterday, after the murder of Winston Bishop. The murder of Gerald Finklestein today confirms it. These murders are part of a series."

Richard could contain himself no longer. "You said three murders. You've mentioned two."

Clark looked at him. "The third murder took place last year. The murder of Darryl Jackson."

Richard looked at me. Richard knew about the murder of Darryl Jackson, of course. The cops had given him a hard time about it. And he knew I'd been involved, though he didn't know how deeply, and he didn't know what I had done. As far as Richard knew, I'd gotten into a little trouble because I'd found the body, but the cops had let it drop because the murder had been solved. But he knew enough to know that my involvement in the affair had not been

62

entirely kosher. So the name Darryl Jackson was a warning signal. And Richard's look to me when he heard it asked a silent question.

I answered it with a hard, steady stare.

Richard took the hint, good lawyer he. He turned back to Clark and said, simply, "Go on."

"In a case like this," Sergeant Clark said, "we must consider all the possibilities. The murder of Darryl Jackson and the murder of Winston Bishop could have been coincidence. I don't believe in coincidence, but as I say, we must consider all the possibilities. Against the theory that the crimes were related, we have the fact that the methods were different—one was stabbed and one was strangled—and the fact of the interval of an entire year. Plus the presence of a confessed killer, now residing in jail. None of these are conclusive.

"In favor of the theory we have the fact that two black men living in Harlem called Rosenberg and Stone asking for appointments, and were subsequently found murdered. The discrepancy is the fact that, as I understand it, Darryl Jackson's purported injury, a broken leg, turned out to be spurious, whereas Winston Bishop's broken arm was genuine."

I found myself stirring in my chair. It occurred to me to give myself a good cold, hard stare to hold my peace.

"Now we come to the third murder," Clark said. "Here we see the pattern repeated, and yet broken. Once again Rosenberg and Stone is called, an appointment made and a client found dead. In this case, the injury is genuine, as in the second murder. The victim has been strangled, as in the second murder. Yet the location is different—Queens. And the victim is not black."

I could bear it no longer. "And doesn't that suggest something to you?" I blurted out.

63

"And what might that be?" Clark asked.

"That while the second and third crimes may indeed be related, the first one is not. That being black and living in Harlem is obviously not part of any pattern. As proved by the third murder. And therefore, the fact that the first two gentlemen were black and lived in Harlem is merely coincidental and therefore does not imply that they are part of the same series."

"Try to keep calm," Clark said.

I must admit I had gotten rather heated toward the end of my statement.

"I'm sorry," I said. "I will try to be calm. It is just hard for me to hear things that I know to be untrue stated by you as fact."

"I'm not stating anything as fact," Clark said calmly. "I told you we must investigate all possibilities. And that's what we're doing—investigating all possibilities. And now, if I may continue."

I kept my mouth shut, which was what Clark had intended.

"Now," Clark said, "I was discussing the third murder. I am willing to concede that it is possible that the first two murders were not the work of the same person." Here he looked at me. "Even though you are not willing to concede the possibility that they were—but let that pass.

"With the second and third murders it is somewhat different. Both men were injured, both men called here for help and both men were found strangled."

Clark looked at Richard. "Who was it who took the calls?"

"That would be one of my secretaries."

Clark nodded. "Could we have them in here, please?"

"You may have them in here one at a time," Richard said.

"I'm still attempting to run a business here, and I need my switchboard manned."

"That will be fine," Clark said.

Richard picked up the phone and pressed the intercom. "May I see you in my office, please?" he said.

He hung up the phone.

"Who was that?" Clark asked.

"Wendy or Janet," Richard said.

Clark gave him a look. "Don't you know?"

"I'll know when I see her," Richard said.

I must admit it was nice to see Sergeant Clark confused.

Moments later the door opened and Janet came in. To say she came in hesitantly would be an understatement. It looked as if she wanted to wrap her hair around her and hide in it. She'd been sitting at her desk, of course, when Sergeant Clark brought me in. He wasn't in uniform, and I wasn't in handcuffs, but he had to stop at the desk to ask Wendy to tell Richard that Sergeant Clark wanted to see him. Janet had been close enough to overhear, and of course, she and Wendy must have been talking things over ever since we went into the room. So she knew he was a cop. And between the two of 'em, even Wendy and Janet must have had brains enough to realize that Sergeant Clark wouldn't be escorting me into Richard's office to sell tickets to the policemen's ball. So Janet was rather flustered.

"Janet," Richard said abruptly. "This is Sergeant Clark. He'd like to ask you a few questions."

Janet went white as a sheet. Answering questions was not one of her strong suits. She probably had trouble answering her boyfriend's questions about where she'd like to go out to eat. So answering a police sergeant's questions was bound to throw her a little.

"Well, now," Sergeant Clark said. "Miss?..."

"Fishbein," Janet said, and then tittered slightly, either because her name struck her as funny or out of relief at getting the first question right.

"Miss Fishbein," Sergeant Clark said. "Were you on the switchboard this morning?"

That threw her for a loop. Even a mind as slow as Janet's had to have figured this had something to do with yesterday's murder, seeing as how she didn't know about today's murder.

She gawked. "This morning?" she said.

"Yes, this morning. Were you on the switchboard?"

"Of course," she said. "Wendy and I are always on the switchboard."

She punctuated the remark by looking at Sergeant Clark as if he were an idiot for not knowing that.

"I see," Sergeant Clark said. "And did you take a call from a Gerald Finklestein?"

Janet's jaw dropped open. I have to admit the girl had more brains than I gave her credit for, because she made the connection.

"My god," she said incredulously. "Is he dead, too?"

12.

Eventually Sergeant Clark got it all sorted out.

Janet had, indeed, taken the call from Hard-sell Finkles-tein.

However, Wendy had taken the call from Winston Bishop.

Therefore, it was my privilege and pleasure to witness both of those fair damsels submitting to the interrogation of Sergeant Clark.

I can't say it was the worst time I'd had all day. Looking at Hard-sell Finklestein's body kind of edged it out. Actu-ally, if I hadn't been in such deep shit, and therefore not in the best of moods, I actually might have enjoyed it, cause it was rather funny. Watching Sergeant Clark try to pin down Wendy and Janet on the time element was sort of like watching a man try to pick up a ball of mercury with chop-sticks.

From Janet, the best he could get was this: The phone call from Finklestein was after she came to work, not before, which put it after nine A.M. It was before she went to lunch and not after or during, which put it before noon.

Aside from that, Sergeant Clark had to extrapolate. He had Janet's virtuous assurance that she had beeped me as soon as the case came in. He had my unsubstantiated word that I had called in in response to that beep at approximately ten-thirty. He had the benefit of his own knowledge that he had called Rosenberg and Stone looking for me shortly after ten-thirty. He had Janet's solemn hyperbole that she had beeped me the instant she got his call, and my corroboration that that beep had come shortly after I had called the office to get the Hard-sell Finklestein assignment.

Working from the other end, he had the fact that the Tessie the Tumbler case had to have come in first, since I was there signing it up when I was beeped about Finklestein, assuming he was willing to take my unsubstantiated word for that. Knowing Sergeant Clark, I figured he wouldn't. I figured Tessie the Tumbler was due for a grilling. But letting that pass, he had the fact that apparently she had called for an appointment, and one had been duly given.

Unfortunately, Tessie the Tumbler's call had been handled by Wendy, which was too bad, since, had it been Janet, she might have been able to remember which call came in first. As it was, Wendy's best recollection was this: the call had been after she came to work, and before she left for lunch, which pinpointed it between nine A.M. and one P.M.

Nonetheless, barring certain reservations, and pending certain witnesses still to be interviewed, I'm sure even a meticulous man such as Sergeant Clark would have been willing to venture to say that the call from Hard-sell Finklestein had probably come in between ten and ten-thirty.

With regard to the call from Winston Bishop, even less was known. The lapse of an additional twenty-four hours had muddled the otherwise vivid memories of both Wendy and Janet. A severe jogging led to the conclusion that, of the calls from Winston Bishop and Jesus Pagan, Wendy had taken one and Janet the other, though neither was quite sure which was which.

Sergeant Clark found this less than conclusive.

He also found he had only my unsubstantiated word for what had happened there.

I suggested that he apply to Sam Gravston, who had rejected the Winston Bishop job before it was offered to me. That jogged my memory to recollect that Sam Gravston had also rejected the Hard-sell Finklestein case, which jogged Janet's memory to recollect that she had, indeed, offered Sam the case before offering it to me, making her instantaneous beeping of me an even more extraordinary feat. Or maybe it was after Sergeant Clark's call that she beeped me instantaneously—by that time my own recollection was getting pretty muddled.

As I'd feared, Sergeant Clark also inquired about the Darryl Jackson phone call. I had hoped that that call had been taken by the long-departed Cheryl, but just my luck, Wendy had taken it. However, with the passage of a year's time, it was all Wendy could do to remember that she had taken the call at all, even with the gentleman in question having been murdered. The only detail that seemed to have stuck in her mind was the fact that at one point in the inquiry she had been strip-searched, a fact for which she had still not forgiven me. (Please don't get the wrong idea—I did not strip-search her, a matron did, but she blamed me for it.)

Eventually Wendy and Janet were dispensed with, and the conversation returned to some semblance of sanity.

"There we are," Clark said, and I had to admire him for it. After all that, I couldn't imagine where we were. "Dispensing with the Darryl Jackson case for a moment,"—I practically applauded—"let's look at the other two cases. In each case a man calls your office and is immediately killed. Strangled. The men have no connection with each other whatsoever, and I doubt if one can ever be established. Except for the fact they called your office. This fact, and this fact alone, leads to the inescapable conclusion that they were both killed by the same person and that we are dealing with a serial killer. No other explanation seems possible."

"I have one," I said.

Sergeant Clark stared at me.

So did Richard.

"You do?" Sergeant Clark said.

"Yes, I do."

Sergeant Clark favored me with his thin smile. "You're saying you have a logical explanation—barring, of course, coincidence—that accounts for these two murders being identical and *not* being the result of a serial killer?"

"Yes, I do," I said.

Sergeant Clark looked at me expectantly.

I said nothing. Fuck him. If he could play that game, with, "I have a problem," I could play it, too. He could damn well ask me.

He did.

"Well, what is your explanation?"

"Copycat crime."

He looked at me. "What?"

"Copycat crime," I said. "Don't tell me you've never heard of it. If the evening news is to be believed, the police use that expression all the time."

"That's right," Richard said. "Like when they were throwing rocks at cars."

"Exactly," I said. "You recall when someone threw a rock on a car from an overpass on the West Side Highway? Then there were several similar incidents in the Bronx? It was stated that it wss not known if these incidents were the work of the same people or if they were copycat crimes committed by various people reacting to the media coverage."

"Yes, yes," Sergeant Clark said impatiently. "I know what copycat crimes are. I fail to see how it has any relevance in the present case."

"Then perhaps you haven't read today's *Post*," I said.

I opened my briefcase and pulled it out. I flipped the page open and handed it to him.

"You'll find the whole thing in here, treated as a joke. Rosenberg and Stone are mentioned by name. I am also mentioned, in a manner that falls just short of being libelous. Which is one of the many reasons why I am not in a particularly good mood."

Sergeant Clark read the article and frowned.

"Now," I said, pointing to the article, "it is just this sort of publicity, done in a slightly humorous vein, that inspires copycat crimes. Some punk reads this and says, "Hey, that's really funny, man, listen to this." And someone else says, "Hey, I happen to know someone who's callin' those guys. Wouldn't it be a goof, if ...""

Sergeant Clark looked at me and shook his head. "I see your point," he said, "but I find that incredibly farfetched."

"No fair," I told him. "The fact that it's happened *at all* is farfetched. The minute you accept the supposition that someone is running around bumping off Rosenberg and Stone clients, any solution you come up with is going to defy plausibility."

"I still find it hard to buy," Clark said. "The copycat killer thing. For someone to strangle someone because he saw it written up in the paper and thought it would be fun, he would have to be out of his mind."

71

"Whereas your serial killer is perfectly sane," I said sarcastically.

"Don't get huffy about it," Clark said. "You have your theory. I've taken note of your theory. I'm not rejecting it out of hand. I'm just telling you where it rates in my estimation."

"So you're not going to act on it."

"I didn't say that," Clark said. He picked up the telephone receiver on Richard's desk. "If I might use your phone," he said. It was a formality, not a question, for he was already punching in the number. "Hanson, Clark. I want a media blackout on the Gerald Finklestein case. You can give out his name and the fact that he was killed, nothing else. In particular, I want no mention of Rosenberg and Stone, no mention that he had consulted a law firm at all and no mention of the fact that he had been injured. Got that?...I know there's another county involved. I didn't ask you how hard it was gonna be, I just want it done."

Clark hung up the phone and turned back to us. He didn't say, "There, are you satisfied?", but he might as well have.

"Now," he went on, as if there had been no interruption, "as I've said, there are a number of possibilities. I would now like to consider the possibility that there is a serial killer. In the event that that is true, I see only two connections." He turned to Richard. "One, of course, is Rosenberg and Stone." He turned to me. "The other, of course, is you."

I said nothing.

"Or, in other words," Clark said, "the reason these people are being killed is, one, because they called Rosenberg and Stone, or, two, because they were visited by Stanley Hastings." He smiled the thin smile at me. "You realize, of course, that the second supposition would make you the killer."

"Of course," I said.

"I'd like to explore those possibilities," Sergeant Clark said. "To begin with, Mr. Rosenberg, I am in the process of obtaining a search warrant empowering me to go through your records. What I'll be looking for, of course, is a disgruntled client, someone who would have reason to have a grudge against you and your company. I will be looking in particular for some client whose case you lost, or whose case you refused to handle."

Before Richard could even respond to that, Sergeant Clark had swung around to me. "The second thing is, of course, you. Now one way to go about it would be to charge you with something and put you in jail. Then, if the crimes ceased, it would be a pretty good indication that you were guilty. But if another crime occurred, you'd be vindicated."

I said nothing. It was not a tactic this time. In the face of that, I could think of nothing to say.

"Because the crimes *will* continue," Clark said. "That much I'm sure of. Because, whether you believe it or not, what we are dealing with here is a serial killer. And a serial killer will not stop. Not until he's caught."

Clark took a breath. "But I'm not going to do that," he said. "Hold you in jail, I mean."

I was about to give the man credit for compassion, before he added, "Too inoffective. It doesn't cover all possibilities. What if you are not the murderer after all, but merely the catalyst? What if, for some reason, someone is killing clients upon which Stanley Hastings calls? You see what I mean?"

I shook my head. "I see what you mean, but—"

"In that case, we would have to look, not for someone who had a grudge against Rosenberg and Stone, but for someone who has a grudge against you. Can you think of any such person?"

"That's ridiculous," I said.

"As you have stated, the whole situation is ridiculous. Therefore, we must examine any possibility, no matter how ridiculous it might seem."

I considered. The only people I could think of who would have a grudge against me were in jail, or at least I thought they were. I made a note to check on it. Aside from that, I was stymied. Had I been a successful writer or actor, there might have been someone jealous enough to hold a grudge, some actor I'd aced out of a juicy role, or some writer who thought his talent greater than mine and my success undeserved. But being a failure on all fronts, I could inspire no envy.

Unless Frank Burke were jealous of the fact that I could handle signups and he couldn't, which in the first place, was utterly absurd, and in the second place, was utterly untrue, for if the truth be known, even after two years I'm sure I'm still just as scared as he is most of the time.

Anyone else?

Sure. The kid in high school I aced out of playing goalie on the soccer team nurses a grudge for twenty-five years, and reaps a hard-earned revenge.

My father-in-law, the renowned plastic-bag manufacturer, miffed at my refusal to enter the family business and my insistence upon pursuing a disreputable career in the arts, pays me back for forcing his cherished daughter to live with a nitwit.

I racked my brain and could only dredge up absurdity after absurdity.

"There's no one," I said.

"So you say," Clark said, "and it may well be true. But, as you have pointed out, since a serial killer is most likely insane, his motive may not be rational. At least not to us. It might be perfectly rational to him, though we would find it absurd. So we can't discount the possibility."

"Fine," I said. "I accept the possibility. Now what?"

"Now we begin eliminating possibilities," Clark said. "The first one I'd like to eliminate is the possibility that you are the murderer."

"I'd like that myself," I said.

"Good," Clark said. "Then I'm sure you'll have no objection to the arrangements."

"Arrangements?" I said.

Sergeant Clark turned to Richard. "I would like to have Mr. Hastings carry on business for you as usual. Alter nothing. Let him handle the cases he would normally get. No more, no less. I want him to simply go about his business and carry out his job."

"Fine," Richard said. "But what will that accomplish?"

"It will eliminate the possibility that he is the murderer."

"How will it do that?" I asked.

Sergeant Clark looked at me. "Because when the next murder occurs—and believe me, it *will* occur—it will exonerate you."

"Why?"

Sergeant Clark smiled the thin smile. "Because one of my detectives will be riding with you all the time."

I must say, much as I would have liked to have been cleared as a serial killer, I didn't like the idea.

Richard liked it even less. He didn't want cops sitting in on interviews and messing in his affairs. Hell, sometimes the people Richard was suing were cops. And some cases even involved alleged police brutality. No, Richard wasn't happy at all.

But there was no help for it. Without actually making it a threat, Sergeant Clark managed to convey the message that, if I didn't agree to this idea, he would have to adopt the less effective method of charging me with something and locking me up in jail. Eventually he prevailed, and eventually he left.

Leaving Richard and me looking at each other like two lost souls in a Theatre of the Absurd play. One about people's inability to communicate. After Sergeant Clark's exhaustive interview, there was nothing much left to say. Richard and I both agreed that, one way or anther, the killings had to stop, but that was about it.

We sat in silence for a while. Finally Richard sighed, leaned back in his chair, scratched his head and put the whole thing in perspective.

"Something like this," he said judiciously, "could be bad for business."

B.

I parked my car on 103rd Street, on the bad side of course, so I could get out in the morning, and walked up West End Avenue toward home. It was supper time, and the mild September night air was filled with oriental men bicycling in all directions. In our neighborhood, a new Chinese or Japanese restaurant seems to open up every week, and all of them seem to be doing well. No one cooks anymore. Alice and I are guilty of ordering out about twice a week, which is probably less than average.

I went into my building and rode up in the elevator. I acknowledged to Jerry, the young elevator man, one more time that the Mets had, indeed, beaten the Red Sox in the World Series.

I got off at my floor and unlocked my front door.

I expected to find my son, Tommie, waiting for me in the foyer, demanding to play baseball, which I was in no mood to do. But it was after six, so he was in the living room watching reruns of "The Monkees" on Nickelodeon.

Alice emerged from the kitchen.

"It's late and you didn't call. What's wrong?"

I took her in my arms and hugged her. I needed a hug.

"It happened again," I said.

She pulled back and stared at me. "Sam got *another* TV show?"

I laughed. I couldn't help it. "No," I said. "There was another murder."

We sat in the kitchen, eating an incredibly good veal stew, and in between mouthfuls, I told her the whole story.

Alice stared at me. "That's incredible."

"Yes," I said. "Everyone seems to agree on that."

"But you're not involved. Not really. And this Sergeant Clark seems to have everything in hand."

I looked at her. "What?"

"Well, he seems to have a pretty good grasp of the whole situation."

I stared at her. "Were you listening to me? Did you hear what I just said. That man thinks the Darryl Jackson case is part of the series."

Alice shrugged. "Yes, but aside from that—"

"Aside from that, Mrs. Lincoln, what did you think of the play?" I said. "This is not a tiny error in judgment. This is a major goof. This is a man flying in the face of logic, and going off on a tangent that's going to lead in the wrong direction."

"But you said he was considering all possibilities."

"Yes, but—"

"Then soon he'll eliminate it as a possibility. He sounds like a reasonable man."

That was too much. "A reasonable man. You have no idea. You don't know what you're talking about."

"No, I just know what you told me. And from what you told me, he sounds very reasonable. Isn't the first thing he's doing trying to exonerate you?"

"Yes, but—"

"There you are."

I shook my head to clear it. My wife has many qualities, and one of them is the ability to make me feel like a total idiot on any given occasion on any given subject. Once again, she was reducing my brain to Jell-o.

"There I am," I said. "Didn't you hear me? The man thinks I'm a murderer."

My wife smiled at me reasonably, which I find devilishly annoying. "He doesn't know you," she said. "Why shouldn't he suspect you of the crime? And he doesn't really suspect you."

"He's having a cop ride along and nursemaid me."

"In order to clear you."

"Yes, but—"

"But nothing," Alice said. "I've heard everything you told me. What's so bad about it?"

I shook my head. "Jesus Christ. There's no way to make you understand. If you just met the man, and talked to him for a moment—"

"Ah!" Alice said. "Now we come to it. You don't *like* him."

"Well, now—"

"Oh, no," Alice said. "That's it. You don't like him. You don't have to protest. There's no reason why you should. You don't have to like everyone. So, you don't like the man, right?"

"Well..."

"Do you?"

"No."

Alice smiled prettily, as she always does when she wins a point. "There you are. You can go on and on about his methods and his abilities and all that, but what it comes down to, basically, is, you don't like him. He irritates you.

He grates on you. You don't like him, so you don't like anything that he does."

I felt that was putting it a little strongly. I also felt it wasn't entirely fair. I also felt I didn't have a leg to stand on in terms of the argument. So I kept quiet.

However, another of Alice's traits is, she doesn't stop arguing just because she's already won.

"See, he irritates you so much because you know he's wrong, you know you're smarter than he is and what you'd really love to do is solve these murders before he does and show him up."

She may have been a little right. Just a little. It's hard to be objective in a situation like that. I mean, I wouldn't go as far as all that, but maybe there was a grain of truth in the idea that maybe somewhere in the back of my mind was the vague notion that it sure would be nice to watch Sergeant Clark eat his words.

I sat there, thinking about it. Thought about solving those murders. Thought about walking into the police station with the cases all wrapped up, turning the killers over to a bewildered Sergeant Clark and saying, "Here, schmuck. Here's what really happened." I had to admit it was a pleasant thought.

From the living room, filtered in the strains of the Monkees, singing "Daydream Believer."

14.

It wasn't that bad.

For one thing, the officer was Detective Walker. I met him the next morning at the East Side Day School when I dropped Tommie off for school. Tommie never knew it. There was no sign of Walker until Tommie had gotten out of the car and gone in the front door. The moment the door closed, Detective Walker materialized out of nowhere and slid into the front seat.

"All right," he said. "Let's go."

The question, of course, was, go where? The thing is, aside from signups, I have no fixed schedule. I make up my own. I have pending photo assignments, and when I get a chance, I knock 'em off. Generally what I do is, I do what I feel like. It doesn't matter.

But suddenly it did. I'd been instructed to do what I normally did. Which is like saying, "Don't think of an elephant." Suddenly, subconscious thought became conscious thought. What would I *normally do?*

The thing was, when Walker said, "Let's go," I felt the

way you do when someone shoves a microphone in your face and you think you have to say something.

I immediately started thinking, and suddenly, something that had always been incredibly easy, choosing which case to do next, became incredibly hard. Suddenly it seemed like a momentous decision. Which case should I choose with this cop watching me, and does it make a difference?

I realized that was utter rubbish. I could work on whatever I wanted, and it couldn't possibly matter. I knew that intellectually, but that didn't help me at all. I felt terribly on the spot.

I could pinpoint the feeling just fine; it was one that was left over from my old acting days.

I had stage fright.

Which was ridiculous, but true. A cop, a homicide detective, was about to observe me in my role as a private detective, or ambulance chaser, or what you will, and I felt foolish as hell.

What saved me, after that flash of paranoia, was realizing what was really going on. What was really going on—aside from the fact a bizarre string of murders had occurred, of which I was prime suspect, but in which I was not involved and would soon be cleared—was I was a working stiff with a wife and kid to feed, who hadn't been making any money lately, what with taking time out finding dead bodies, and who needed hours on the clock.

I popped open my briefcase and pulled out my assignment sheets. The three photo assignments I'd had to postpone were still pending.

"All right," I said. "Let's go to the Bronx."

"Fine," he said. "Let's grab some coffee and doughnuts on the way."

"Great," I said.

I headed up Madison Avenue, pulled in at a coffee shop and Walker hopped out and went in.

It was nice.

I have to explain. Ordinarily, I couldn't have stopped for coffee and doughnuts. Not that I don't have the time—as I said, I make my own schedule. I simply couldn't have parked. Because, while parking on the West Side of Manhattan is hard, parking on the East Side is impossible. At least as far down as the Eighties, anyway. You just don't do it. There's no legal place to park, the meter maids are quick as greased lightning, the tow trucks materialize from nowhere and if you blink your car is gone. It's so bad, when I get beeped near Tommie's school, I drive out of the neighborhood before I risk pulling into a pay phone and calling the office.

But I had Walker. And I could sit in my car while he ran in. What a luxury. See, the thing about ambulance chasing is, it's a lonely business. You drive around by yourself all day, and the only people you see are the occasional clients. Now that's great for someone like me who is supposed to be thinking about what he wants to write while he's driving, but the thing is, I rarely do, and I'm often bored.

But now I had a partner. And his stopping for coffee and doughnuts was so stereotypical it reminded me who he was. A cop. I was partnered with a cop, and my partner was grabbing the doughnuts, and then we were gonna cruise on up to the Bronx and kick some ass. Son of a bitch. Here we were, the Hill Street Blues. Hill and Renko. But no, they're uniformed cops, and Walker was plain-clothes. All right, we're Larue and Washington. And as soon as Washington gets back with the coffee I got this scheme to lay on him about how we can make a bundle on the side, backin' this friend of my brother-in-law's who's startin' a CD plant, not to mention a terrific practical joke to play on Belker.

Walker got back in the car, and pulled out the coffee and doughnuts. I wondered if he'd had to pay for them, with all you keep reading about policeman's perks. I figured the thought was uncharitable, and accepted my coffee with good grace. It wasn't half bad.

I pulled out and headed for the Bronx.

The address I wanted was on Plimpton, which is in that no-man's land up near the bridge where the number you're looking for can be on either side of the Cross Bronx Expressway, and getting from one side to the other's a bitch. I could recall getting dorked by one-way streets that didn't go through. And with Walker, who undoubtedly knew the city like the back of his hand, sitting next to me, I didn't want that to happen.

I got lucky. The street was one-way the right way. The number I wanted was on the near side of the Cross Bronx. I pulled up in front of the dilapidated brownstone with a feeling of relief.

I left Walker sitting in the car, hopped out and shot a roll of film of the front steps, of which the second step from the top was badly cracked.

I hopped back in the car, feeling pretty good.

"What was that all about?" Walker asked, as I whipped out my paysheet and made notation of the time and mileage.

"A guy fell on those steps," I said. "I'm taking the accident pictures. See the cracked step?"

Walker pointed to the fact sheet for the assignment.

"According to this," he said, "the guy fell last February on those steps due to ice and snow."

"That's true," I said, "but the cracked step is a contributing factor. Had the step not been cracked, the ice and snow might not have built up on it, and the crack itself may have contributed to the injury."

Walker merely grunted.

I could feel my self-esteem oozing away. I realized my initial fear was justified. It was going to be no fun chasing ambulances in front of a homicide cop.

My next assignment was on Barnes Avenue. I pulled out the Hagstrom map. I figured having to consult the map probably dropped me a few notches in Walker's estimation, too, but there was no help for it. I found the address, started the car and pulled out.

And immediately got beeped.

Well, no problem with a cop in the car. I didn't even need a parking space. I spotted a pay phone on the corner and pulled in next to a fire plug.

"Gotta call the office," I said.

"You don't have a car phone?" Walker said.

I realized any resemblance between me and a Hill Street Blues detective was entirely coincidental, and not to be inferred.

"No," I said, and got out.

I called the office. Wendy/Janet answered.

"That was quick," she said.

"I believe in service," I told her. "What's up?"

"I have a new case for you," she said. "It just came in."

"Whereabouts?" I asked.

"West 150th street, Manhattan."

Jesus. Not again.

"What about Sam?" I said.

"Sam's taking the morning off. He got a callback for that TV series, and ..."

I gave up. I took down the info and got back in the car.

And panicked again.

I have to explain. See, the West 150s in Manhattan are an iffy proposition. For instance, on West 150th Street I could give you two street numbers that would appear to be next door to each other. They're not. They're actually miles apart. The reason is, Manhattan at that point has an upper and lower level, and the only way to get from one to the other is to go way out around by the 155th Street Bridge.

I yanked out the Hagstrom map. The number I wanted was right on the borderline. A toss-up. If I got it wrong I'd be fucked, and I'd be driving around for an hour, trying to find the address, and Walker would think I was a total moron.

"What's the problem?" Walker said.

"I gotta go to West 150th Street, and I'm not sure whether the number's up or down."

I expected some scathing retort, but Walker just said, "Oh yeah, I can never figure that out myself."

I realized the guy was a human being. I also realized he'd been pretty nice when he'd taken my statement that day.

"What are we going there for?" Walker asked.

I consulted my notebook. "A new case came in," I said. "A Diane Johnson fell on a city bus and broke her arm."

"Fine," Walker said. "That's what I'm here for."

I blinked. And I felt once again, as I often do, like a total asshole.

Yes, that was what Walker was here for. And that was what we were doing. And I'd been so self-conscious and so uptight about the fact that he was observing me in the performance of my job, that I'd completely lost sight of it.

Two people had been murdered. This was not a case of observe Stanley Hastings and make value judgments on his life and work. This was a murder case. And bizarre as the whole thing might be, it was very, very real.

I stopped thinking about myself for a moment and started thinking about someone else.

I thought about Diane Johnson.

I wondered whether Diane Johnson had been strangled.

15.

She hadn't.

Diane Johnson was alive and kicking when we got there. In fact, very much so. Diane Johnson turned out to be a feisty black woman of about twenty-five who was righteously indignant at the bus driver, who had failed to get close enough to the curb on Eighth Avenue for her to have descended safely from the steps.

Detective Walker, whom I had introduced as my assistant, interrupted her tirade long enough to inquire if he could use the phone. I felt a chill when I realized his purpose was to report in that Diane Johnson was, in fact, still alive.

By the time he'd returned from the kitchen, where the phone was located, I had taken down all the pertinent facts about the bus mishap, and had moved up to the top of the form to take down Diane Johnson's personal data.

"Married or single?" I asked.

"Single," she said.

Which made me hate to ask the next question. Which

was, of course, "Do you have any children?" It was a relevant question. You have to know who a client's dependents and next of kin are, in case the client should die before the action is settled. And a mother with dependent children can get extra compensation for child care. In point of fact, at least half of Richard's single clients had children. So there was nothing unusual about asking.

But with Walker sitting there, being black, and the client being black, I somehow felt that asking the question would brand me as a hard-line racist who immediately assumed that any unmarried black woman would be likely to have a few children.

But I had to ask, so I did.

Walker never blinked. And it turned out Diane Johnson did indeed have two children, ages five and seven. I took their names, birth dates and Social Security numbers.

I finished up the fact sheet. Then I had Diane Johnson sign the hospital release forms to get her medical records; an assignment to the hospital, assuring them that if we got a settlement, they would be paid, so that they would give us the records without us having to subpoena them; and a Request for Aided Accident form, to get the police report of the accident.

Then I hit her with the biggie: the retainer. It empowered Richard Rosenberg to act in her behalf, and in the event he got a settlement, to retain one third of it, after first recouping his expenses.

She signed it without reading it, which was not unusual. Most of my clients do. I always give them the retainer last, so by the time they get to it they've already signed half a dozen papers, and it's just another form. That's not to say they shouldn't sign it, or that they're getting rooked, or anything of the sort. The retainer is a standard form that all attorneys use, the percentage is always the same, they can't do better elsewhere and if they want to get any money, they have to sign.

But still, I always feel a pang of guilt when they sign it without reading it. It's as if I've sold them something, which, in a way, I have.

I gathered up the forms, took pictures of her broken arm and Walker and I got out of there.

I was glad to have Walker with me. Diane Johnson lived in a fifth-floor walk-up in a particularly undesirable building. It was nice having a cop along.

As if he read my mind, Walker said, "That's one thing I like about police work. I would sure hate going into some of these places alone."

God, the guy was human. It occurred to me he was wearing a gun, too.

We left the building and got in the car.

"Nice lady," I said.

"Yeah," he said. "And alive, too."

I grinned at that, pulled out and headed back toward the Bronx.

By now I had calmed down enough to start thinking like a human being instead of an uptight schmuck. And I found it was only natural to start discussing what any normal person would have been discussing to begin with.

"Well," I said. "What do you think?"

"What do you mean?" Walker said.

"About the murders. You think it's gonna happen again?"

"Sergeant Clark seems to think so," Walker said.

That sounded like an opening to me. I went for it. "I'm not entirely sure that Sergeant Clark knows what he's doing," I said.

That certainly gave Walker all the opening he needed. But he merely pursed his lips and said, "Clark's a good man."

Frankly, I was getting pretty sick of hearing that. First MacAullif, then my wife, and now Walker. In Walker's case, I wondered if he was really sincere. It occurred to me, it would not be politic for a detective to speak ill of his sergeant. Particularly to a murder suspect.

"Is that right?" I said. "Well, I have a few problems with his theories."

Walker seemed perfectly willing to talk theory. "Oh yeah," he said. "And what's that?"

"Well, his theory is the killer is some disgruntled client who's got it in for Richard."

"Yeah?" Walker said.

"It doesn't hold water," I said. "It seems like it's entirely off on the wrong track."

"Why do you say that?"

"It's illogical."

"What's illogical about it?"

"It's farfetched."

"That I'll grant. But the whole thing's farfetched, so that argument's no good."

"But it doesn't make sense," I said. "If someone had a grudge against Richard, they wouldn't kill his clients, they'd kill him."

"That's a thought," Walker conceded. "And it's one that might well occur to the murderer. However, with cops in his office going over his books, it would be difficult. And we're having him escorted to and from work."

I looked at him. "Then you've thought of that?"

"Of course," he said. "We have to cover all possibilities. It's entirely possible that if someone really does have a grudge against Richard Rosenberg, the only reason they haven't killed him is because he's inaccessible, whereas his clients are not." Walker shook his head. "Personally, I don't hold much with that theory. I think Rosenberg's safe. I think whoever's killing clients is killing clients not because he can't get to Rosenberg but because he wants to kill Rosenberg's clients. Which would indicate that the next victim would be, not Mr. Rosenberg, but a client."

"So you're saying you think there'll be another killing too?"

"Yes, I do."

"Just because Sergeant Clark says so?"

"No," Walker said. "Clark and I have our own opinions. They don't always coincide. But in this case, they do."

"I see," I said.

"So, go on," Walker said. "Tell me why you think this theory's absurd."

"Well," I said. "I can give you one simple reason. It couldn't be done. It's physically impossible. It couldn't have happened that way."

"Oh? What couldn't have happened that way?"

"Someone with a grudge against Richard Rosenberg could not be going around killing off clients as soon as they call in for appointments."

"Why not?"

"Because, how would he know?"

"Know what?"

"That they were calling in," I said. "Now look, taking the bull by the horns here, much as I hate to say it, it makes much more sense that *I* killed those people than a disgruntled client did. Because I have the opportunity. That's what you look for, right? Motive, method and opportunity. Well opportunity is the big stumbling block here. I could have done it, because I got the calls giving me those people's names and addresses and telling me they called in. This phantom serial killer we're envisioning—this enraged former client, or whatever—how would he have known? There was no way he could have found out that these people had just called Rosenberg and Stone. Those murders happened right after the calls.

"This is your theory, yours and Sergeant Clark's. So you tell me. How could the murderer have possibly done it?"

"Simple," Walker said.

I gawked at him. He smiled.

"See," he said, "your problem is you're not a cop, so you don't think like a cop. Somebody tells you something and you believe it. You take note of it and base your theories on it.

"Now Clark and I are cops. Someone tells us something, the first thing we do is discount half of it. Then look at the other half with extreme skepticism."

I was getting tired of being lectured to. "And what the hell does that mean?"

"In this case, you say, 'How could the murderer have known that those people were going to call Rosenberg and Stone? He couldn't have, therefore he couldn't have killed 'em.' Right?"

"Right."

"In saying that, you're going on the unsubstantiated word of what people have told you."

"What do you mean?"

"You just told me both of the murdered clients called Rosenberg and Stone. How do you know that? You know that because two ditsy secretaries, whose accuracy is very much in question on almost any subject, told you so. But you buy it as fact. Mr. Bishop and Mr. Finklestein called for appointments. You're taking those girls' word for that. And what do they know? At best, they know that a voice on the telephone told them such and such a person wanted an appointment. Is this identifying Mr. Bishop and Mr. Finklestein? Those girls never met them before in their lives, and never heard their voices."

I looked at him. "You mean?..."

"Of course I do," Walker said. "You ask me how the killer could have done it. Very simple. All he had to do was go out, find someone with a broken arm or leg, follow them home, kill them and call Rosenberg and Stone and ask for an appointment."

Jesus Christ. It *was* simple. So simple. And I hadn't even thought of it. And what made it worse was, in the Darryl Jackson case, I'd *used* a bogus phone call in just that way. And I *still* hadn't thought of it.

But Walker was right. It *could* happen. It *had* happened.

I felt a sudden chill as I realized that meant it could happen again.

My beeper went off.

16.

This time I was nervous calling in.

I'd been in the middle of the 155th Street Bridge when the beeper went off. I was cruising along, talking to Walker about the case and then, bam! Suddenly I wanted to get there. If I'd have had a siren, I'd have used it. I gave it the gas, bobbed and weaved, aced out a taxi, sped off the bridge and pulled up by a bank of pay phones under the train trestle by Yankee Stadium.

I hopped out and called the office.

Wendy/Janet answered the phone.

"Rosenberg and Stone."

I was in no mood for the Wendy/Janet bit. For once, I wanted to know who I was talking to.

"This is Stanley," I said. "Who is this?"

"It's Wendy, of course," she said. She sounded offended. "Don't you know my voice by now?"

I didn't want to go into that.

"Is this a new case?" I said.

"That's right. Just came in."

"O.K. Let me have it."

She did. The client's name was Jake Odell. He'd fallen on the sidewalk and broken his leg. He lived on 126th Street between Lenox Avenue and Adam Clayton Powell. He wanted an investigator to come right over.

"What's his phone number?" I asked.

"Client has no phone," Wendy said.

"Then how'd he call in?" I demanded.

"What?" Wendy said incredulously.

It *was* a stupid question. Many of our clients had no phone. They'd call from a pay phone on the corner, or they'd have some friend call in, or whatever. It made no difference, and I'd never thought about it before. But I was sure thinking about it now.

"You said he's home now, waiting for me, and you also said he has no phone. So did he call in, or did a friend call for him?"

"He did."

"You sure?"

"Sure, I'm sure."

"How do you know?"

"He told me so," she cried in exasperation.

I realized Wendy thought I was an idiot. I also realized how right Walker was about on what flimsy grounds I had been basing my theories.

"Well, let's double check the address," I said.

We did, and this time Wendy had gotten it right. At least, she'd given it to me right. Whether she'd gotten it right from Jake Odell, or whoever the hell had called in, was another matter.

I slammed the phone down, hopped in the car and pulled out.

"What's the hurry?" Walker asked.

"A new case," I told him. "Jake Odell. 126th, between Lenox and Adam Clayton Powell."

"So?"

"That's Harlem."

Walker looked at me. "I thought your theory was that Harlem was a coincidence and had nothing to do with it."

"It is. It is," I said. "I just don't like it. After what you just told me, any new case makes me nervous."

"Case just come in?" Walker asked.

"That's right."

"Client have a phone?"

"No."

"Too bad."

"Why? You'd stop and call him?"

"No. But if the gentleman's murdered, and the client had a phone, it would be interesting to find out if the call to Rosenberg and Stone came from that phone or from somewhere else."

I looked at him. "You're tracing the calls?"

"Of course we're tracing the calls."

"And tapping the phones?"

"I didn't say that."

"But you are, aren't you?"

"It would be nice to have a voiceprint of the murderer, don't you think?"

"It certainly would."

"Well," Walker said, "if Odell is dead, we probably will."

It occurred to me, if it came to that, having a voiceprint of the murderer probably wouldn't mean that much to Jake Odell. I didn't know Jake Odell, but I must say I felt rather anxious about his safety.

I went back over the 155th Street Bridge and worked my way down into Harlem.

The address was a project. As I've said, projects make me nervous. This probably marked the first time I'd gone into one when I wasn't concerned with my own safety. For one thing, I had Walker with me. For another thing, I was preoccupied with my concern for the safety of Jake Odell.

The apartment number was *8H*. The project had odd/even elevators, the designer of which has to get the Dumb-Shit-of-the-Year award. Those elevators are so slow and infuriating that, no matter what floor people are going to, when an elevator arrives, everyone piles in. As a result, the elevator has to stop at floors people aren't even going to, and thus makes almost as many stops as if it had gone to every floor in the first place. The added bonus is that people have to use the dimly lit stairwells to get where they are going, and sometimes they fall in them, and then I have to come and see them in their nice projects so these people can sue the city for building them in the first place.

In this instance, as so often happens, one elevator was broken, and as it was the even one, Walker and I rumbled up to the ninth floor in the odd, then walked down to the eighth floor.

Where we played find the apartment. Walker found *D* and I found *A* and we took our bearings from that and counted along till we got to *H*.

I banged on the door with no result. No answer. No sound of footsteps. Nothing.

I had a terrible sense of déjà vu. I also had a terrible sense of dread.

Jesus Christ. Not again.

I tried the doorknob. It turned easily and clicked open.

I looked at Walker.

He looked at me.

We bolted through the door.

It was a large apartment, and we did it fast. Kitchen. Dining room. Living room. No results, but none expected. It wouldn't be there.

The hallway to the bedrooms. As we went down it I noticed Walker had his gun out. I hadn't seen him pull it, but it was there, and frankly, I was glad.

I let him lead, but I was right behind. Like glue.

First bedroom. Empty.

Second bedroom. Empty.

One more to go.

Walker slithered in, gun first, flat against the wall. I came in behind him low and flattened against the wall too. I was scared as hell, but I wasn't going to miss it.

No sign. The closet checked out. Even under the bed.

That left only one place. The hall bathroom.

I had a premonition. It was like in the movies. They kill them, then prop them on the john. We'd find a large black man with a cast on his leg, strangled and sitting on the toilet.

The door was shut. Walker approached it from the side, flattened against the wall. He turned the knob, jerked it open. He came around fast, with me right behind.

He was sitting there, just as I'd envisioned. A large black man with a cast on his leg.

Only he hadn't been strangled, his pants were around his ankles and he looked up at the two men in suits, one of whom was holding a gun on him, and said, understandably enough, "Who the fuck are you?"

17.

I count it to my credit as a seasoned, professional ambulance chaser that after all that Jake Odell still signed the retainer. It occurred to me to ask Richard for a bonus on the case. After all, signing a client at gunpoint ought to be considered something special. But then it occurred to me I hadn't gotten a bonus when I'd served the divorce papers on the guy who was holding a gun on me, so I didn't bother to bring it up.

I stopped by Richard's office at the end of the day's work. That wasn't normal procedure—I usually stop in biweekly to turn in my cases—but I didn't care. I wanted to see what was going on. Besides, we'd never worked out where I was gonna drop off Detective Walker, and Richard's office seemed as good a place as any. Particularly since there were two cops there already, the ones going over Richard's books.

The atmosphere in Richard's office was somewhat less than jovial and somewhat brighter than funereal. Wendy favored me with a cold look, my punishment for not having recognized her voice. I felt that was being a little hard on a person who even has trouble recognizing people's faces, but I let it go.

Janet was just as cold. I hadn't insulted her that I knew of, though maybe she felt my not recognizing Wendy reflected on her as well, which, indeed, it did.

Jack and Alan worked in somber silence. They were working on the files, and the cops were working on the files, and I think somehow they had put two and two together and figured out that meant *they* had done something wrong. Either that, or they had finally figured out just how little they were getting paid. At any rate, they were glum.

Even the irrepressible Sam Gravston did not look happy. He was seated at a desk in the back of the office, and I wondered what he was doing there. Then I saw he was ID-ing photos, and realized this was his day to turn in assignments. Which meant my day was next week.

I left Walker jawing with the other two officers and went over to talk to Sam.

"How's it going?" I said.

He seemed preoccupied. He almost didn't hear me. Then he looked up.

"Oh, hi," he said.

"How did your audition go?" I asked him.

I had a feeling it hadn't gone well, and perhaps there was a bit of malice in my asking. If so, it vanished when I saw his reaction. He frowned and rubbed his forehead.

"I don't know. I don't know," he said. He looked up at me. "I don't know if they like me. I just don't know. I'm so afraid I won't get it, you know?"

I knew. I knew damn well. I felt compassion for him then. I realized it was a horrible way to feel—lose the part and I'll like you.

"Look," Sam said. "I'm sorry this is all happening at

once. The auditions, I mean. You're really getting loaded up with the shit, huh?"

"Not that bad," I said.

"What came in today?"

"Five signups."

His jaw dropped. "Five? And Frank's gone, right?"

"Since yesterday," I told him.

"You did five signups by yourself?"

I jerked my thumb over my shoulder. "No, I had a cop helping me."

"No, I mean—"

"Yeah, I did five," I said. "It's all right. I need the money."

"Don't we all," Sam said.

"Did they tell you anything? At the audition, I mean."

"Yeah," Sam said flatly. "We'll call you."

The kiss of death.

"Maybe they will," I said.

Sam smiled ironically. "Yeah, sure," he said. "Well, tell you one thing. I'll be out with you tomorrow. I need the bucks, too."

The door to the inner office opened, and Richard Rosenberg appeared in it.

"Stanley," he hissed through clenched teeth.

I rolled my eyes for Sam's benefit. "Catch you later," I told him.

I went into Richard's office. He closed the door behind me, then wheeled on me as if the whole thing were all my fault.

"This has got to stop," he snapped.

"What?" I said.

Richard pointed to the door. "This! This!" he said. I could feel the energy level rising. "I have *cops* in my office. I have *cops* going through my files. I have *cops* following me to work. I have a *cop* riding around with one of my investigators. I have *cops* coming out my ears. I am sick to death of *cops*." He lowered his voice slightly. "I don't *like* cops. This has got to stop."

"Richard—"

"Don't Richard me. I am in a very bad mood."

"I hadn't noticed."

Richard's eyes narrowed. "You think it's funny? You know what those cops are doing? Those cops going through my files? They're looking for *failure*. They're looking for cases I *blew*." Richard shook his head and exhaled noisily. "It's humiliating. And it's unfair. You know what my success ratio is? It's incredible. It's over ninety-nine percent of the cases I take. Because I can judge 'em and pick 'em and choose 'em and weed 'em out. Ninety-nine percent. There's no lawyer in the city that can touch that." Richard jerked his thumb over his shoulder. "But those fucking cops in there are busting their humps to find one failure. Just one. And then they're gonna grab it, and hold it up, and point to it and say, 'Look. Rosenberg failed. We did it. We cracked the case.' And then they'll plaster it all over the papers and suddenly I won't be the lawyer with the ninety-nine percent success rate, I'll be the lawyer who fucked up and blew a case!"

"That's not going to happen," I said.

"Oh yeah," Richard demanded. "Why's that?"

"Because the cops aren't going to let out any publicity until they catch the murderer."

"Assuming they catch him."

"True. But until they do, they're not."

"But when they do, they'll fry me."

"No they won't. That's just because Sergeant Clark thinks the murderer is a disgruntled client. Personally, I think that's bullshit."

"Of course it's bullshit."

"Right. So when they catch the murderer, assuming they do, he won't be a disgruntled client. So there won't be any publicity about any case you blew. The cops aren't going to publicize the fact they had a bum theory that didn't pan out."

Richard thought that over. "That's right," he said eventually.

I couldn't believe *I* was the one calming *Richard* down. After all, *I* was the one who'd found the dead bodies. *I* was the one riding around with the cop. *I* was the one being pushed out front like a sacrificial lamb, the one blundering into the buildings just waiting for another grisly corpse to jump out at me.

"So you've got nothing to worry about," I said.

Richard bit his lip. "Yeah. Maybe. But business is going to suffer."

Jesus. What a prick. But then, if I had a business, I'd worry about it too.

"It hasn't so far," I told him. "I had five new cases today."

"You did?" Richard perked up a little. I realized he'd been so worked up about the cops in his office he hadn't even thought about the day's cases. Somehow that made me like him a little better.

"Yeah," I said. "So we're doing OK."

Richard considered that. He nodded.

"Could be worse," he said.

It was.

18.

Walker met me at Tommie's school again the next morning. Alice and I used to have a car pool with another couple from the neighborhood, but they'd moved away, and now we had to go it alone. Either that or fork over eleven hundred dollars for the bus. Not on my salary. I drove Tommie every morning, and Alice picked him up every afternoon.

"Morning," Walker said. "What's on for today?"

"More of the same," I told him. "Only it shouldn't be as bad as yesterday."

"What do you mean?" he asked.

"Five signups is a little much. Particularly spread out like that." (Besides the one in Harlem, we'd had two in Brooklyn, one in the Bronx, and one in Queens.)

"Today should be slow."

"How come?"

"Well, for one thing, Sam Gravston's working today. He'll handle half the load. For another, they'll group the assignments. If a new case comes in, they'll give it to the investigator in the area. So we won't be chasing around all over."

"OK. So what's first?"

"How about coffee and doughnuts?" I said.

Walker grinned. "Sounds good."

"My turn to buy," I said.

We got coffee and doughnuts, then, as no new cases had come in yet, headed out to the Bronx to shoot some photo assignments. It being the second day and all, Walker and I were old pals by now, and we were sipping coffee and eating doughnuts and having a grand old time.

"How old's your kid?" Walker asked.

"Six," I told him.

"What's his name?"

"Tommie."

Walker grinned. "Same as me. Thomas."

"Detective Thomas Walker," I said.

"That's right."

"You got any kids?"

Walker grinned and held up three fingers. "Two boys and a girl. Six, four and two."

"That's planning," I said.

"You could set your watch by it," Walker said.

"Does that mean another one's due?"

"Not on my salary," Walker said. "Maybe later on."

I caught the note in his voice. "You lookin' to make sergeant?"

"I'm lookin' to make lieutenant or captain."

He was grinning, but I could tell he really meant it. I had a feeling he had a pretty good shot, too.

We drove on up to the Bronx so I could shoot the steps of the subway station at Brook Avenue and East 138th Street. There was a parking spot right there, so I invited Walker to come with me, and he did. It was nice having a cop with me, 'cause the station was dark and deserted, and I hate whipping out my camera under those circumstances. Walker watched while I shot the northeast-corner stair.

"You'll pardon my asking," he said, "but what's wrong with these stairs?"

"Take a look at the garbage on 'em," I said.

"Yeah, but the client fell two months ago. This garbage wasn't there then. That's yesterday's newspaper, for Christ's sake."

"I know," I said. "But the general conditions apply. Plus the lights are out. The bulbs are smashed."

"It doesn't mean they were out two months ago."

"Again, the general conditions apply. These steps are not being properly maintained."

Walker grunted.

"You don't think much of this job, do you?" I said.

Walker shrugged. "Well, I suppose *someone* has to do it."

"I don't know about that," I told him. "But *I* certainly do."

The beeper went off while we were still in the station, which was nice, because there was a pay phone there. I called in and spoke to Wendy/Janet. She had a signup in Queens. A Phillip Lester, of Astoria, had fallen down at a roller skating rink and broken his leg. That made him one of my less favorite clients. In my opinion—which, of course, counts for nothing—people who go roller skating should *expect* to fall down and should not blame the rink when they do.

Still, I didn't know Phillip Lester, and I certainly wished him no ill.

In other words, I hoped he hadn't been strangled.

He hadn't. But it certainly wasn't his fault. Phillip Lester was sixteen, and he was one of those teenagers who inspire people to acts of violence. How his parents had managed to live with him for that long was beyond me. Phillip Lester answered every one of my questions about his skating accident with either a shrug or, "I dunno."

It went something like this:

"Well, what do you think made you fall?"

"I dunno."

"Was the floor slippery?"

Shrug.

"Was there anything on the floor that you tripped on?"

Shrug.

"Did anyone bump into you?"

"I dunno."

It was a bad signup, and what made it worse was that Detective Walker sat there grinning like a Cheshire cat the whole time. It was a great relief when I finally got the facts, what there were of them, taken down, and had the mother sign the retainer, which she had to do since Phillip was under age. I shot pictures of the sullen punk's broken leg, and Walker and I got the hell out of there.

He was still grinning when we went out the front door.

"This mean you're gonna have to go roller skating?" Walker asked me.

I shook my head. "I'll give it to Sam. He can take a girl friend with him and snap pictures of her at the rink."

"And what will those pictures supposedly show?" Walker asked.

I shrugged. "The condition of the rink, such as it is. That's not my problem. Nor is it Sam's. We're paid to do the assignment. We shoot what's there. Sometimes it's nothing. Frankly, just between you and me, it's a lousy case and Richard will probably reject it. But that doesn't concern me. I was assigned the job, I did it, so I get paid."

"Right," Walker said. "And then everything's fine unless this kid gets mad about being rejected and starts murdering people."

"There's always that," I said.

My beeper went off just as we got to the car. There was a phone on the corner so we walked down to it and I called the office. Sure enough, Wendy/Janet had a new case.

One thing about my job is, after a while you find things tend to run in cycles. That is to say, I'll get a string of octogenarians, one right after another. Then I'll get a run of amputees. Then I'll get one client after another who doesn't speak English.

Now it appeared I was getting a run on minors. The client was eight years old. His name was David Dressler. He'd fallen on a swing on a school playground, and had ten stitches over his left eye.

"What's the address?" I said.

She gave it to me. A project on West 135th Street.

"That's Harlem," I said.

"That's right."

"I'm in Queens. What about Sam?"

"I'm sorry," she said. "I beeped Sam and gave it to him. He called back all excited. His agent called and said they want to see him again. He still may have a shot at that series."

My head was spinning.

I hate to admit this, but I do get premonitions. I'm not superstitious, and I don't believe in that junk, but sometimes something hits me. I'm a writer, so often it's words.

And that's what hit me now.

Sam's got a shot at a series.

Series.

Series.

Series.

I gave it to Sam....He can't take it...audition... Harlem...shot at a series.

STRANGLER

Jesus.
No.
Not a kid.
Please.
Not an eight-year-old kid!

19.

David Dressler was fine.

In fact, he was more than fine. He was intelligent and vibrant and helpful. Though half the age of Phillip Lester, he was more than twice as swift. Though, to be fair, by the time he was sixteen, David Dressler could turn out to be quite a punk, too. But fortunately, I didn't have to find out. I took down the information, signed him up and Walker and I headed back to the Bronx.

We never got there.

Because, with Sam Gravston off to another audition, I was shouldering the whole load again, and despite Richard's concerns about losing business, the phones at Rosenberg and Stone were ringing off the hook.

In the course of the day, Walker and I called on Natalie Woodridge of College Point, Queens, who had slipped on the sidewalk and broken her leg; Albert Winestock, of Bensonhurst, Brooklyn, who had been in a car accident and fractured his collarbone; Bob Dawson, of the Melrose section of the Bronx, who had been hit by a car and broken his hip; and George Webb of Harlem, who had been strangled.

20.

Which cleared me.

I realize that's a horribly selfish way to look at it, but from my point of view, that's what I saw. The demise of George Webb cleared me of suspicion of murder. For which I was duly grateful.

Thanks, George.

George Webb lived in a second-floor walk-up on Adam Clayton Powell. His body was lying half in, half out of the bedroom. The legs and feet were in. The shoulders and head were out. The stomach straddled the doorway. One of the legs was wearing a cast.

George Webb was a black man of about thirty. He was lying on his back, so we could see his face just fine. It was not a pretty sight.

It was a first for me. I didn't throw up. I looked at his body and I didn't throw up. I felt numb, I felt weak, I felt nauseous, but I didn't blow lunch. The seasoned investigator. The tough P.I.

Walker didn't blow his lunch either. I was still huffing

111

and puffing and swaying queasily and congratulating myself on the strength of my stomach when he was already
calling it in. He pulled a walkie-talkie unit I hadn't even
known he had out of his belt, snapped it on, barked some
police code or other into it that I was too far gone to copy,
and before I knew what was happening, there were cops all
over the place.

"Downing, you call this in to Clark?" Walker said.

"Already been done," the cop called Downing said.
"Clark's on his way."

"How long has this place been sealed."

Downing whipped out a notebook. "Thirty-five minutes
now. Call came in at four-fifteen. First cop on scene at four-
twenty-two. Backup three minutes later, four-twenty-five."

"Anyone in and out since then?"

"Woman with a baby carriage left at four-thirty-three.
She's being tailed. That's it."

My head was buzzing. All this was happening around
me. I was there, but I wasn't there, if you know what I
mean. What with the shock of finding another dead body,
and the sudden appearance of a million cops, I had a little
catching up to do in the thinking department. Concerning
the significance of what had just happened, I mean.

As I've said, my initial reaction was just the realization
that I had been cleared. If you've never been a murder suspect you probably can't understand that, and I couldn't
even begin to explain. But after the thrill of that had begun
to wear off, I started coming back to my senses and thinking about someone other than myself, and then I realized
what was going on. And what it meant.

The cops were here. They'd been here *before* us. Ever
since the call came in. They'd been here sewing up the
apartment and keeping tabs on everyone who went in and

112

out. Before we got here. Before they knew George Webb had been murdered.

Which meant they'd been everywhere. At Phillip Lester's. At David Dressler's. At Diane Johnson's. At every client we had called on in the past two days. Every phone call that had come in to Rosenberg and Stone, Sergeant Clark's men had sewed up the apartment. And kept it sewed tight until Walker had called in to report that the client was still alive.

For the past two days there had been cops everywhere I went. And I hadn't seen one of them. Never even suspected. Though, on reflection, it was a shrewd and logical move. But I hadn't even considered it.

Some detective.

My thoughts were interrupted by the arrival of Sergeant Clark. He breezed in as usual, crisp, efficient and cold as ice. Not a word of greeting, not a word of well-done for Walker.

"Where is it?" he snapped.

"In there," Walker said, pointing over his shoulder.

"Strangled?"

"Yes."

"Black?"

"Yes."

"This is Harlem, isn't it?"

"Yes."

Sergeant Clark looked at me. "What a coincidence," he said, ironically. He looked back at Walker and jerked his thumb at me. "He been with you the whole day?"

"Since eight-thirty this morning."

Sergeant Clark grunted, and nodded toward the bedroom. "Medical examiner in there?"

"Not here yet," Walker said.

"Is that so?" Clark said. "*I'm* here, and I had farther to come."

He managed to say it as if it were Walker's fault.

Before Walker could respond, the pudgy medical examiner I'd seen at Winston Bishop's came bustling in the door.

"Where is it?" he said.

"Well, took you long enough," Clark said. "It's in there." Clark jerked his thumb toward the door. "And get me a prelim right away, wouldja?"

I swear the medical examiner smiled as he went by.

"My pleasure," he said.

Sergeant Clark turned his attention back to Walker. "They trace the call yet?"

"I don't know. I've been with him."

"Let's find out. Who's on the phone tap?"

"Donaldson."

"All right. Check with him. This apartment have a phone?"

"Yes, it does," Walker said.

That startled me. I'd been told the client had no phone, and I hadn't noticed one in the apartment. But Walker had.

"Is it working?" Clark said.

"I haven't touched it. I didn't want to mess up any prints."

Clark nodded. "Not that they'll do us any good," he said, sourly. "Prescott," he shouted to one of the detectives.

"Sir?" Prescott said, coming in from the hall, where the body was.

"Dust this phone for prints, willya, so we can use the damn thing."

"Yes, sir."

"Make it snappy, willya?"

"Yes, sir."

I thought Sergeant Clark should know about the discrepancy. "I was told the client had no phone," I said.

"Yeah, but you've been told a lot of things," Sergeant Clark said. "You probably believe 'em all, too." He snapped over his shoulder, "That phone ready yet?"

"Working on it," Prescott called. "It's lousy with prints."

"Then photograph 'em, lift 'em and get on with it," Clark said. "I want to use the damn thing."

A young detective emerged from the direction of the bedroom. "Sir?"

"Yes?" Sergeant Clark said.

"The dead man, sir. He was tentatively ID'd as George Webb."

"So?"

"There was no identification on the body. But we found a wallet in one of the dresser drawers."

"Yes?" Sergeant Clark snapped. "Are you rehearsing for some TV thriller? Spit it out."

I couldn't help feeling sorry for the young detective, who was obviously flustered by Clark's overbearing manner.

"Yes, sir. Sorry, sir. From the identification in the wallet, the victim is actually Clarence White."

"You sure it's the victim's wallet?"

"Yes, sir. I found a photo ID."

"What kind?"

"Driver's license."

Clark nodded. "Probably valid. What address?"

"Here."

"Phone ready yet?" Clark shouted over his shoulder.

"One minute," called back Prescott.

"Damn it, I—"

"Ready, sir."

Clark strode to the phone, picked it up and punched in a number.

"This is Clark. Get me Donaldson." There was few seconds wait, then, "Donaldson. Clark. Did you get it?" Another wait, then, "Hell!"

Clark slammed down the phone and strode back to us.

"A pay phone on Broadway and 125th. They sewed it up, but no one's there."

I just stood there, taking it all in. The client had a phone, but his phone had not been used. The call had come from a pay phone many blocks away. The guy had given the right address, but the victim's wrong name.

What the fuck was going on?

I had just had time to think all that when the medical examiner emerged from the bedroom.

"Got the prelim," he said. He looked at me, then at Clark.

"It's all right," Clark said. "We're all family here. Let's have it."

"Well, he was strangled, all right."

"I know that," Clark said, impatiently. "The question is when?"

"You understand this is preliminary, and not very accurate."

"Come on, Murray, I don't want excuses, I just want an answer. When was the guy killed?"

The medical examiner rubbed his chin. "Well," he said, "best I can tell you is, the guy's been dead at least twelve hours."

21.

Which fucked me again.

I'd had a series of jolts. It was like watching layers of reality being stripped out from under me. First George Webb clears me of murder. Then George Webb turns out not to be George Webb, but some other guy named Clarence White. Then Clarence White puts me back on the hook for murder again.

I could have killed Clarence White. I realized it the minute Murray, the medical examiner, said twelve hours. Walter gave me an unimpeachable alibi from eight-thirty in the morning on.

But not before.

My wife is a sound sleeper. And she goes to sleep early. Usually, she passes out before the end of the eleven o'clock news. So there was nothing to stop me from waiting until Alice went to sleep and then getting up, putting on my clothes, going out to Harlem and strangling Clarence White. Then going back, climbing into bed, getting up in the morning, taking my son, Tommie, to school and waiting there,

117

oh so innocently, for my friend Walker to hop in the car with me and give me an alibi for rest of the day.

I hadn't done that, but I could have.

The only thing that saved me was the phone call. I couldn't have made the phone call. I was in the car with Walker when it came in. And the cops would have a recording of that call. We could play it back and hear the caller's voice.

Hope flickered for a moment.

Then.

The voice of my accomplice. That's what Clark would think. Or some stooge on the street I'd slipped a few bucks to and told to make the call. Yeah, that's what they'd think.

Sergeant Clark had taken the medical examiner off in the corner of the room and was chewing his head off. I had no idea about what. Apparently, he wasn't too happy with the diagnosis. Or is that right? Can you have a diagnosis of a dead body? I guess not. You have an autopsy, don't you? But that's in the morgue, when you cut it up. So what was this? A preliminary examination. Prelim. Or was that a preliminary report? I don't know. How about a postmortem? Is that what this was? A postmortem?

Who gives a shit. The fact was, whatever you called it, George Webb, or Clarence White, or whatever you called him, had been dead for more than twelve hours, and I was fucked.

Sergeant Clark finished with the medical examiner and strode back to me.

"Walker," he barked.

"Sir," Walker said, striding up.

Clark put his hand on my shoulder and I knew what was coming. The ride downtown.

"This man can go," Clark said. "Send him home."

"Yes, sir," Walker said. "And do I pick him up again tomorrow morning?"

"No," Clark said.

I blinked. A double whammy. Clark wasn't having me arrested. And he was taking off my nursemaid.

What had the medical examiner told him? Was I cleared after all? What was going on?

"You won't be meeting him tomorrow morning," Clark said, "because he'll be meeting you." Clark turned back to me. "I want to see you and Richard Rosenberg in Rosenberg's office, first thing tomorrow morning, at nine A.M. sharp."

22.

"Gentlemen, we have a situation."

The gentlemen Sergeant Clark was referring to were Richard Rosenberg, Detective Thomas Walker and me.

The situation was obvious.

But that didn't stop Sergeant Clark from stating it.

"Mr. Rosenberg, someone is killing your clients. Or your potential clients. Or more to the point, someone is *making it appear* that someone is killing your clients.

"Because, you see, there is no evidence to the fact that these people were ever your intended clients at all.

"But leave that for now. The fact is, we have a situation. And regardless of whether the clients are really clients or are only being made to look that way, or regardless of why, the fact is that the situation we are dealing with is that of a serial killer,"—Sergeant Clark looked at me—"and *not* the case of a copycat crime. There have been no leaks to the press. None. And yet the crimes continue. We have a serial killer committing a series of crimes.

"And it must stop. And that is why I am here."

Richard had been controlling himself with an effort. Now he snapped. "I'm glad to hear it," he said sarcastically. "So far all you've done is take over my office, harass my staff and bird-dog me. And meanwhile the killings go on. I must say, your methods, such as they are, seem to be totally ineffective."

Sergeant Clark regarded Richard as if he were a particularly odious beetle with which he was reluctant to stain the heel of his shoe. "You, sir, are a lawyer. Presumably that presupposes that you are possessed with the ability to reason. Though, considering some of the attorneys I've met—but let that pass. The point, sir, is that the latest victim, Clarence White, alias George Webb, did not call your office. He had, in fact, been dead for several hours before the call came in. In light of that, perhaps you would care to suggest to me how the murder might have been prevented?"

"Simple," Richard snapped. "By catching the killer, that's how. By doing something constructive, instead of just rooting around in my files."

"I think you'll find that we have been quite busy," Clark said. "As to your files, I am still convinced that we will find the answer there. In point of fact, my own opinion is that the only reason we haven't found it before now is that your files are in such deplorable condition that finding anything is next to impossible. Which is not surprising, considering the young men you have doing your filing. If you're paying those two boys what they're worth, then you're guilty of violating the labor laws, and if you're paying them minimum wage, then you're being taken."

Richard, recognizing a no-win situation, contented himself with a contemptuous snort.

"But we're not here to bicker," Clark said. "We're here to solve a series of murders. Now you can bitch all you want about what the police aren't doing—though when I tell you what we *are* doing I think you'll change your tune—but the fact is, I want to do more. And that's why I'm here."

Clark walked to the door, opened it, looked out and closed it again. It was so hopelessly theatrical I almost laughed. He was checking to see if anyone was listening at the door.

"Now then," Clark said. "Whatever else we may know about the killings, one thing we know for sure. They are connected in some way with Rosenberg and Stone. And there must be a reason. And if there is a reason, it is possible that one of you knows it." Sergeant Clark held up his hand. "Now don't protest. You wouldn't *know* that you know it. But you might know some small thing, that when added to everything else, would fit in and make a pattern. If so, I want to find out what it is."

"And how do you propose to do that?" Richard said.

"Simple," Clark said. "I'm going to tell you what we have so far, and you are going to tell me if anything rings a bell."

Whatever Richard had been expecting, it wasn't that. He couldn't think of a single thing to say.

And neither could I. The last thing in the world I'd expected was that Sergeant Clark would want us to listen. A grueling interrogation had seemed entirely more likely.

Sergeant Clark pointed his hand and snapped his fingers. "Walker," he said. His manner was as if calling a trained dog.

Walker appeared to take no offense. He opened a briefcase and pulled out a file.

"Start with Clarence White," Clark said. "It's the most recent and the most relevant."

"Yes, sir," Walker said. He flipped the file open.

"Before you do, let me summarize the situation," Clark said. "Now then, we've had four killings." I groaned, but said nothing. "Darryl Jackson, Winston Bishop, Gerald

122

Finklestein and Clarence White, or George Webb, if you will. The killings form a pattern, the pattern of a serial killer. As in any serial killings, we look for similarities in the pattern.

"The last killing tends to bear out a theory I have held. The victim was black and lived in Harlem. As were the first two victims. It is my contention that black and Harlem is part of the pattern.

"The third victim, Gerald Finklestein, was white and lived in Queens. I suggest this is not consistent with the pattern as we know it, but may be consistent in some other way. Or it may turn out we do not have the complete pattern yet.

"At any rate, that is my present contention. That black and Harlem are part of the pattern, and relevant to our current discussion.

"All right, Walker. Clarence White."

"Yes, sir," Walker said. "Clarence White. Six feet, one inch, one hundred ninety pounds, black. Taxi cab driver. Has been off and on for seven years. Present employment, operates a gypsy cab for Fascab, a fleet of ten cabs operating out of an establishment on West 125th Street. The proprietor is one Joe Black, who, incidentally, is white."

That was something. A black man named White, working for a white man named Black. That had to mean something. It was a shock to realize it didn't.

"Unmarried. No children. Mother, Clarissa, lives in Bedford Stuyvesant with boyfriend, Harold Johnson. No brothers. Two sisters. One in Bed-Stuy, one in Queens. Sister in Queens married with three children. Husband of sister in Queens, mother living, five brothers, two sisters, seventeen nieces and nephews. None ever injured, none ever contacted Rosenberg and Stone."

My jaw was open. All that in one night. Sometimes it

had taken me a week and a half just to *find* one of Richard's clients.

Walker looked at Clark. "You want all the names and addresses?"

"No. They can go over the list later. Just the essentials."

"OK. Girl friend, Julie Bainbridge. Harlem. Twenty-five years of age. Lives in project with mother. Two sisters. Two children by a previous marriage. Ex-husband, Ronald Bainbridge, reportedly living in New Jersey, possibly Newark, have not yet been able to trace."

That made me feel a little better. For all their efficiency, the police had not yet been able to find the ex-husband of the victim's girl friend.

"From all reports, Ronald Bainbridge has not been seen or heard from for at least three years. Julie Bainbridge is, quote, devastated by the news. She had not seen Clarence White in the past two days. That is to say, since the morning of the day before yesterday. They had quarreled, apparently over a boyfriend of Julie Bainbridge's, although this is surmise, as she is reticent on the subject. All attempts to identify her outside interest have been futile. She's not talking, and the family either knows nothing or isn't talking.

"Regarding the injury. Clarence White broke his leg in an automobile accident a week ago Tuesday. It was a two-car accident involving a cab and a private car. Clarence White was driving the cab, and he appears to have been at fault. Officers on the scene reported finding open alcohol in the cab, and subsequent blood tests lead to Clarence White being charged with D.W.I. He was taken to Harlem Hospital, from which he was released three days ago. No friend, relative, neighbor or anyone at the hospital has any recollection of Clarence White saying anything of having any intention of calling Rosenberg and Stone."

"What?" Richard said, leaping to his feet. "Just a minute. Just a minute here. What are you doing? Are you trying to ruin me?" Richard glared at Sergeant Clark, then pointed his finger at Walker. "That man has just read off a list of over fifty people, all of whom you say state that Clarence White had no intention of calling Rosenberg and Stone. Is that what you're doing? Going around and asking the friends and relatives of all the victims if they ever called Rosenberg and Stone? You might as well close me down. You might as well put a full-page ad in the paper, warning people against calling Rosenberg and Stone."

Sergeant Clark eyed Richard coldly. "I have thought of that, Mr. Rosenberg. I have considered it. It may well be that that is exactly what the killer is after. Exactly the result the killer is attempting to bring about. The closing of Rosenberg and Stone. If so, by doing what you say, the killings would stop. We could potentially save lives."

Richard blinked. It was not exactly a threat, but it might as well have been. Sergeant Clark, by giving information to the press, could do exactly that.

"It's a tough decision," Clark said. "There's a homicidal maniac out there. If I in effect shut down Rosenberg and Stone, that will stop him from killing Rosenberg and Stone clients.

"But will it stop him from killing? That's the question. The thing is, I think not. It's a disease, you see. The serial killing. The homicidal mania. And it feeds on itself. It gets easier every time. And it becomes a compulsion.

"So my opinion is that the killings would not stop. The pattern would merely change. The killer would transfer his attentions elsewhere. Perhaps start a different series.

"Which would put us back to square one in the investigation. And potentially cost us more lives.

"The only solution is to nail the killer. So my decision is

to proceed as we are doing. And maintain media silence. And close the net on the creep."

Sergeant Clark looked at Richard Rosenberg with some distaste. "So, to answer your question, no, we have not been asking everyone if the victims in question ever mentioned calling Rosenberg and Stone. We have asked very casually, among several other things, if they had consulted or mentioned intending to consult a lawyer with regard to their accidents. A perfectly routine question under the circumstances. The law firm of Rosenberg and Stone has never been mentioned. Not by us. With the exception of the early publicity linked to Winston Bishop, which has since been curtailed.

"However, discrete inquiries have elicited the information that Winston Bishop did express an intention to call a lawyer, though no one can remember which one. Gerald Finklestein was known to have had the intention of calling Rosenberg and Stone. Clarence White, to the best of our knowledge—which is somewhat limited, since we have only been working on this since last night—had expressed no intention of hiring an attorney, though a brother-in-law states he had intended to recommend Davis and Lee.

"So your fears are groundless. Your law practice, such as it is, for the moment is not in jeopardy."

"Thank you," Richard said coldly. "You will pardon my saying so, but for a police sergeant engaged in an impartial murder investigation, you seem to express personal animosity toward me."

"Is that so?" Clark said. "You'll pardon it, I'm sure. I believe I stated that your files, such as they are, may eventually prove illuminating. They have in one respect already."

"What about my files?"

Sergeant Clark smiled coldly. "I note that you are attorney of record for one Enrico Hernandez. In the case of *Her-*

nandez vs the City of New York, the Police Department of the City of New York, and officers Morris and Beame."

Richard was incensed. "You're supposed to be looking for evidence of murder. You have no business simply pawing through my files."

"Perhaps, Mr. Rosenberg. Though we're all human beings, aren't we? Let me refresh your memory with regard to Enrico Hernandez. The gentleman in question has a number of priors, including sale of narcotics, assault and rape. The incident in question occurred when the officers attempted to arrest Mr. Hernandez for the rape of a twelve-year-old girl. A charge, by the way, of which he has subsequently been found guilty. In the course of the arrest, Mr. Hernandez pulled a knife and slashed the face of Officer Morris, a wound requiring forty-four stitches. According to the arresting officers, Mr. Hernandez then leaped from a second-story window onto concrete, fracturing his left leg.

"You, sir, have filed a five-million-dollar suit against the City of New York, the police department, and the officers in question, alleging police brutality."

"That's my job," Richard said. "I file the complaint, the city contests it and the court will rule."

"Perhaps," Clark said. "But more than likely, in the interest of expediency, the matter will be settled for a compromise figure. It won't matter to Hernandez, as the state will garnishee his share of the settlement to pay his past debts to the city. On the other hand, you will make a fat fee, and the names of the officers will be blemished."

Clark took a breath. "Now, Mr. Rosenberg, in spite of any personal animosity you might feel I have for you, I am doing everything in my power to keep your business open. So would you kindly hold your tongue and let us get on with it?"

23.

I felt bad.

You see, I'd signed up the Enrico Hernandez case myself. I'd been working for Richard about four months when the case came in. And I had reason to remember it, 'cause for me it had been a big case, particularly after a steady diet of trip and falls.

The case was something substantial. Something important. Police brutality. You hear about police brutality all the time. It's phrase in our language. It's one word: police-brutality. And suddenly here it was, and I was investigating it.

I was properly awed.

I remember it very well. I was in the Bronx doing an INV, (that's investigation), looking for one of Richard's clients who had to be in court for a pretrial hearing. The client had no phone, so I had to go to her apartment, only when I got there I found out she hadn't lived there in a year and a half, and no one seemed to know where she was. I was on my way to the post office to pay a buck to see if she'd filed a change of address when she left, when I got beeped.

I called in, and Kathy, who was one of Richard's secretaries at the time and who had a disposition like a jackhammer, gave me the assignment.

Enrico Hernandez. Broken leg. Case involves police brutality. Client has been charged with rape and resisting arrest. Client currently at Montifiore Hospital under police guard.

"What?" I said.

"Enrico Hernandez. Montifiore Hospital," Kathy snarled. "Go sign him up."

"Wait a minute," I said. "This is a case of police brutality and the guy is under police guard. How am I gonna interview him with a cop there listening?"

"I don't know," Kathy said sarcastically. "Would you like me to come hold your hand?"

That prospect did not thrill me. But I would have liked someone.

You gotta understand. I'd had very little experience with cops back then, and cops had always intimidated me.

But it was a job, and I had to do it, so I went.

There was no problem. They gave me a visitor's pass at the front desk and sent me on up. They didn't ask if I was a lawyer, nor did they tell me that the patient was under police guard.

But when I found the room, there was a cop in uniform sitting on a chair right outside the door.

I didn't know the procedure. I wondered if I should speak to him. But I figured if that was the procedure, he'd speak to me. So I walked on in. He didn't stop me. I just walked into the room.

There were two beds in the room, but only one was occupied. The bed by the window. Lying in the bed was a twenty-five-year-old, emaciated Hispanic, with a mustache, a two-day's growth and watery eyes. There were scratches on his face, and a tooth was missing. His left leg was en-cased in a cast and suspended above him in traction.

But all those things were secondary.

The thing that I noticed, the thing that got me, was the fact that his right wrist was handcuffed to the headboard of his hospital bed.

"Mr. Hernandez?" I said.

He looked up at me. "Who are you?"

"I'm Mr. Hastings, from the lawyer's office."

There was light in his eyes and he tried to sit up in bed, impossible with the handcuffs and his leg in traction.

"Yeah, yeah," he said excitedly. "Beat me up, man. Cops beat me up."

As he said it, the cop came strolling in from the hall, pulled up a chair and sat down.

And stayed there for the whole interview. Stayed there while Enrico Hernandez told how he'd been out on proba-tion and had noticed some cops following him. And how he didn't want to get in trouble with the cops, 'cause he was on probation, so he ran. Only the cops chased him and caught him. And when they caught him, they were angry at him for running away, so they beat the shit out of him.

I can't tell you how I felt in that hospital room. Listening to the guy tell the story, with the cop there, listening too. I mean, there I was, representing Hernandez's attorney, which made me on his side. In a case of police brutality. Which made the cop on the other side. Which made it a hostile situation. And I'm not good at hostile situations. And I was even less so back then.

The cop never said a word. He just sat there while I took down all the information. Sat there while I had Enrico Her-nandez sign the retainers. He never said boo.

But I sure knew he was there.

After all that, I took out my camera. I figured I was taking

a good chance of getting it impounded, but I figured I had to try. I took out my camera and snapped on the flash, to see what the cop would do.

He did nothing. He just sat there.

So I aimed the thing and snapped off shots of Enrico Hernandez. I shot his missing tooth. I shot his scratched face. I shot his broken leg.

But most of all, I shot the handcuffs. The handcuffs chaining his right wrist to the headboard of the hospital bed.

See, I figured that was the key. I figured it was a case of police brutality. And in the case of Enrico Hernandez, the most brutal thing I could think of, the most telling visual, the most glaring example of oppression, was the sight of those handcuffs, chaining a man in traction to his bed.

And that was it. That was the end of the case as far as I was concerned. I turned in the signup and the pictures, got paid for it, and my job was finished. As far as I was concerned, that was it.

But the thing is, I felt good about it at the time. It had been a tough assignment, one that I had been nervous to do, but I'd done it. And I'd done a good job. I'd done a good job signing up the client, and I'd done a good job taking the pictures. I was particularly proud of those. Because I was doing a job for Richard, for Richard and the client, and I'd got just what Richard would want.

It never occurred to me to question Enrico Hernandez's story at the time. Or if it did, it didn't bother me. That's the thing. The client had made a charge of police brutality, that might or might not be true and I had covered my end of it well.

But at the time, I had thought of the arresting officers as cops. Not people. Cops. Not as human beings who might have been hurt by what I'd done. Assuming they were, in fact, innocent. Just cops. A word on a piece of paper. An element in the story.

So it hadn't bothered me at the time.

But now I felt bad.

And I was angry at Sergeant Clark for making me feel that way. Because, damn it, I was only doing my job. And Richard was only doing his job. And if Enrico Hernandez was lying, I wasn't at fault. And Richard wasn't at fault. But Sergeant Clark was making us feel that way. And I felt sorry for Richard for being put in that position. And I felt I should defend him. But I could think of nothing to say. And I felt I should defend myself, too. Though I could think of even less to say there.

And Sergeant Clark had already asked specifically that we be quiet and get on with it.

I looked at Richard.

And Richard held his tongue. He smoldered. He fumed. He looked about ready to jump out of his chair and bite Sergeant Clark in the neck.

But he kept quiet.

And I kept quiet.

And we got on with it.

24.

Sergeant Walker resumed.

"Gerald Finklestein. Sixty-three years of age. Widower. Door-to-door vacuum-cleaner salesman. For Electrovac. Company in Brooklyn. Two grown sons. One lives in Florida, one in Michigan. Owns a car. Eighty-one Chevy. Sells vacuum cleaners door to door in New York City, Long Island, Connecticut and New Jersey. Neighbors report him as quiet, mild-mannered, respectable. Express the usual shock and surprise.

"Finklestein's one hobby seems to have been bridge. He was a member of the Hillsdale Social Club in Queens. Played duplicate there Wednesday nights. Members of the club report Finklestein took the usual amount of good-natured ribbing about his accident, and noted stated intention to call Rosenberg and Stone, increasing the likelihood that his phone call was, indeed, genuine."

Walker turned the page.

"Winston Bishop. Black. Forty-two years of age. Single. No children. Parents deceased. No known brothers and sisters. Occupation, construction worker. Unemployed at time of death. On public assistance.

"Drug paraphernalia, including hypodermics, found in apartment. All indications user, not pusher. Two priors, both possession.

"With regard to the accident. Winston Bishop fell on the subway steps at 135th Street, officers on scene, treated at Harlem Hospital for broken arm."

Walker flipped the page.

"With regard to Darryl Jackson—"

With regard to Darryl Jackson, I didn't want to hear it. But I had to. I had to sit there and listen while Walker went through the whole thing. It was infuriating, of course, seeing as how I knew the Darryl Jackson case had absolutely nothing to do with what we were talking about. But there was nothing I could say.

Eventually, Walker finished.

"Fine," Clark said. "That's the picture. At least that's the general picture. We have some details, and we've been able to draw a few parallels. Go ahead, Walker."

Walker flipped another sheet.

"With regard to Clarence White. He had been known to frequent a bar known as Duke's Place, on Lenox Avenue. At least three people remember seeing him in there the day before the murder. They remember because he had a cast on his leg. However, no one seems to know any more about it than that. Apparently, he was not in a particularly talkative mood. As we understand it, he had quarreled with his girl friend, was in a blue funk and was sitting off in a corner by himself getting soused. As far as we know, he spoke to no one in particular, and no one in particular spoke to him. Nobody even seems to know how he injured his leg, let alone whether he intended to call an attorney to do anything about it. The best we can get is that he was there.

"And there's a link—Winston Bishop also used to frequent the same establishment."

The first hard clue. I straightened up.

"Is that right?" I said.

"That is right," Walker said. "In the Winston Bishop case, even less is known. The best we have is that the bartender and two customers identify Winston Bishop as someone they had seen in the place. None knew his name, none recall seeing him recently, none recall seeing him with a cast on. In his case, you must remember, it was his arm that was broken, not his leg. Therefore he could come and go without notice. A man on crutches coming in the door, everyone would see. Whereas a man with a cast on his arm, perhaps even covered up with a coat, could go unnoticed. At any rate, no one saw it.

"No one recalls any discussion about hiring a lawyer for any purpose whatsoever." Walker smiled. "With the exception of one gentleman whose brother was a crack dealer, and who was concerned with raising bail."

"And there you are," Clark said. "It's a thin lead, but it's there. We're running it down. We're doing everything we can. But if there's anything that Duke's Place brings to mind, please let me know.

"What's next, Walker?"

"Next is Harlem Hospital. Bishop and White were both treated at Harlem Hospital. I know that's nothing to write home about, seeing as how both live in Harlem and their accidents occurred there.

"But here's the thing. Finklestein was injured in Long Island. He was treated at Good Samaritan Hospital in West Islip. Nothing special there. But a check into his background shows that approximately two years ago he was a passenger in a taxi that was in a motor vehicle accident in Harlem, and he was taken to Harlem Hospital for observation."

"So what?" I said. "I fail to see how that means anything."

"I'm not saying it does," Clark said. "I'm merely listing coincidences. The coincidence in this case is the fact that the doctor who treated Gerald Finklestein in emergency was the same doctor who treated Winston Bishop."

"What?" I said.

"For what it's worth," Clark said. "Those are the facts. Now, with regard to the phone calls." Here he looked at Richard. "And I must say, your secretaries have not been particularly helpful on this point. However, this much is known. The phone call from Winston Bishop, which neither of your secretaries will positively admit to taking, was received at a time when the gentleman in question presumably could have been alive. In other words, it's entirely possible Winston Bishop actually made that call.

"We have indirect evidence to the effect. Winston Bishop was black, he was a dope addict and he was not particularly well educated. Presumably, his English would have been recognizably black. Or what can be colloquially referred to as jive. In other words, his speech could not be mistaken for white English, like Walker here. However, had the speaker been white, calling up and giving an address in Harlem might have been an unusual enough occurrence that one of those girls might have remembered it."

"I doubt it," Richard said.

"It's a very slim chance, and I say, might," Clark said. "Now, with regard to Gerald Finklestein, the reverse is true. We have the testimony of Janet Fishbein that she took the call. Presumably with a man named Finklestein, had he sounded like a black man, that would have rated some notice. We also have the corroborating testimony of Mr. Hastings here, to the fact that he called Mr. Finklestein to postpone the appointment. The gentleman answered, claiming to be Mr. Finklestein. And though there is nothing to substantiate this, there is every reason to believe that he was. The medical examiner's report concludes that he could have indeed been alive at that time.

"Now we come to Clarence White. There is no need to speculate here. We have a tape recording of the actual call. Walker."

Walker opened the briefcase and took out a small, battery-operated tape recorder. He set it on Richard's desk. He took out a cassette, slipped it in and punched play.

There was a crackle of static, and then the dulcet tones of Wendy/Janet filled the room.

"Rosenberg and Stone."

It was so familiar I almost smiled. But this was no laughing matter. There was an instant of dead quiet while we waited for the next voice.

It came.

"Is this the lawyer?"

It was a high-pitched voice, and so typically black as to be almost a caricature of itself, as if a stage comedian were doing a jive black man.

In contrast, came the coldly oblivious tones of Wendy/Janet.

"This is the law firm of Rosenberg and Stone."

CALLER: "Tha's it. Tha's what I want. I hurt myself. Broke ma leg. Want a lawyer."

WENDY/JANET: "And how did you break your leg?"

CALLER: "Fell down."

WENDY/JANET: "And where did you fall, sir?"

CALLER: "Stairs of my building."

WENDY/JANET: "What is your address?"

The voice gave the address and apartment number of Clarence White.

WENDY/JANET: "Your phone number, sir?"

CALLER: "Ain' got no phone."

WENDY/JANET: "Your name, sir?"

CALLER: "George Webb. My name is George Webb."

WENDY/JANET: "All right, Mr. Webb. If you are going to be home, I will schedule you an appointment with our investigator."

CALLER: "I be home. Ain' goin' nowhere. Broke ma leg."

WENDY/JANET: "How would four o'clock be?"

CALLER: "Don' matter. I be here. Sen' him over."

WENDY/JANET: "And could I check your address, please?"

There came a click and then a dial tone. The caller had hung up.

Walker snapped off the recorder.

"Well," Clark said. "That gives us a pretty clear picture. That caller was not Clarence White. It was either the murderer or some stooge hired by the murderer to make the call. Personally, I think it was the murderer."

"So," Clark continued, "our picture of the murderer becomes clearer. In all likelihood, he is an uneducated black man, living in Harlem, in fact, the man whose voice we just heard. In which case, the murderer was at a phone booth on the corner of Broadway and 125th Street yesterday afternoon at exactly four-fifteen."

"That's a guess," I said. "All that is is a guess."

"Granted," Clark said. "A guess. A deduction. Whatever you want to call it. As far as we're concerned, we take it as a supposition. Not the only supposition, but certainly one."

Clark shook his head. "Now, the secretary who took the call, this Janet Fishbein, has been somewhat less than helpful. The question, of course, being whether she had ever heard this voice before. She claims as far as she knows she hadn't. It would help if we knew if she was the one who took the Winston Bishop call, but we don't, and having talked exhaustively with both of the young ladies in question, it is doubtful if we ever will. In addition, Miss Fishbein claims a lot of these black voices, the ones talking jive, all sound the same to her anyway. So there we are.

"At any rate, we were building a picture of the murderer. So we have a black man. Uneducated. Strong—to have strangled the victims. And probably poor."

"Why poor?" I asked.

"That's the other thing," Clark said. "The bodies had all been robbed."

"Oh, really?" I said.

"Yes. And you see what that means. None of the victims was affluent. They would not have been carrying much cash on them. But what they had, was taken. Now, admittedly, that could just be a ploy by the murderer to throw us off the track. But taken at face value, it tells us the murderer was someone who was hard up, even for small amounts of cash. That would tend to indicate a junkie. It would also tend to indicate that the murderer was someone who had killed before to get money. By before I mean before all this started. But the thing is, these killings are so typical of the routine murders committed by junkies to get money to feed their habits that if it hadn't been for the fact that the victims called Rosenberg and Stone, the connection might have gone unnoticed."

Sergeant Clark took a breath. "But we have the connection. And that is why I believe that what we have to look for is a black client whose case was lost or rejected"—Richard shifted restlessly—"or on the other hand, a black man who Rosenberg and Stone successfully sued."

"Entirely more likely," Richard said. "Though still far-fetched."

"Perhaps," Clark said. "But that is the premise on which I am working. So let me tell you how we intend to proceed. We

shall continue very much as we have been. We shall keep the
lid on publicity. In other words, there will be no mention of
Rosenberg and Stone. Meanwhile, we shall continue going
through your files, we shall maintain the taps on your phones
and we shall attempt to trace every call that comes in.

"Now, with regard to that. I have not instructed your secretaries to attempt to keep the people who call in on the
phone until we can trace the call and get to them. In the
first place, I don't want those girls to know we're doing it.
As far as they know, we don't even have taps on the
phones. In the second place, they couldn't do it. They're
not swift enough. They would tip the guy to what they
were trying to do right away. Then we'd have lost him. So
we'll keep trying this way. We're tracing the calls pretty
fast, we got men out all over the place. If there's a chance of
nabbing them through the phone calls, we'll do it. To keep
him talking longer wouldn't help.

"As I said, I don't want the girls to know what we're
doing. I also don't want anyone else who works here to
know what we're doing. This is just between you and us."

He pointed his finger at me. "Now this joker here
wouldn't know what we're doing, but he happened to be
there when the last one went down. So now he knows. And
now you know. We're staking out the address of every call
that comes in. But I don't want anyone else to know that.
Your other investigator, this Mr. Gravston. Your secretaries.
Your file clerks. No one. I don't want this leaking out.
'Cause everyone knows someone, and everyone talks. And
eventually the word gets to the person you don't want to
have hear. So you keep the lid on.

"Now, as for Mr. Hastings here."

I knew what was coming. Walker would be riding with
me again.

"For the time being," Clark said, "we may consider Mr.

Hastings provisionally cleared. As it happens, the time element on the Clarence White case doesn't do that. From what the medical examiner has told us, Mr. Hastings still could have killed him. But I don't think so. I have to go with the best information I can get. And Walker here tells me Hastings didn't do it. He bases that on an assessment of his character after having ridden around with him for two days. Says he's not the type of guy who would have committed these murders." Clark shrugged. "Personally, I take that with a grain of salt. I think murderers come in all kinds of packages. But Walker has one convincing argument. He says Mr. Hastings simply wouldn't have the guts. That I can buy.

"So, for the time being, Mr. Hastings, you can consider yourself temporarily cleared. Detective Walker will not be riding with you today. It's not really that I think you're so innocent. Frankly, he has more important things to do.

"So that's it. The main thing is, if anything should come up, or if you should remember anything that ties in with what we've told you, contact me at once. You may not like the way we're going about this Mr. Rosenberg, but the sooner we clear this up, the less chance there is of your business going under."

During this, Walker had packed up his briefcase. Now he and Clark turned and walked out the door. I started to follow.

"Stanley," Richard barked.

I turned around.

Richard's face looked murderous, as if *he* wanted to strangle someone.

"You stay," he said.

25.

"That man is a moron."

I could have hugged him. Finally. Another person who shared my opinion of Sergeant Clark. It had been getting depressing, one person after another telling me what a good man he was. At last, a sane, rational human being who could see the obvious.

But the thing was, from the look on Richard's face when he'd asked me to stay, I had thought he was going to tear into me for some reason. As if somehow I was to blame for all this. But no, he wanted to cut up Sergeant Clark. It was almost too good to be true.

"The man's a complete idiot," Richard said. "He has this insane idea that somehow I've wronged a client, and he's basing his whole investigation on that. And this other idea, that the killer might be someone I've successfully sued, that seems more likely until you think about it. And when you do it's just as stupid. I mean, everybody carries insurance. It's not the individual, it's the insurance company

142

that eventually pays. So why should anyone hold a grudge?"

Richard had been holding this all in for a long time, so he was getting more and more excited and worked up as he went on.

"And this idea that the killer is some poor, uneducated, black man in Harlem. I mean, come on, give me a break. How does that tie in with someone I've successfully sued? A poor, uneducated, black man in Harlem doesn't have any money. How the hell could I have sued him?"

"I know. I know," I said.

"You know. I know. We know. Of course, we know. It's that moron who doesn't know. He's a fool. He's out chasing his own shadow. Meanwhile, I'm in danger of losing my business."

"No, you're not, Richard. At least they're controlling the publicity."

"Yeah. No thanks to him. If you hadn't come up with the copycat killer theory, they'd be spreading it all over the papers. That was an inspired piece of bullshit, by the way. But it's only a stopgap measure. It's only temporary. If this goes on, the publicity is going to get out. It's only a matter of time. Meanwhile, that moron is running around in circles."

"I know. But what can we do about it?"

"What we can do about it is do what he ought to be doing. We can investigate this thing right side up."

"You mean—"

"I mean we can't wait for that moron to solve this crime. We have to take matters into our own hands."

"You mean—"

"I mean we have to take an intelligent look at what's happening here."

143

I knew what that meant. Richard, having had two days to do nothing but sit and stew it over, was now going to tell me *his* theory of the case. Which wasn't necessarily brilliant, and wasn't necessarily right. But as far as I was concerned, it had one big thing going for it.

It wasn't Sergeant Clark's.

"All right," I said. "What do you think?"

"All right," Richard said. "Here's the thing. This Sergeant Clark is going about the whole case ass-backward. I mean, looking for some wronged client. That's bullshit.

"Now I'll tell you what I think. If someone is knocking off the clients who call in, that means to me just one thing."

"What's that?"

"There's a leak."

"A leak?"

"Yeah. A leak. Here. At Rosenberg and Stone."

I stared at him. "You suspect one of your staff?"

"No, no, no," Richard said, shaking his head. "At least, not necessarily. The person who's doing it probably doesn't even know he's doing it. But here's the thing. The calls come in here. All the information is right here. About the clients, I mean. And someone is leaking it out."

"Who?"

"Well," Richard said. "The most likely person would be you."

"What?!"

"I'm not saying you did, I'm just saying you're the most likely. After all, you get beeped and told the whole story. That gives you the information to use.

"The second would be Sam. As I understand it, he was offered some of those jobs before you were.

"Then there's Wendy and Janet. They took down the information to begin with. They could easily have passed it on to somebody else."

144

"Yes. But why would they do that?"

"I don't know," Richard said. "But look at it this way. Suppose either Wendy or Janet had a boyfriend. A boy-friend who didn't like her working here. Who thought it was a waste of time. Who thought I wasn't paying her enough."

I saw Richard's eyes blink as he recognized a touchy subject. He hurried over it.

"Who wanted her home so he could put the old pork to her instead of her coming to work every day. Suppose this guy was a psychopath who took a notion about closing down Rosenberg and Stone."

I wrinkled up my face. "I'm afraid that doesn't sound too logical to me."

Richard's eyes narrowed. "I suppose it sounds more logical to you that I would have fucked over some client."

"No, no, of course not," I said. "The thing I have to keep remembering is the whole thing is absurd."

"You do that," Richard said. "And then there's those two file clerks, whatever the hell their names are. Wendy and Janet can't leave here. They're on the phones all day long. But those two guys. They do so little work here. They could have heard the call come in, rushed out, killed the guy and got back here, and nobody would have known the differ-ence."

I frowned. "Well, maybe."

"Maybe is right," Richard said. "But maybe is all we got to go on here. So that's it. I want you to check this out."

"What?"

"Yeah, you heard me. I want you to check this out. I'm not happy with what Sergeant Clark is doing. I want some-thing else done. You've had some experience in these mat-ters, so you're the man to do it."

"You're kidding?"

145

"No, I'm not. Look, I want you to go out, go on your rounds as normal today. You've got to anyway. Sergeant Clark will be expecting it, and you can't do anything different. Besides, everyone else will be here. Then tonight, after you get off, I want you to poke around."

"Poke around?"

"Yeah. I want you to call on those people. Wendy, Janet, Sam. Those two guys."

"You're kidding?"

"Not at all."

"What'll I tell 'em?"

"I don't know. Make something up. Tell 'em as much of the truth as possible. That's always easiest. Tell 'em I'm not happy with how things are going, I think the cops are messing everything up and I've asked you to ask some questions to try to straighten things out. Yeah, that's it," Richard said brightly. "It's not a question of my suspecting them. It's a question of feeling the cops have got their information wrong."

"I see," I said.

Already in my mind I had agreed to the project. Actually, it was what I felt like doing all along. I agreed one hundred percent that the cops were off on the wrong scent. I wasn't sure this was the right one, but whatever I was going to do couldn't hurt. And Richard did have a point. The motive of this thing could well be internal. So it was something that should be done.

Also, Richard had never asked me to do anything like this before. And this was not your ten-buck-an-hour, thirty-cents-a-mile job. This was serious stuff.

I wondered what it was worth. I was tempted to say, "All right, Richard. Two hundred bucks a day plus expenses." But I couldn't quite see doing that. Not seeing as how I was spending most of the day working for him in the regular job. It would be like getting paid twice. I decided I'd have to wait and see what he'd offer.

"All right," I said. "I guess I could see what I could do."

Richard smiled. He walked over, shook my hand, clapped me on the shoulder.

"Good man," he said. "I knew I could count on you. I appreciate it."

Then, before I even realized what had just happened, he turned and walked out the door to see what the cops going over his files were doing.

26.

I thought about it all day as I drove around and signed up
my three cases. There were only three because Sam was
working today. Somehow or other, his agent had not managed to get him another audition, so I had it relatively easy.
Three signups, two in Queens and one in Brooklyn.

It was kind of weird going out on them. It was weird
because I knew the cops were there. I'd get beeped, call in,
get the address and know before I even got started that the
cops would be there before me.

I'm only human. I looked for them. I looked for them at
every address I went. And I never spotted one. But I knew
they were there. And I knew that if the person I was calling
on happened to be dead, all I had to do was walk out the
front door and wave my arms and cops would suddenly
materialize from everywhere. It was kind of freaky.

But none of my clients were dead. It was a perfectly routine day, and I had nothing to do but drive around leisurely
and think about the case.

And the job I was going to do for Richard. That was kind

of exciting somehow. Even if Richard didn't pay me for it, it was kind of nice. The secret agent. The man on the inside.

It was nice that Richard shared my lack of faith in Sergeant Clark. It was nice, too, that he shared my fantasy of beating Clark to the punch, of cracking this stupid case.

Although, on reflection, I had to admit that Richard's ideas were even more stupid than Sergeant Clark's. I mean, come on. A leak at Rosenberg and Stone? Wendy/Janet, the spy within our ranks? Give me a break. The paralegals, Frick and Frack, who probably didn't have an I.Q. of a hundred between them. Frank Burke, the frustrated investigator, seething because he can't cut the job, sets out to destroy Rosenberg and Stone from within. Hey, there's a great theory. The guy doesn't have the guts to go into bad neighborhoods to do signups, but he's got the nerve to strangle people. Sam Gravston. Well...

Sam Gravston.

I started thinking about Sam. Sam was working Manhattan and the Bronx today. I wondered if he'd get any assignments. I wondered if he'd get one in Harlem. I wondered if he did, if he'd walk in and find the client dead. So far, I'd been the only one to do that. But what if Sam did?

I thought about that. I thought about that a lot. And once again, words began to haunt me. This time it was Richard's words, Richard saying, "He was offered some of those jobs before you were."

Jesus. He certainly was. In every single case. No, that wasn't right. But in the Winston Bishop case and in the Gerald Finklestein case, they'd been offered to Sam before they'd been offered to me. So he had the names and addresses. They hadn't offered him the Clarence White case, but that didn't matter. Because that wasn't an actual call-in. Clarence White had been killed the night before. And then the murderer had called in the next day to make the appointment. Sam could have done it. But the call had been from Broadway and 125th Street. And Sam was downtown at an audition. But wait. The call had been late in the day. Four-fifteen. Presumably the audition would have been over. Sam could have rushed uptown to make the call. He'd have gone uptown because he was smart enough to have figured out the police might start tracing the calls, and if so, he'd want them to trace the call to Harlem.

But wait. I was being stupid. I'd heard that phone call. That call had been made by an uneducated black man, and—

A chill ran down my spine. I remembered what I'd thought at the time. A voice so typically black as to be almost a caricature of itself, as if a stage comedian were doing a jive black man.

Jesus.

Sam Gravston was an actor. And presumably a good one. And he did dialects. And did them with ease. I remember when I was an actor and had to do an accent, I would take two or three weeks to work into the voice. But not Sam. He could slip in and out of voices at will. I'd heard his French, his Spanish, his German. And what could be easier for him than jive black? And high-pitched to boot, to further disguise his voice.

I realized I was being ridiculous. Good god, I didn't have a motive. I mean, why the hell would a young, eager, aspiring actor with an agent and everything, and presumably on the eve of a sort of breakthrough, decide to indiscriminately start killing people? It made absolutely no sense. No, there was absolutely no motive.

The more I analyzed it, the only motive I could come up with was my own. Much as I hated to admit it, the only reason I could think of for maintaining a case against Sam

Gravston in this matter was because he was a young actor who had succeeded in getting an agent and succeeded in getting himself auditions, and I couldn't bear his success and wanted to be able to think something must be wrong.

I thought about that for a while, and I laughed about it, and I laughed at myself, and I laughed at Sam and I laughed at the whole situation. If that seems heartless, it's just that, when a situation gets too grim and your senses just can't take it anymore, the defense mechanism is to laugh. "All right, gang, I'm sorry, so people are getting killed. Sorry about it, but I just can't see the horror in it anymore. I'm just wonderin' who's gonna bite the big one next."

I actually started giggling as I was driving along in my car. I do that every now and then, particularly in tense situations. I just hold myself together as long as I can, and then I sort of lose it.

In this case I really lost it. I got the giggles pretty good. By the time I got to my last assignment, it struck me so funny that the person I was calling on was actually alive that it was all I could do to keep a straight face through the signup. The line I thought about, but did not actually say when the client opened the door, "Oh, you're alive," kept running through my head, and every time it did I had to bite my lip to keep from going to pieces. It was a huge relief when I finally shot the client's picture and got the hell out of there.

When I did it was after five o'clock, and seeing as how I hadn't been beeped, by then it was time to head back to the city.

Ordinarily, I'd have headed home, but tonight I was on special assignment for Richard. Richard's switchboard shuts down at six, which meant by the time I hit Manhattan the office would be closed and the staff would be heading home. Time for supersleuth to swing into action.

But first, supersleuth had to clear it with the powers that be.

I hunted up a pay phone and called Alice. It was Friday night, and had Alice managed to line up a baby-sitter for us, I might have been in deep shit, but as it happened, she hadn't. She wasn't at all pissed at my not coming home. In fact, when she heard what Richard had in mind, she thought it was rather neat.

"And you're just the person to do it, too," she said. "It's right up your alley. You're good with people. They like you. They'll tell you things. You'll see."

I was glad for her support, but I wished I shared her optimism. As far as I was concerned, I was a fool on a fool's errand, with little or no expectations of success.

But a job's a job, whether for pay or not, and I had undertaken it, and it was up to me to carry it out.

So I girded my loins, fired up the ancient Toyota and headed into Manhattan. Mr. Secret Agent. The man behind the scenes. The man under cover.

Come to save the day.

21.

Everything you always wanted to know about Wendy/Janet but were afraid to ask.

Correction. More than you wanted to know about Wendy/Janet. More than *anyone* could *ever* want to know about Wendy/Janet.

Jesus.

I tried Janet first. She was the lesser of two evils. After all, she'd been at Rosenberg and Stone a shorter amount of time, so I had less to resent her for. Plus, the fact that she was newer made her more of a suspect, if such a ridiculous concept could really apply.

Janet had a one-bedroom apartment in a brownstone on Bleeker Street in the Village. It was a fairly nice building. Janet was too young to have lived there long enough to be paying very low rent, and with what Richard Rosenberg was paying her, there was no way she could afford it. I figured she must have some outside source of income, probably rich and indulgent parents.

It was around seven o'clock when I got to Janet's. She'd

been home long enough to have got undressed, 'cause she came to the door in a robe and slippers.

"Stanley," she said. "What are you doing here?"

"Sorry to bother you," I said. "But I need to talk to you. It's about the murders."

"The murders?" she said. She seemed hesitant to let me in the door.

"It will only take a few minutes," I told her.

She opened the door then.

"Well, it better," she said. "I have a date."

That figured. I followed her into the living room, wondering why it was when women went out on a date, they always got ready for it by taking their clothes off.

"What's this all about?" Janet said.

Janet was clearly ill at ease and unhappy to have me there, and it couldn't be just that I was a pain-in-the-ass investigator that she had to deal with. I figured her date was with someone special.

"As I said, it's about the murders. Or rather, about the murder investigation. Richard is not happy with what the police are doing."

"I should think not," Janet said. "You think it's easy working in that office with the police crawling around all over the place? They make me so nervous I can't think straight."

It occurred to me that the presence of two policeman was not a necessary prerequisite for that occurrence.

I didn't point that out. I merely said, "That must be annoying."

"Annoying," she said. "It's insufferable. How'd you like a police officer looking over your shoulder all day?"

"I've had one," I told her.

"Oh, that's right," she said. "So you see what I mean."

"Yes, I do. You don't like it. And Richard doesn't like it.

In fact, he's so dissatisfied that he's asked me to do something about it."

"Oh really?" she said.

"Yes. He thinks the police are botching up the case and not getting anywhere. He thinks their theories are stupid. He thinks they're off on the wrong track. He's asked me to try to straighten things out."

She looked at me. "You?"

"Yes."

Her face showed utter puzzlement. "Why you?" she said.

Clearly, she hadn't the faintest notion the remark could be the least bit rude.

"I'm a private detective," I told her. "I've had some experience in these matters."

Usually, I blush to tell people I'm a private detective, but in Janet's case I didn't mind. The result was astonishing. Her eyes widened.

"You're a private detective?" she said.

My first thought was, Jesus Christ, what did she think I was, a dishwasher? Then I realized she wasn't really being stupid. She was just another person brainwashed by television. To her a private detective meant "Spenser For Hire." She kept staring at me, as if wondering how she'd missed seeing my muscles and my gun.

"That's right," I said. "And I've helped the police on other murder investigations. For instance, the Darryl Jackson case that they were talking about the other day. So Richard has asked me to look into this. And that's why I've come to you."

Her eyes got even wider. "Me? Why me?"

"Don't be alarmed," I told her. "No one suspects you of anything. But Richard feels the police have the facts all mixed up, and he wants them straightened out. You know that Sergeant Clark, the guy who questioned you?"

Wendy drew herself up. "I certainly do."

Her antagonism was so blatant I decided to play off it. "Well, Richard feels the way he questioned you was a disgrace."

"Oh?" she said, brightening.

"Yes. Richard feels the way he questioned you was totally unfair, and as a result, Clark got his facts all balled up. So he wanted me to chat with you and straighten things out."

A frown creased Janet's brow as she realized she was going to have to remember again. "About the phone calls, you mean?" she said.

I decided to win her heart. "No," I said.

You'd have thought I just crowned her Miss America.

"Well," she said, practically giggling in relief. "What, then?"

"Well, let's go back to the day of the first phone call."

Storm clouds appeared.

"Never mind the phone call itself. Just that day."

"All right," she said.

She sat there expectantly.

This is the point at which I wanted to be brilliant. I wanted to say something seemingly irrelevant, like, "What color dress were you wearing?" And then her eyes would widen, and she would say, "That's it! That's it! I remember!" And then she'd blurt out the one crucial fact I needed to crack the case.

The thing was, I couldn't think of one fucking thing to ask her. I felt like a total moron. There I was with the girl all softened up, all primed, all ready to tell me anything I wanted, and I was bone dry. The actor'd gone up on his lines.

Some detective.

I was saved by the front doorbell.

"Oh, my god," Janet said, jumping up. "That's Barry. He hates it when I'm late." She ran for the bedroom. "Let him in, tell him I'm sorry, I'll be right there."

She slipped inside and slammed the bedroom door.

I went to the door and opened it. There was no one there. Of course. He'd rung the downstairs bell. Janet hadn't told me how to deal with that, but the button on the wall looked promising. I pushed it, and I heard a faint buzz below.

I closed the apartment door again. I figured I'd give Barry a little shock. It would be kind of amusing somehow. I do look a little younger than my years, and Barry would probably take me for a rival. That might get a rise out of him, and I might find out something.

I heard footsteps and then a knock on the door. I opened it.

It was a shock for both of us. Barry was about 6'4", 220 pounds. He and the diminutive Janet must have made quite a couple. He was about her age, with a good-looking, goofy face, and sandy hair.

He gawked at me.

"You must be Barry," I said. "Come on in. I'm Stanley. Janet will be right out. She's getting dressed."

Barry followed me into the living room. I must say he was regarding me peculiarly.

"Sit down," I said. "She'll be right out."

Barry sat on the couch. I sat in the chair across from him. We looked at each other.

"So," I said. "You been dating Janet long?"

It was none of my business, of course, and he could have told me to go to hell, but he just gulped, and said, "Yeah. About a year."

I looked at him, and suddenly I realized the question I should have asked Janet before, when I'd gone up on my lines. And I realized I could ask him, too.

"You work in Manhattan?" I said.

"Yes I do."

"Oh yeah? What do you do?"

"I'm a shipping clerk. Down on Hudson."

"You like it?"

He looked at me. "It's not bad."

"You got a phone in your office?"

"Office?"

"The room you work out of," I said. "You got a phone there? They let you make calls?"

"Yeah, I can make calls," he said.

"And get calls?"

He was looking at me very funny. "Yeah," he said.

"Janet ever call you there?"

"Sure."

"How about this Tuesday?" I said. "She call you there this Tuesday?"

His eyes were wide open now. "Why you wanna know that?"

"I was just wondering," I said. "You work on Tuesday?"

"Yeah."

"All day?"

"Yeah. All day."

"When is that? From when to when?"

"Eight-thirty in the morning to five-thirty at night."

"You worked all day? You never took a break?"

"I took off lunch," he said.

"Did Janet call you that morning?"

He shrugged his shoulders. "How could I remember that morning?"

"You couldn't," I told him. "Listen. Tell me. Which of Janet's old friends do you know? Frank Burke? Sam Gravston? Winston Bishop?"

His eyes never flickered.

He shook his head. "I'm afraid I don't know any of them," he said.

I believed him. He couldn't have been that cool. If the name Winston Bishop meant anything to him, I'd have known it. So even if Janet had called him at work that day —which, of course, was the question I should have asked her—she hadn't told him about Winston Bishop. Or if she had, it had made no impression on him. At any rate, in my humble opinion, Barry hadn't strangled him.

I figured I'd nail it down, though, seeing as how Barry and I were getting on so good. Seeing as how he'd taken me as an old friend of Janet's, perhaps someone from her past.

"So," I said. "You're sure you never left work all day Tuesday?"

He blinked twice. Then looked at the bedroom door. Then looked back at me. Then he leaned in, screwed up his face, and asked, almost in awe, "Are you her *father?*"

28.

The address Richard had given me for Wendy Millington was in Chelsea. West 22nd Street. As with Janet, I didn't phone first. I didn't want people anticipating my arrival, thinking about what they were going to say to me, making up stories. Just drop in out of the blue, catch 'em off their guard, that was my plan.

So the thing was, having not called first, when I got there and found a four-story brownstone with apartments in it, I didn't know where Wendy Millington was. The address Richard had given me was just the street address with no apartment number.

I went up the front steps into the foyer and checked the mailboxes. Sure enough, there was a W. Millington. Underneath the mailbox it said apartment 3.

Only there was no bell. There were no bells for any of the apartments. This was one of those buildings where the only way you could get in to see someone was if they came downstairs and opened the door. But there was no bell to tell 'em to come downstairs. So if you were calling on someone, you either had to stand out in the street and shout up at her window, or go to the corner and call from a pay phone.

The prospect of going out in the street and shouting Wendy Millington's name was more than I could bear. I opted for the phone.

Before I went, I pushed on the foyer door, just on the off chance it wasn't locked.

It wasn't. It swung open easily.

And then I saw why. The lock had been broken off it. There was no way it could be kept closed.

The thing was, I couldn't tell when that lock had been broken. It could have been like that for weeks.

But, as I said, sometimes I get premonitions. And I got one now. I guess I just read too many mystery stories. But the thing is, in the murder mysteries, when the detective's going around chasing down clues, just before he calls on someone who has a vital piece of information which could have cracked the case, that witness is silenced.

And when I saw that smashed lock, that's the premonition that hit me.

The premonition that Wendy Millington was dead.

I pushed the door open, started up the stairs.

There was only one apartment to a floor, which made finding it easy. At the top of the first flight was a single door marked apartment 2. At the top of the next flight was a single door marked apartment 3.

Wendy Millington's apartment.

As I reached the landing, I saw to my horror that the door was slightly ajar.

This was more than just a premonition. This had become frightfully, agonizingly real.

Jesus Christ, no.

Wendy Millington was a stupid, infuriating twit of a girl.

161

I had never liked her. But still, I didn't wish her dead.

I could be wrong. Please let me be wrong. Some doors are really locked and just *look* ajar.

I pushed against it.

It swung open. Silently. Ominously.

I crept in. Slowly. Carefully. Dreading what I would find.

And then I heard it.

The sound of a scream. Not the long, drawn-out scream of someone in horror. No, a short, high-pitched, immediately muffled scream.

The scream of someone being strangled!

Jesus Christ! Now! He's in there! It's happening now!

It was a situation I had never encountered before. Confronting a killer in the act of killing. Preventing a murder from being done.

I was scared. Jesus, was I scared. And I was angry at myself, too. I mean, Jesus Christ, here was a murder being committed, and I could stop it, and yet here I stood petrified. But I couldn't help it. The man had killed three times already and here he was going for four, and this was the man I had to stop.

My eyes darted quickly around the room. Looking for a weapon. A blunt object. Something to hit him with.

No object caught my eye.

All right.

With my bare hands.

Jesus.

My bare hands?

I stood there like an asshole, vacillating.

Another muffled scream from the bedroom tipped the scale.

I crossed the room in a flash with quick, quiet strides. I reached the door to the inner room, turned, raised my fist and—

Stopped dead in my tracks, gaping.

Facing me was Wendy Millington. She was not being strangled. Nor did she appear to be in any immediate danger. She was on the bed. She was also stark naked. A young man was lying on the bed. Wendy Millington was straddling him. Her head was thrown back and her eyes were closed in ecstasy, her surprisingly large breasts were flopping to and fro, and her ass was pumping up and down like some crazed jockey straining for the finish line, as she impaled herself on the young gentleman's cock.

29.

If Wendy Millington's young gentleman had stayed the whole night I might have strangled him. I know I said I was going to stop using that expression, but in this case I make an exception. 'Cause if he'd stayed the night, I would have had to stay the night, too, because, of course, I had to find out who he was. Fortunately, he left shortly after eleven, so I was able to tail him back to his apartment on West 74th Street and peg him as David Cooper.

He never saw me. And thank god, neither did Wendy Millington. I'd never have been able to live that one down. I'm not sure Wendy would have either. But fortunately, I'd managed to back out of the bedroom and slip out the apartment door without anyone being the wiser. After that I'd staked out the front door of her apartment, hoping I'd be able to recognize the gentleman in question when he came out of the building. Which wasn't a sure thing, seeing as how I'd only seen his face from the point of view of looking sideways across the profile from somewhere near the top of his head. Plus, when I'd seen him his face had not been his most recognizable feature.

However, the gentleman coming out the door at five after eleven had to be him, even though it was the first time I got a really good look at his face. He wasn't that bad looking, and I couldn't help wondering what attraction Wendy Millington held for him. I mean, everybody loves somebody sometime and all that, but everybody doesn't love Wendy Millington. But somebody did.

And if the nameplate on his apartment door was to believed, that somebody was David Cooper.

I wondered about David Cooper. I wondered if David Cooper was using Wendy Millington as a source of inside information to Rosenberg and Stone. I realized it was an absurd thought. The only thing that made it seem less absurd was that that would explain his involvement with Wendy Millington. Yeah, I was gonna have to check David Cooper out.

But it sure wasn't gonna be that night. By the time we got back to his apartment on West 74th Street it was close to midnight. And the thing was, he'd gone home on the subway. And I'd had to follow him on the subway. Which meant there I was on 74th Street with my car still down in Chelsea. By the time I took the subway back downtown, got my car and drove back uptown, it was close to one o'clock.

Alice was still up when I got home. I was surprised— one o'clock was late for her. But she knew I was working on the case. And she couldn't wait to hear what I'd found out. The inside dope on Rosenberg and Stone. Did I have anything to report?

Did I ever.

I must say, the Wendy Millington adventure was the chief topic of conversation. Which, I suppose, was only natural. I don't know about you, but it is not every day that I see people copulating. It is not a daily occurrence for Alice, either. She was understandably interested.

"She was doing *what*?" Alice asked.

I described the scene in Wendy Millington's bedroom to the best of my ability.

"Why don't you show me?" Alice said.

I must say, in this particularly draggy case, it was not the worst time I'd had.

30.

I spent Saturday chasing down the two paralegals, Jack and Alan, and also Frank Burke. I say chasing down because that's what it entailed. It was a day fraught largely with frustration. I'd abandoned my drop-in-and-surprise-'em routine, partly through expediency, and partly due to the Wendy Millington fiasco. So the frustration was largely due to unanswered phones.

I started calling at ten in the morning. None of the three was home. Frank Burke and Jack didn't answer, and Alan's answering machine said he was out.

I left a message for Alan to call me, and took Tommie down to Riverside Park to play baseball. He beat me fourteen to nothing, which was par for the course.

By the time we got back home it was eleven-thirty. I made my phone calls again. Alan was still an answering machine, and Frank Burke wasn't home, but Jack was. I told him Richard wanted me to talk to him and I'd be right over.

He sounded shocked as hell, and for a while I thought I

was on to something. I was excited when I hung up the phone. A guilty reaction. Could this be it?

Then I realized that the way I'd phrased it, the poor guy probably thought he was being fired.

Jack's last name was Winthorp, and he lived in the College Point section of Queens. I took my beeper, so Alice could beep me in case Alan called in in response to the message I'd left on his answering machine, and drove out there.

On the way, I wondered what the hell I was going to do when I got there. I realized my knowledge of Jack and Alan was less than encyclopedic. In fact, my conversation with Jack on the phone was the first time I'd ever talked to either of them. This was not because I was a big investigator and they were just puny file clerks, but simply because they were so new, and in the normal course of my business I only get into the office once every other week. Jack's voice, high-pitched and nasal, confirmed my impression of him as a somewhat nerdy type of guy.

I was in for a bit of a shock. When I got there I discovered my knowledge of Jack and Alan was even worse than I thought. Jack wasn't Jack. Well, he was, of course, but what I mean is he wasn't the nerdy one. He was the one who looked like a football player. He just happened to have a nerdy type of voice.

He also lived with his parents. I suppose that shouldn't have surprised me so much—after all the guy wasn't much older than twenty—but it did. That's because I have a habit of being blinded by my own preconceptions. And I hadn't ever thought of Jack even *having* parents, let alone living with them. That, coupled with finding out Jack wasn't Jack, so to speak, really threw me. Jack had parents, a mousy, thin mother, and a bull of a father, both of whom seemed deeply concerned with their son's welfare. Jack introduced me to them with all the appearance of a dog who expects to be whipped. We all sat down in the living room and I began my spiel.

The relief on Jack's face when he found out what I was there for cleared him in my mind, even though none of the rest of the conversation did. The conversation, such as it was, went on for a good forty-five minutes, and I would feel safe in saying it shed no light what so ever on the situation.

A random sample went something like this:

ME: "We're just trying to help the police clear up this matter."

MOM: "The police! What do the police want with my boy?"

JACK: "Nothing, Mom."

MOM: "But you said there were police in the office."

ME: "Yes, but they're just going over the files."

DAD: "Files? The files you worked on, boy?"

JACK: "Yes, Dad, but—"

DAD: "You done something to them files, boy?"

JACK: "No, Dad, I—"

DAD: "He mess up them files?"

ME: "No, sir, you see—"

JACK: "No, Dad, honest—"

DAD: "Shut up, boy! Don't you interrupt the man."

MOM: "Hank!"

DAD: "Well, he shouldn't interrupt. You'd think we never taught him anything."

JACK: "Aw, heck, Dad—"

DAD: "Again? You're doing it again?"

JACK: "No, Dad, I—"

MOM: "You're picking on him again."

DAD: "Picking on him? Who's picking on him? I just want him to be quiet."

MOM: "Yes, but—"

DAD: "And you be quiet, too."

JACK: "Dad!"

MOM: "Now, Jack, he didn't mean anything."

DAD: "No. That's right. I don't mean nothing. All I mean is I want everyone to be quiet so I can hear what the man has to say. Now then, what were you saying?"

I had no idea. And by the end of the conversation I had even less idea. By the time I got out of there braindrops were dribbling out my ears, and I was happy just to be on my way.

My beeper went off before I got to my car, which is usually a blessing, only in this case, there wasn't a phone to be found, and I had to get in and drive around anyway. Eventually I found one and called Alice, and as I had suspected, she had beeped me to tell me Alan had just called in. I called Alan and he told me to come right over.

Right over was Park Slope in Brooklyn, so it took me a little time to get there, even with fairly good traffic. When I did, I discovered Alan's address was a brownstone in the process of renovation. Alan didn't own the brownstone; he had rented a room in it, and the renovation was going on around him. How he lived in all that chaos was beyond me, but then I guess if you can work in Richard Rosenberg's office, you can get used to anything. At any rate, Alan didn't seem to mind the clutter.

Nor did he mind my questions. He took no offense and seemed to take nothing personally. He was respectful and cooperative. He was also more intelligent than I had given him credit for. I must confess, I found that a rather suspicious circumstance, and it alone elevated him on my suspects list.

Nothing else did, however. Alan stated that he had been at Rosenberg and Stone all day on the days in question, those being, of course, the days on which Winston Bishop and Gerald Finklestein had been killed. He also vouched for Jack, whom he said had not left the office either. I wished Jack could have vouched for him, but poor Jack, at the mercy of his parents, had been lucky to get a word in edgewise.

There was, of course, the possibility that Alan could have gotten the information and phoned it to an accomplice, and this was a possibility that I could not rule out. He was certainly smart enough to have done it. Why he would have done it was beyond me, but then I didn't understand anything in this case, so why should I understand that? At any rate, as I say, I couldn't rule out the possibility.

I also couldn't confirm it. I couldn't even think of any way to try. I left Alan's place feeling like one hell of a private detective.

I called Frank Burke from a pay phone on the corner, and this time he was in. He told me to come right over.

Right over was—you guessed it—back up in Queens, so I got in the car and headed out.

Frank Burke lived in an apartment over a storefront on Hillside Avenue in Jamaica. It was a fairly nice building, with a locked outer door and a buzzer system to call up, and I had a feeling if the assignments Frank Burke had gone out on had been to buildings as safe as his own, he'd have still been working for us.

I buzzed up, and Frank buzzed me in.

He was grinning in the doorway as I came up the stairs.

"Well, well, the supersleuth," he said. "How's it going?"

"Not too good," I said, and stepped by him into his apartment.

It was a modest but neatly furnished one-bedroom affair, with a living room and a kitchen alcove.

"Sit down," Frank said, trailing me into the room. "Can I get you a beer?"

171

I noticed he was holding a half-finished bottle of Heiniken. "No thanks, nothing for me," I said.

He shrugged. "Suit yourself." He flopped into an easy chair. "So what's this all about?"

I looked at him. Frank Burke was about twenty-three or twenty-four. He was about my height and weight, which is to say, about average, but he had a deceptively lean and wiry look. I figured he might be strong. Strong enough to have strangled someone.

I paused while thinking all this, and the result was that I didn't answer him immediately. And by doing so I inadvertently stumbled upon an interrogation technique, one that the police use deliberately and to good effect.

Because he got nervous. He started fidgeting, and then he grinned in a manner that was obviously forced.

I was fascinated. Was I getting something? I didn't know, but having lucked into it, I decided to play it. I hadn't told him anything on the phone, just that I wanted to see him, so he had no idea why I was there. So I kept quiet, to let him stew, and see if he'd crack.

He did.

"Now look," he said. "I know why you're here."

"Oh?"

"Sure. You want me to come back to work. I'm sorry, but I can't."

"Oh," I said, utterly disappointed that that was what was worrying him.

Of course, he misunderstood.

"I know, I know," he said. "You're really overworked with just you and Sam, and him having auditions all the time, and you must be going nuts racing around trying to cover everything, but the thing is, I just can't do it. See—"

I cut him off. "No. You don't understand. I don't want you to come back to work."

"You sure?"

"Absolutely. That's not why I came out here. I just need to talk to you."

"About what?"

"To begin with, when did you quit?"

"So it is about that."

"No, it isn't. I just want to know when."

"Well, last week, of course. But when? Let me see." He thought a moment. "All right. The day the guy got killed. The day Richard was joking that you strangled him."

"You quit then?"

He shook his head. "No. The next morning. I came in the next morning and turned in my kit." He took a pull on the beer bottle. "I went home that night and I thought about it, and I decided I just didn't want to do it, you know." He took another sip. "The truth is, I had a bad signup that day. In Queens. You know, out toward the airport, and then get off the Van Wyck and take Linden Boulevard east for a while, and then some side street out in there. The client was this black guy who was very drunk and kept trying to borrow money off me to buy a bottle. It wasn't that scary, really, you know, it just made me uncomfortable." He took another swig. "And then it was something Sam said."

"Oh?"

"Yeah. Remember, when he came in all excited about his audition? Well, after that I got talking to him and I told him about the signup, you know, and he laughed and said, yeah, they always gave the trainees the easy ones. And it was a joke, you know, but I realized it was true. And I got to thinking, Jesus, if these are the easy ones, what the hell are the hard ones like? So the next morning I turned in my kit."

"What time?"

"What?"

"What time did you come in?"

173

"First thing. Nine o'clock."

"Did you talk to Richard?"

He shook his head. "He wasn't in yet. I talked to one of the girls. She said he didn't usually come in till ten. I didn't want to wait around until then, so I left the kit with her."

My mind was racing. The Gerald Finklestein case hadn't come in until after ten. If he'd really left he office before ten he couldn't have known about it, so he couldn't have done it. Unless, of course, he'd raced out there, strangled Finklestein and made the call himself. But I'd presumably talked to Finklestein. And while I didn't know if it was really Finklestein, I didn't think it was Frank Burke. Not unless he had a talent for dialects that I wasn't aware of. And not unless he had a strong enough stomach to strangle someone, and then wait there by the body until the phone rang so he could impersonate him. Which would be so bizarre there was no way I could see him doing it.

I tried to come back to earth and zero in.

"So you left your kit with one of the girls?"

"Yeah. Is there a problem? Is the signup missing?"

"No, no. Nothing like that. Which girl did you leave it with?"

"I can't remember their names. The skinny one."

"Janet."

"If you say so. Why is it important?"

I realized something that, of course, I should have realized before. If Frank Burke really had turned in his kit as he said, and hadn't been back to Rosenberg and Stone since, then he knew nothing of the murders, aside from Winston Bishop. He didn't know that Gerald Finklestein or Clarence White had been killed.

Unless he killed them.

And if he didn't know, I wasn't going to tell him.

174

"It's not really. I'm just wondering. Did you get paid?"

"No. Rosenberg wasn't in yet to sign the check, and I didn't want to wait around. They said they'd mail it to me."

"You didn't go back later and get it?"

He shook his head. "No. I didn't have that much coming, you know. I'd only been there a couple of days. And trainees only get half-time for training. What's this all about?"

I couldn't put him off much longer. "Nothing. I'm just making small talk. What I really came to see you about was the guy who got killed. Winston Bishop."

His eyes got real round. "No shit!"

"None. See, the cops are giving me a hard time about it, 'cause I found the body and everything, so I wanted to talk to everybody who was working that day to see if anybody knows anything that would back up my story. I wouldn't put it past those clowns to decide I was the one who did it."

He was grinning like a zany. "You? That's a laugh. You? And after everything Richard said that day about you strangling the guy. And we're all laughing. And he's talking about getting you off. And now the cops think so, too. Jesus."

Frank Burke's laughter was quite genuine this time, and his relief was very apparent. I couldn't tell if he was relieved to find out that that was all I wanted, or if he was relieved to find out the cops suspected me instead of him, but he sure was relieved.

"I'm sorry," he said. "I shouldn't be laughing at your troubles. I know this can't be any fun for you. But it's just so absurd. And you know, I have to tell you, I'm so glad you're not trying to talk me into coming back to work. Because I couldn't do it. I got another job. A better job. Steady. Better money. I start tomorrow."

"Oh?"

"Yeah. I was lucky to get it. I wouldn't have, but I knew someone, you know, and he got me in."

"Oh?"

"Yeah. See, so I wouldn't come back to Rosenberg and Stone, no matter what. So I'm glad that wasn't it."

I smiled, but inwardly I groaned. Jesus, everyone was doing better than me. All these young kids. First Sam Gravston with his auditions, and now Frank Burke with his better job. I wondered what it was that was better than Rosenberg and Stone that Frank had been so lucky to get.

I shook my head. "No, that wasn't it. So you got a better job, huh? Who's it with?"

He was grinning from ear to ear, he was so happy.

"The Sanitation Department."

31.

I'd saved the best for last. The best, of course, being Sam
Gravston. Sam was the best because he was my own pet
project. My prime suspect. The man most likely.

The way I saw it, Sam had the means. He was a big,
strong guy, and could easily have strangled those people.

And he had the opportunity, and opportunity was a biggie. Not many people would have had the opportunity. But
Sam would have. He was offered the Winston Bishop and
Gerald Finklestein cases before I was. And the Clarence
White case wasn't a real signup. The man had been strangled the night before. And then there'd been the bogus
phone call, pretending the guy was calling in to make the
appointment. Which Sam, with his acting talent, could
very well have made.

Yeah, Sam had the opportunity all right.

That left motive.

Small problem there.

Why the hell should a young man with everything going
for him go on a rampage and begin indiscriminately killing

the very people he was supposed to be helping? Unless he was crazy. But that was no answer—even a crazy man has some rationale for what he is doing. It may be totally bizarre and not make sense to a rational mind, but it would still make sense to him. And the thing was, I couldn't even come up with an *insane* motive for Sam Gravston to kill those people.

But that didn't stop me from thinking it. Because I'm smart enough to realize that I'm not that smart, and that there might be a perfectly logical explanation, and the only problem was that I was too stupid to see it.

So I was eager to talk to Sam.

I didn't reach him till late Sunday afternoon. I tried to call him Sunday morning, but as with Alan, all I got was his answering service. Sam called back about four o'clock, and I gave him the usual spiel. I can't say he seemed particularly concerned. But then some murderers aren't. At least in the books I've read. If they were to be believed, a lot of murderers were self-assured and cocky. At any rate, Sam didn't seem alarmed, just slightly exasperated. He had a date that evening, and he'd just got back from playing tennis, and he had to shower and change and all that, but if it was really important and I came right over, we could talk while he was dressing.

It was really important and I came right over. On the way I thought about Sam—the successful actor with the agent and the auditions. Sam—the carefree bachelor who played tennis all afternoon and then rushed back to his bachelor pad to prepare for his dinner date with a young lady. Sam —who could give me a few minutes if I rushed right over.

Sam—the potential murderer.

How could I trap him? The obvious things came to me: check times, alibis; drop hints, watch for reactions; get him to advance *his* theories of the case. That was a good one—I think Columbo used to do that a lot.

I wondered if I could trick him into talking black jive for me. I realized it would be dangerous to try. That would be one thing he would be sure to be wary of. I could think of no way to bring it up without putting him on his guard. I was hoping something would come to me.

It hadn't by the time I got there.

Sam Gravston's address was a loft in SoHo. That figured. There was something glamorous about a loft in SoHo. It was entirely in keeping with Sam Gravston's image as a rising young actor that he would have one. A loft in SoHo. An artist's residence. To which he would bring back the attractive starlet after a night of dining and discotheques.

As I pulled up in front of Sam Gravston's address, I got a rude shock. I realized my knowledge of SoHo was rather limited. Apparently there are lofts and there are lofts. Sam Gravston's building was a narrow, four-story affair squeezed in between two larger loft buildings. It was almost as if the other two buildings had joined forces and were attempting to squeeze it out. The other two buildings looked clean, new and in good repair. I realized they weren't. That was just by comparison. Sam Gravston's building looked as if the condemned sign must have just fallen off. Cracked, dirty windows, with rusting bars. A cellar grating caving in, with only half a sawhorse warning people not to tread. Horrid graffiti, as bad as I'd seen in the worst of projects. And the outer door flopping open on one hinge.

I went in and up the narrow, unlit stairway to the second floor, where a hallway divided the thin building into two, thinner halves. Two metal doors faced me. Sam had said the one to the right. I banged on it. There was no answer. I banged louder. Then I heard footsteps, and then the sound of a deadbolt and then Sam Gravston, dripping wet and with a towel around him, opened the door.

"Come on in. I'm in the shower. I'll be right with you," he said.

He ushered me inside, slammed and locked the door and disappeared through a door in the back of the loft.

Leaving me to look around.

And feel, as usual, like a total asshole.

So this was the life of luxury I had envisioned Sam Gravston living. I'd always thought of lofts as spacious expanses with floor-to-ceiling windows letting in copious quantities of light. Sam Gravston's loft was no more than twelve feet wide and twenty-five feet long. It had two small, dirty windows overlooking the street, and that was it.

The door through which Sam had disappeared in the back appeared to be to a small, stall shower/toilet enclosure. Along the back wall were a stove, refrigerator and bathtub, vintage 1950. There was also a kitchen sink without cabinet, a free-standing unit coming out of the wall, supported only by it's pipes. A dilapidated card table next to it held the drainboard.

The loft had not been painted in years. It appeared to be furnished largely with furniture gathered from off the street. A mattress on the floor served as the bed. I sincerely hoped Sam had at least bought that, not tugged it out of some junk heap somewhere, as he'd obviously done with the other stuff. There was a sofa with a cushion missing and a spring coming out; a coffee table with three legs and a hunk of two-by-four for the fourth; an old metal dresser that looked like a reject from some boarding school; next to it, a broomstick suspended on wires from the ceiling, serving as a clothes closet; and a bookcase with a shelf missing, crammed with cheap paperbacks.

I walked over to it and looked. I smiled. Sam Gravston was a mystery buff, as was I. The books were mostly murder mysteries. I saw that his taste ran largely to British authors. I noted a large number of Simon Brett, Josephine Tey, Patricia Highsmith. And an entire shelf of well-read Agatha Christies.

I was still looking at the titles when Sam Gravston emerged from the bathroom. He had dried himself and was dressed in jockey shorts. As he came he grabbed a shirt from the clothes rack and began to put it on.

"So, what's up?" he asked.

I felt bad. What was up was I was about to question him to determine his involvement in the Rosenberg and Stone murders. Only now I didn't feel like it. I'd do it, of course, but my heart wasn't in it. Because half an hour ago Sam Gravston had been my prime suspect in the case.

And now he wasn't.

And I realized that made no sense at all, but it was true.

I knew intellectually that a man's life-style should make no difference—that a poor man could kill just as easily as a rich one, and would probably even have more motive. But that didn't matter. Before I had envisioned Sam Gravston as an arrogant, aggressive young man, clawing his way up the ladder to success. And now I saw him as a poor schmuck like me, just scratching out a living. Rosenberg and Stone wasn't just a lark for Sam. Despite his agent and his auditions and his lofty aspirations, Sam Gravston had nothing going for him but hopes and dreams and the profits from broken arms and legs.

And somehow that made all the difference in the world.

I gave Sam Gravston the prepared spiel, most of which I'd already been over with him on the phone. He continued dressing, and was up to his socks and shoes by the time I'd finished.

"That's all well and good," he said, "but, frankly, I don't see how it's gonna help."

"I don't either," I said. "But Richard wants it done, so if you'd just bear with me."

"Oh, sure. Whaddya want to know?"

"The Winston Bishop case. You were given it before me."

"Right. And then I got the audition." He grinned. "Sorry about that."

"Not your fault," I said. "But if I could jog your memory a little?"

"No problem. I've already been over all this with the police."

"I know. It's just that Richard wants it first hand, not what the police feel like giving out."

Sam shrugged. "OK."

"What time did you get the case?"

"I got beeped around nine-thirty."

"Where were you?"

"Out in Queens, shooting a photo assignment."

"By nine-thirty you were already out in Queens?"

"Yeah. Why not? You gotta move the car at eight. No sense double parking and hanging around. I had a photo assignment in Astoria I wanted to knock off. There's a restaurant there, right over the Triboro Bridge, with a parking lot—you know the one I mean? I drove over there, caught breakfast and was out shooting the sidewalk when the beep came in."

"And that was at nine-thirty?"

"Near as I can make it."

"You called in right away?"

"There was a pay phone on the corner. Astoria's not that bad with pay phones. Most of them work. Not like Bed-Stuy, you know? I called in right away."

"Who did you talk to?"

182

"Wendy or Janet."

"You don't know?"

Sam grinned. "No, and they don't know either, and the cops don't know, and they're kinda pissed off about it."

"Anyway, you took the assignment and said you'd do it?"

"Right. And Wendy/Janet said the client was waiting and to go right over. And you know a signup takes precedence over everything, so I hopped in the car and took off."

"So what happened?"

"I got beeped again in the middle of the Triboro Bridge."

"Oh?"

"Yeah. By my agent."

"Oh?"

"Yeah. You know how the beepers got two tones, the regular beep and the steady tone?"

"Sure. My wife has the other tone."

"Right. I gave out mine to my agent. So he beeps me on the Triboro Bridge. Which is a real pain in the ass, cause I figure it's important, but I can't call him till I get off the damn bridge, and there's a traffic jam. Anyway, I get to Manhattan and I call, and it's about an audition, and you know the rest."

"Yeah, I sort of do," I said. "What time was the audition?"

Sam had been answering my questions right along. For the first time, he looked at me funny. "Why?" he said.

I was embarrassed, but I figured the only thing to do was to go right for it.

"For an alibi, of course," I said. "To prove conclusively that you couldn't have done it."

That didn't throw him any. If anything, he looked reassured, as if he'd just thought of it. "Oh. Of course. Well, I'm afraid it won't do it. The audition was for noon."

"Oh?"

"Now, I know what your thinking," Sam said. "If it wasn't till noon, why couldn't I just knock off the signup first? Well, I could have. But I had to change, you know. For the audition. It was the part of a young college kid. You know how it is. I couldn't walk in looking like a plain-clothes cop. So I had to get all the way downtown and change and then catch the subway uptown. As it was, I barely made it."

"At noon?"

"Right. And then it was the usual bullshit. I sat around and they didn't get to me till after three."

"OK," I said. "So much for Winston Bishop. What about Finklestein?"

Sam sat down on the couch and rubbed his head. "Let's see, I had a meeting with my agent that morning."

"Who's your agent?"

"Manny Rothstein. You know him?"

Never having had a theatrical agent myself, my knowledge of them was sketchy at best. "Sorry. I don't."

"Yeah, well he's supposed to be good. At least, he hustles. You know?"

"Yeah. What time was your meeting?"

"Ten o'clock."

"Where?"

"His office. West 44th Street."

"So what happened."

"Well, I left word at the office that I had the meeting, and not to schedule me anything early, and I'd call in as soon as I was through. But they beeped me anyway, right in the middle of the meeting. So I called in from there and they gave me the Finklestein case—at least, asked if I could do it. But Manny'd just lined me up a commercial audition for that afternoon."

Sam sighed, shook his head. "I wanted the signup—I

needed the money—so I asked where it was. If it'd been close I'd have squeezed it in, but it was way the hell out in Queens, so I had to let it go."

"And you went to the audition?"

"Yes."

"What time?"

"Two o'clock.

"Where?"

"Fillmore, Roston and Brown. On Madison Avenue." Sam shook his head. "Which was a waste of time. I wasn't right for it, and I knew it the minute I looked at the story-board. I didn't get a callback."

"I see," I said. "And the day of the Clarence White killing? You had an audition then, too."

Sam looked at me in surprise. "I thought he was killed the night before."

"He was. I'm talking about when the body was discovered."

"Why?"

I didn't want to say the real reason. Which was, of course, the phone call. "Because if you hadn't had an audition, you'd have been the one who discovered him."

Sam grinned. "That's right, isn't it? Say, you must have really felt put-upon."

"It was not a great week," I told him. "At any rate, you had an audition."

"Yeah. A callback. Kept me there all day."

"Till when?"

"I don't know. Four o'clock, maybe."

I smiled and nodded, but that wasn't what I'd wanted to hear. Four o'clock was cutting it close, but Sam still could have got uptown in time to make the phone call. If only he'd said five.

Sam reached for his shoes and socks and started pulling

them on. "Anything else you need to know?"

I wished there was. But I couldn't think of anything. Other than that I'd been wasting my time.

"Not really," I said.

"Oh, yeah. Well, listen. Let me ask you something."

"What's that?"

"Is it true about IBs?

IB stood for "Incentive Bonus" or "Initiative Bonus"—no one was ever really sure which. But in any case, what it meant was that Richard would pay a bonus to anyone who found a new case, which he accepted. I'd stopped chasing IB's long ago, having found them distasteful. But they still existed.

"Is what true?"

"Richard really pays a hundred and fifty bucks if you bring him a new case?"

"So they say."

He looked at me. "You never had one?"

"Actually I did. But not for a long while. But you do?"

He nodded. "Yeah."

"So sign it up and turn it in."

"And I'll get a hundred and fifty bucks?"

"Well, that depends."

Sam looked alarmed. "On what?"

I shrugged. "The case itself. Where it came from. Some things disqualify it. Like if it arose out of another signup. Say you sign some guy who was in an automobile accident. He tells you there was another passenger in the car who was injured. That person didn't call in, but signing them wouldn't get you a bonus, because the source is really the client who called in in the first place."

"But if you find it yourself it's all right?"

"Usually. Why don't you tell me what the case is?"

"It's my uncle," Sam said. Then added, apprehensively, "Is that all right? If it's a relative, I mean?"

"Relatives are fine."

"Well, it's a relative. My only relative, actually. The guy brought me up."

"None of which disqualifies him. What's the case?"

"Simple. Slip and fall. Tripped on a crack in the sidewalk and broke his leg."

"Fine. You sign him up yet?"

"No."

"Does he want to sign?"

"Yeah. I talked him into it."

"So what's the problem?"

"Well, I just want to be sure. Let me tell you what happened. The accident was about two weeks ago. Marvin— that's my uncle, Marvin Gravston—told me about it over the phone, and I talked him into letting me sign him up. Only thing was, I couldn't do it 'cause he was leaving town. He's out in Texas now. The guy's got oil wells out there. He's stinking rich." Sam couldn't help a glance around his loft. "Tight as hell, but stinking rich. Anyway, I didn't want to take a chance on him changing his mind, so I had him make an appointment."

"What do you mean?"

"I have an appointment with him this Tuesday to sign him up."

I frowned. "What do you mean, appointment? He's your uncle. You see him by appointment?"

Sam shook his head. "No. I wanted to tie him down, you know, so it wouldn't get away. So I had him make the appointment."

"What do you mean?"

"Before he left for Texas. I had him call Rosenberg and

187

Stone and make an official appointment to see me."

I frowned. "Oh."

"What's wrong?"

I didn't want to panic him. "Well," I said. "It's all right, but you shouldn't have done that."

I panicked him. "Done what?"

"Had him call in. See, if you just sign him up and bring in the retainers and Richard takes the case, that's it, you get the bonus. But if he called in and asked for an appointment, it's not automatic. 'Cause it's just like a regular call-in and signup."

"So I don't get the bonus?"

"No. You do. You just have to be careful. Make sure Richard knows it's your referral and not a call-in. What you do is, when you sign him up, have him write, "Referred by Sam Gravston" on the retainers. And you write it on the fact sheet. And star it and circle it and write a big "IB" on the top of the sheet. You do that and it'll be OK."

"You sure?" Sam asked.

"Yeah, I'm sure."

His relief was boundless.

So was mine.

I know it makes no sense at all, but as far as I was concerned, Sam Gravston's uncle clinched the case. In my book, this poor schmuck, who wasn't concerned at all about what he was doing at the time three people were murdered, but who was desperately concerned about whether he'd get his hundred and fifty bucks, could not have killed those people.

32.

Monday was a hodgepodge. I started off by dropping Tommie off at the East Side Day School and rushing back to West 74th Street to stake out David Cooper's apartment. It was eight-twenty-five when I got there, and I was really afraid the son of a bitch had gotten up and left for work. By twenty-of-nine I'd just about convinced myself I'd blown it when out he came, dressed in suit and tie.

He set off down the street, unfortunately not in the direction traffic was going. I left my car double-parked and set off after him. I wondered if Richard would pay for it if I got a parking ticket. I realized that was idle speculation.

He walked over to Broadway, and up two blocks to a bank. He banged on the front door and a guard with keys came, unlocked it, let him in and then relocked the door. It wasn't nine o'clock yet, so I figured that had to mean he worked there.

I rushed back to my car, drove around, found a meter and sat there until it ticked off till nine o'clock. Then I got out, fed a quarter in and walked back to the bank.

I went inside and looked around. Sure enough, David Cooper was the third teller from the left.

I didn't go up and talk to him, however. Instead I detoured over to the other side, where the bank officers were. It was early, and there was no line at the counter yet. A smartly dressed young woman of about thirty-five left her desk, came up to the counter and smiled at me.

"May I help you?" she said.

"I certainly hope so," I said. "Could I talk to whomever's in charge of personnel?"

She frowned slightly. "Is this with regard to a job application?" she asked.

"No, no," I said. "Nothing like that." I flashed my ID at her briefly and put it back in my pocket. "I've been sent out by the main office to conduct a random survey on worker turnout. In other words, how often is the bank operating at full capacity, and how often is it understaffed due to sick leave, vacation time or what have you."

She looked at me. "I beg your pardon?"

"You see what I'm getting at, of course," I said. I thought that was a good ploy—to imply that the person you were talking to was astute enough to comprehend your absurdity.

Unfortunately, she didn't.

"No, I don't see what you mean. Could you be more explicit?"

"Certainly," I said. "Let's take last week, for example. Talking specifically about the tellers now. How many days last week were you at maximum capacity? Did you have all tellers working full-time?"

I don't know what it was that I did or said that tipped her off. All I know is, one way or another, I blew it.

Because she frowned, cocked her head at me and said, "Could I see your ID again, please?"

No, she couldn't.

I turned on my heel and walked out of the bank as fast as I could. And felt, as I often do, like a total asshole.

Which sort of set the tone for the day.

I had three signups, all easy, all in the Bronx. When I say all easy, it shows you where my head was at. One of them was actually in a pretty hairy building, and under normal circumstances I would have been terrified out of my mind. But as it was, I was so obsessed with my job for Richard, I couldn't really concentrate on it. Couldn't focus in on the terror, if you know what I mean.

In between those signups, I made other stabs at my Rosenberg and Stone investigation. All of them were about as fruitful as my escapade in David Cooper's bank.

I drove down to the packing plant where Janet's boyfriend worked. I went in and wandered around until I spotted him working in the shipping room. Thank god he didn't spot me. The poor guy wouldn't have known what to make of that. I wondered what clever ruse I could come up with to find out if the guy had actually been working on the two days in question. I couldn't think of a damn thing. And after my adventure in the bank, I was too nervous to even try. That hadn't exactly been a real confidence booster.

I called the Sanitation Department and tried to ascertain if they had a Frank Burke working for them. That was a joke. If you want to aggravate yourself some time, try calling the Sanitation Department. It took me a half hour to get anyone on the phone. After that I got transferred three times and cut off. I tried again with much better results. It took me only ten minutes to get someone on the phone, and I got transferred two times and cut off.

PARNELL HALL

Third time's the charm. That time I managed to get transferred to the proper person, who not only had the information but also had the authority to be able to inform me that he was unable to give it out.

That was enough for me. I wasn't sure what confirming that Frank Burke really had a job with the Sanitation Department was going to do for me anyway. It was just confirming his story. But would the fact that he told me the truth about that be any indication that he hadn't strangled three people? Not really. But I wanted to check out Frank Burke, and I couldn't think of anything else to check.

And I checked out Sam Gravston. Again, to the best of my ability.

I called his agent. I represented myself as an independent movie producer and told him I wanted to check Sam Gravston's availability.

Now, I know this is a no-no. Actors are fragile enough things to begin with, and you shouldn't fuck with their emotions by misrepresenting the possibility of work. But this was murder, and I had to know.

Not that I found out. I gleaned the information that Sam Gravston was currently up for a TV series, and I learned the name of it, "Shake the Tree," but that was it. I couldn't really ask the agent what specific auditions Sam had been to in the last week. The question just didn't make any sense.

Nor did it make any sense when I considered asking it of the woman who answered the phone at Telvue Productions, which was casting the sitcom. To her I represented myself as an agent representing a young actor whom I thought would be perfect for the show. That turned out to be a good opening tack, for it got me the information that the show had been auditioning all last week, that they were

192

already well into callbacks, and that the cast was close to being set.

But that was it. I didn't know what to ask next. I mean, I knew what I wanted to ask next, which was which auditions had Sam Gravston been at. But there was no way to ask the question without sounding like a total moron, which wouldn't have bothered me if I'd thought there was any chance of the woman answering it. But there wasn't. And on top of that, it occurred to me that by inquiring specifically about Sam Gravston, I would lead her to believe that I was in some way lobbying either for or against Sam, which might result in costing him the part. For which, I realized, there was no way I would ever be able to forgive myself.

So, as I said, it was a draggy day, and not one that really boosted my morale as a demon investigator. It was a big relief to me when I finally finished giving Alice a blow by blow description of my misadventures, and was able to tumble mercifully into bed.

33.

Black Tuesday.

I'd had Blue Monday, so it was only natural that I would have Black Tuesday. But I didn't think of it at the time. Never even suspected. Which gives you a good idea of how perceptive I am.

It started off routinely enough. I dropped Tommie off at his school and immediately got beeped. I couldn't call in right away because I didn't have Walker in the car with me, so I had to drive out of the area to where I could park. I sped up to 125th and Madison, which turned out to be a shrewd move, because when I called in Wendy/ Janet had a signup in the Bronx. I went on up Madison Avenue, over the bridge and to the address on Webster Avenue.

Which was where things started going wrong. I couldn't find the address. I'd called the client to verify it, and the building number he'd given me was the same one Wendy/ Janet had given me. But it wasn't there. No such building. No such number.

I hunted up another pay phone and called the client again. He was indignant. Of course that was the right address—where the hell was I?

I was at a pay phone in the Bronx feeling stupid and getting pissed off.

It only took me a good five minutes on the phone to eventually ask the right question, which was, of course, "Is that Webster Avenue in the Bronx?" And, of course, it wasn't. It was Webster Avenue in Mt. Vernon.

I wondered how Wendy/Janet could have made that mistake. Mt. Vernon does not sound like the Bronx to me. But there was no sense arguing with the client. He had every right to live in Mt. Vernon if he wanted, and it was my job to go see him.

I did, and it was a disaster. When I got there the guy turned out to be a crotchety old fart who had decided since talking to me that he was so irritated by my inefficiency and my hassling him about his address that he wasn't going to sign.

Fine by me. I slammed out of his rented, two-story frame house, being careful not to break my leg on the perfectly sound-looking porch steps that had somehow incapacitated him, got in my car and drove off.

And immediately got beeped again. This time it was the steady tone that meant Alice was beeping me.

And I hate that. I mean, it's nice to have so that Alice can get ahold of me in an emergency. But I hate it when she does. I hate it when the beeper goes off with that steady tone. Because I always think of it as an emergency, and I always think the worst. I tense right up. God, what happened now?

I spotted a pay phone on the corner and I slammed the car into the curb, praying the phone would work. That was the worst of it—sometimes Alice would beep me, and I wouldn't be able to find a phone right away, and when I did it wouldn't work, and I'd go out of my mind.

This one worked. I called her and punched in our calling-card number.

She answered on the first ring.

"What is it?" I said.

"Nothing's wrong," she said. Alice is great that way. She knows I worry, so she always says that first.

"Then why'd you beep me?"

"I'm sorry. I didn't know what to do. Sam Gravston called."

"What?"

"Yeah. I'm sorry, but he's all upset. He asked me to beep you and have you call him. He left a number."

This was a little much. "Why?" I said. "Why you? Why didn't he just have the office beep me?"

"He said he was sorry, but he didn't want them to know about it."

"Jesus Christ. Why the hell not?"

"Hey," Alice said. "Don't shoot the messenger. Why don't you ask him?"

"What's the number?"

She gave it to me. I wasn't sure, but I didn't think it was Sam's home number.

I called it. He answered on the first ring.

"Hello?"

"Sam?"

"Stanley. Thank god."

"What's the matter? What's wrong?"

"Listen. I got a big problem. My agent just beeped me. I got another callback for the sitcom. It's down to two people, me and one other guy."

"What?"

"Yeah. It looks like I really might get it."

I have a slow reaction time, but that was long enough. I was getting really pissed off.

"Sam," I said, rather sharply. "Why the hell did you have Alice beep me?"

"Oh. Oh," he said. "I'm sorry. I hate to ask you. It's just, I'm desperate. I mean, I might get this job, but then I might not, and—Oh. I'm sorry. There I go again. It's just I really need the money, and—"

"Sam."

"Yeah. Yeah. Sorry. It's my uncle. You know, I told you I had a signup with my uncle. My IB case. Well, it's this morning. Between eleven and twelve o'clock. And I can't go. I got the damn audition."

"So reschedule it."

"You don't understand. I can't. You don't know my uncle. He's a really cold bastard, you know. It was all I could do to talk him into this, you know. If I change it, he'll cancel. I'll lose the bonus. I hate to ask, but I really need the money, and—Oh hell."

"I see," I said, rather coldly. "You want me to sign up the case for you, and give you the bonus."

"I know, I know. It sounds bad. But I'm desperate. You'd get time and mileage, of course. Just another signup. I wouldn't even ask, but—"

"Yeah, yeah, you're desperate," I said. "What's the address?"

He gave it to me. His relief was almost comical, his gratitude overwhelming. It was all I could do to get him off the phone.

I hung up in a foul mood. It was the type of favor that, in a perfect world, you wouldn't be asked to do. You know how it is. There are some favors that people ask you for that, on the one hand, you can't really refuse, but on the other, you really resent doing.

This was one of them. Jesus. Do a draggy signup to make Sam Gravston a hundred and fifty dollars. So that he can go to another audition to boot. All right, so I would get time and mileage, just like any other signup, but still . . .

I had just opened my car door when suddenly I stopped dead.

Wait a minute! This was an IB case. You didn't get time and mileage for an IB case! You did it on your own and got the bonus only if Richard took the case. Son of a bitch!

I was stomping back to the pay phone to call the office to tell them to beep Sam Gravston to tell him where he could stick his damn signup when I remembered. He'd had his uncle call in and schedule an appointment. So it *was* a regular signup in the eyes of the office, and time and mileage would be paid.

I resented *that*. Having come to the conclusion that I was getting dorked, and that therefore I had a perfect right to refuse the case, I was infuriated to realize that I wasn't getting dorked, and therefore I had to do it. I stomped back to the car, got in, slammed the door and pulled out.

As I got on the Major Deegan and headed back to Manhattan I began to calm down somewhat. All right, it wasn't as bad as it could have been. Sam's uncle lived in Manhattan, and if I'd started from there the case would have been no mileage, and two hours, tops. But I was in Mt. Vernon. That meant I could charge mileage and travel time from there, and pick up a quick three hours on the clock. And I needed hours on the clock. I was in a much better mood by the time I hit Manhattan.

And immediately got pissed off again. Sam Gravston's uncle lived in a townhouse on East 36th Street. Try parking on East 36th Street sometime. You can't do it. If you do, you'd better have $115 plus taxi fare over to Pier 40, where your car is going to be towed. If that doesn't sound like fun, you'd better have $15 for a garage.

I didn't. I had seven bucks on me. I drove around the East Side, cursing and bitching, and trying to figure out what the fuck I was going to do, and the end result was I finally got a parking meter on Second Avenue and 28th Street.

It was an hour meter, twenty-five cents per thirty minutes. Which meant I'd have to feed two quarters into it, hotfoot it up to 36th Street, sign up Sam Gravston's uncle quick like a bunny and then race back to 28th Street ahead of the meter maid, so that the parking ticket didn't eat up all the profits of the signup. It could be done, but it was an iffy proposition. Particularly, with what Sam Gravston had said about his uncle—if he really was a cold, humorless son of a bitch, he would be apt to ask a lot of questions, take a lot of convincing and not take kindly to being rushed.

All that was floating through my head as I hurried up Second Avenue. That and how I felt about it, and how I felt about Sam Gravston, and the whole bit. And the way I felt was really hassled, and really put-upon, and really pissed off.

And it was all of those personal feelings that clouded my mind and blinded me to the obvious. Because, I must admit, it never even occurred to me. But, as I'm sure you've already guessed, when I got there, Sam Gravston's uncle had been strangled.

34.

"This is intolerable."

Richard was right. Intolerable was the word for it. I agreed, and I'm pretty sure Sergeant Clark and Detective Walker agreed, too.

The four of us were in Richard's office, conducting what was rapidly becoming a ritual postmortem. Discussing how it was that I, Stanley Hastings, had happened to find another body.

It was getting ludicrous. It crossed my mind that if Sam hadn't gotten the audition, if he'd been the one to go on the signup, his uncle wouldn't have been murdered—that it only happened when I went out on a case.

I realized this was just paranoia. I also realized I had a lot to be paranoid about. After all, I'd just found my fourth dead body in two weeks.

As I've said, I'd blundered into the place without a thought in my mind other than that I had to beat the parking meter. Sam Gravston's uncle owned the whole building, so there'd been no apartment to find. I'd gone up the front steps, banged on the door, got no answer, cursed out Sam, tried the knob, found it open, gone in and found the body.

Marvin Gravston was lying in the living room on the first floor. He was a big man, as big as Sam, and apparently he hadn't taken kindly to being strangled, and had put up a bit of a struggle. A coffee table and an end table had been overturned, and various vases, ashtrays and other ornamental objects had been smashed.

I'd managed, once again, not to throw up. I'd staggered, white-faced, to the front door, opened it and waved my arms, and just as I'd imagined it would happen, suddenly the place was lousy with cops. Walker and Clark had shown up ten minutes later, immediately followed by the medical examiner.

I hadn't heard his report. After he'd arrived, I'd been stashed outside in a police car, probably, I figured, because this most recent development had once again elevated me to the position of prime suspect.

Ten minutes later, Clark and Walker had come out of the townhouse, and an officer had chauffeured us down to Rosenberg and Stone.

Where Richard pronounced the situation intolerable. And, just in case there were any doubt as to whether or not he meant it, he said it again.

"Intolerable."

Sergeant Clark nodded. "Yes, sir. It is."

Richard turned on him coldly. "I don't think you understand what I mean. I am referring to your handling of the case."

"I beg your pardon?"

"Yes, of course," Richard said. "It is intolerable that people are being killed. That goes without saying. But what I am saying is the *reason* people are being killed is because you botched the case. And that is intolerable."

"I botched the case," Clark said. "Just how did I botch the case?"

"You and your damn theories," Richard said. "The killer is a client I wronged. The killer is a black man from Harlem. The victims will be black men from Harlem."

"I never said that."

"You implied it. And the thing is, your theory's full of shit. And if you weren't too blind to see it, this murder could have been prevented."

"How?"

"How? How? This case has been on the books for three weeks now, for Christ's sake."

"Yes," Clark hissed. "And no one told me!"

"What?"

Clark was a cold, unemotional man, who probably prided himself on his even temper, but I could tell he was suppressing rage. "No one told me," he repeated. "I've been on this case since last week. I've been monitoring every new case that comes in. When we took over, we checked the assignment log. You know how the log is set up. It's one page per day. When we took over, the log had two pending assignments for that day, and one for the following day, and nothing after that. How the hell were we supposed to know that if we kept turning page after blank page, eventually in the middle of next week we would find one lone assignment that had been made three weeks previously? A case that wouldn't have normally been made so far in advance, but was only done so because the client happened to be a relative of one of your investigators. Now how the hell was I supposed to have counted on that?"

Clark paused, took in a breath and blew it out again. I assumed it was his method of remaining calm.

"Listen," Clark said. "I have a preliminary report from the medical examiner. According to him, Marvin Gravston died sometime between seven and nine this morning."

"What?" I said.

Clark turned to me. "Surprise you?" he said. "Or are you just trying to convince me you're not guilty?" He turned back to Richard. "Yes. Between seven and nine. Do you know what that means? I mean in terms of my intolerable investigation. Well, let me tell you. No new cases came in yesterday for today. Everything that came in yesterday was handled yesterday. Do you know what that means? That means the goddamned assignment log was never turned to today's page until your secretaries got in this morning. They turned the page, and there was this assignment that came in three weeks ago, and my cops saw it for the first time at nine-oh-five this morning. Do you realize how galling that is? Nine-oh-five!"

Sergeant Clark stopped and rubbed his head. "We sewed up the house, of course, and I can guarantee you no one went in or out of there from nine-eighteen until your man here went in at eleven-sixteen this morning. But a fat lot of good that does us, since the guy was already dead."

"I see," Richard said. He was in no way mollified. "Everything you've told me just makes a case for your own inefficiency. You should have known about the case."

"You should have told us about the case," Clark snapped.

"Me?" Richard said. "Me? I'm a lawyer, not a bookkeeper. Not a secretary. Do you think I answer my own phones? Do you think I do the paperwork? The first I knew of the case was when you told me the guy was dead."

"Right," Clark said. "And then you have the gall to tell me I should have done something because, 'The case has been on the books for three weeks, for Christ's sake.'"

Sergeant Clark's imitation of Richard was so good I almost smiled.

My next thought was to wonder if Sergeant Clark could also do jive black.

I shook my head. What a thought. God, this case was getting to me.

Richard was ready with some terrible rejoinder, but Sergeant Clark held up his hand. "Stop. Enough. Bickering is not going to help. The question is, what do we do now?"

"Oh yeah," Richard said. "Well, I have the answer to what we do now. We reexamine our ideas, that's what we do. We take this theory that the killer is some black client in Harlem that I've wronged, and we chuck it in the river. And we take your other theory, that the clients aren't necessarily clients—that someone is just killing injured people and phoning in appointments for them—and we chuck that in the river too. This was a bonafied client. A signup. On the books for three weeks. So that theory doesn't hold."

"That's going a little far," Clark said. "I'll admit we have to rethink certain aspects—"

"Rethink certain aspects!" Richard said. "Come on. Give me a break."

The argument was interrupted by a knock on the door. Sergeant Clark, preempting Richard's authority, barked, "Come in." The door was opened by two plainclothes cops, who ushered Sam Gravston into the office.

Sam was distraught, and I couldn't help wondering if it was because his uncle had been killed, or because he had been unceremoniously yanked out of a crucial audition under circumstances that at best were embarrassing and at worst had probably cost him the part. I immediately regretted the thought, because Sam's eyes darted about the room, fixed on me, and the first words out of his mouth were, "I'm sorry. Jesus, Stanley, I'm so sorry."

"I know," I said.

Sergeant Clark dismissed the plainclothes cops with a

nod of his head. They went out, closing the door behind them. He turned to Sam Gravston.

"Sit down, Mr. Gravston," he said, indicating one of the clients' chairs. "I'm sorry to put you through this, but you understand we have to ask you some questions."

Sam sunk into the chair. He rubbed his forehead with his hand. "Of course," he said. "Of course."

"Now, as I understand it, you were the one who was supposed to meet your uncle this morning?"

"That's right. Then my agent called me about the audition. It was important." His lip trembled. "Very important. Jesus. Oh, Jesus."

"I understand," Clark said. "And I'm sorry we had to drag you away from it. But I'm sure the people there will understand."

"Yeah, sure," Sam said flatly.

"After all, this is your uncle we're talking about."

"I know. I know."

I reaffirmed my first thought. Sam was obviously more upset about his audition than his uncle.

This struck Clark too. "Were you and your uncle close?"

Sam snuffled. Shook his head. "No. Not really."

"Oh? I understand he was your only living relative."

"Yes. That's true. But we weren't close. You can't know, you never met him. But he was a hard man to like. To get close to. And—well, he never liked me much either."

"I see. But you had an appointment with him."

"Yes. He broke his leg. I convinced him he could make some money out of it. That was the only language he could understand—money. He could make some money out of it, and I could make some money out of it. And he'd rather have me earn money than have to give it to me."

"He gave you money?"

"He was my guardian. He felt some sense of responsibility to my father, his brother. Not much, but enough that sometimes I could play on his sense of guilt for a touch. On, Jesus, what a way to think of it now."

"Yes," Clark said, gently prodding. "But you had this appointment?"

"Yes."

"And it was made when?"

"About three weeks ago. I'm not sure exactly."

"I'd like the exact day."

For the first time, Sam seemed to come out of himself. "Why?"

Sergeant Clark smiled his thin smile. "Because, you see, we don't know what's important and what's not. So we want all the facts we can get, however small."

Sam nodded, even though it was an explanation that didn't explain. "I see. Well, I don't know. I have to think. Let's see. I remember, I'd called his office, because"—he broke off, flushed—"because the rent was due, and they told me he wasn't in, he'd broken his leg and gone to the hospital."

"What hospital?"

"Bellevue."

"Go on. So what did you do?"

Sam flushed again. "Well, I was working in the area, so—"

"You called on him at the hospital?"

"Yes."

"And tried to sign him to a retainer?"

"No."

"No? Why not? Wasn't that why you went to see him."

"Well, yes. But, I told you, my uncle's funny. I didn't dare walk in there with a clipboard. He'd have been offended, and—Oh, hell."

Sergeant Clark smiled coldly. "I see. You went there under the guise of friendship, and then proceeded to sell him a bill of goods."

It was an extremely blunt and offensive way to state the situation. But Sam was too overcome to even protest. He just sat there, rubbing his forehead.

"Now," Clark said. "The long and the short of it was you talked your uncle into letting you sign him up. Right?"

"That's right."

"But you didn't do it then because you hadn't brought your clipboard?"

"Yes."

"So you had him call and make an appointment?"

"Yes."

"Did he call from his hospital bed? Perhaps while you were there?"

Sam flushed again. "Yes. He did."

"And why was the appointment made for three weeks later? Why not sooner?"

"My uncle was going to Texas. He had business interests there. The accident actually delayed his trip. He left as soon as he got out of the hospital."

"When was that?"

"I'm not sure. Two or three days."

"I see. And why didn't you como back and sign him up in the hospital?"

Sam flushed again.

"I see," Clark said. "You suggested that, but your uncle wouldn't have it. He wanted to be left alone. His compromise was to make an appointment for later. He probably agreed to it largely to get rid of you."

This was a little much, even for Sam. "Now see here—" he began.

Sergeant Clark held up his hand. "No offense meant, Mr. Gravston. I'm just trying to get the facts. But the fact is, he called from his bed while you were there and made the appointment, the one for this morning?"

"That's right."

"Tell me. The day you saw him at the hospital—was that the day he was admitted?"

Sam thought. "No. The day after."

Clarked nodded. "Fine. Now then, when is the last time you saw your uncle?"

"Then."

"What?"

"That was it. There in the hospital. That was the last time I saw him."

"You hadn't seen him since he got back from Texas?"

"No."

"When did he get back?"

"Saturday or Sunday. I'm not sure. But over the week-end."

"Did you speak to him on the phone?"

"No. I called his office yesterday, to verify the appointment. But I didn't speak to him. Just his secretary. She looked in his appointment book, and confirmed he was scheduled to meet me at his home at eleven o'clock."

"Why at his home? Why not in his office?"

Sam grimaced. "Because he was a big shot. It was his company, you know. He was the boss. He never went in before noon. He'd lounge around home all morning, then go out to lunch at some fancy restaurant, and then breeze in around two or two-thirty and start giving everybody hell."

"All right. At any rate, you had the appointment this morning at eleven?"

"Yes."

"And what happened?"

"Like I said. My agent called, and..." Reminded of it again, Sam once again lapsed into despair.

"So you called Mr. Hasting's wife, asked her to beep him and have him call you?"

"Yes."

"Where were you?"

"At a pay phone."

"Where?"

"On Houston Street."

"What were you doing there?"

"Shooting a photo assignment."

"Then how did your agent call you?"

"He beeped me."

"Oh?"

"I have a second frequency on my beeper. When he beeps me, I call in. That's how I found out."

"So Mr. Hastings called you at this pay phone, and you got him to cover the assignment for you?"

Sam looked at me miserably. "Yes."

Clark looked at me. "Is that right? Is that how it happened?"

"That's right."

Clark frowned and rubbed his head. "All right. That's all for now, Mr. Gravston. But you're going to have to go downtown and make a complete statement."

Clark strode to the door, yanked it open and barked an order to the plainclothes officers who were waiting right outside. They came in and escorted Sam Gravston out.

Clark closed the door and wheeled on me. "All right. Now what about you?"

"What about me?"

Clark jerked his thumb over his shoulder. "About Mr. Gravston. What he said. Was it right? Do you have anything to add?"

"You already asked me that."

"I asked you in front of him. Now that he's gone, is there anything you didn't say?"

"No. Why would there be?"

"I don't know. That's why I'm asking."

"Well, the answer is no."

"Fine. Then let's talk about you."

I sighed. "What do you want to know?"

"When you called Sam this morning. At the pay phone. Was that the first time you heard about this signup?"

Shit. He would ask me that.

"No."

Sergeant Clark stared at me. So did Richard.

"No?" Clark said. "You mean you knew about it?"

"Yes, I did."

"How? When did you find out?"

"I found out on Sunday."

I hated to go into it, but I had no choice. Out of the corner of my eye I could see Richard, who had already figured out how and why that had happened.

"Well," I said. "I was talking to Sam—"

"When?" Clark demanded.

"I told you. On Sunday."

"Sunday. You were talking to Sam Gravston on Sunday?"

"Yes."

"And where was this?"

"At his apartment. His loft, really."

"His loft?"

"Yes. He has a loft in SoHo."

Clark was looking at me as if he'd just cracked the case. "Oh, is that right? Tell me, have you ever been to Sam's loft before?"

"No."

"Sunday was the first time?"

"That's right."

"I see," Clark said. "And could you tell me what was so special about this Sunday that you chose to go to SoHo and call on Sam Gravston in his loft?"

I avoided looking at Richard. "Well," I said. "I got to thinking about the murders, and it occurred to me that Sam had been offered some of those cases before I had, and—"

Clark couldn't wait to hear the rest. "Yes, yes, of course," he said, throwing up his hands. "You got to thinking about the murders and you decided, hell, you were a detective, weren't you, maybe there was something you could do. Something the poor bungling cops were too stupid to think of." Clark shook his head. "Amateurs. God save me from amateurs." He glared at me. "So. You knew about this signup as early as Sunday?"

"That's right."

"You knew it was for Tuesday morning?"

"Yes."

"Did you know what time?"

"I'm not sure Sam mentioned that."

"Oh, you're not, are you? Pretty poor memory for a detective, wouldn't you say?"

I wouldn't say. I sat there and took it.

"So, you knew that the signup was for Tuesday morning, and you knew it was with Sam Gravston's uncle. Did you know his address?"

"No."

"No matter. It's an unusual name, Gravston. You could have looked it up in the phone book."

"Now just a minute," Richard said sharply. "I'm afraid I have to jump in here. This man is my client. If you are suspecting him of a crime, I must point out that you haven't advised him of his rights."

Clark wheeled on him. "Great! Wonderful! What an admirable contribution to the conversation, Mr. Rosenberg. For your information, I am not suspecting this gentleman of a crime. I happen to be suspecting him of gross incompetence."

"I beg your pardon," I said.

Clark turned on me frostily. "No offense intended," he said. "Just a simple statement of fact. Up till now, I had assumed that no one except Sam Gravston was aware of this signup. With the exception of the secretary who took the call three weeks ago, who couldn't be expected to remember that. You'll recall Mr. Rosenberg was complaining about the police inefficiency in not preventing this murder. And I said, the reason was we didn't know. But you knew." He lowered his voice, but spoke with almost fierce intensity. *"Why didn't you tell us?* You've known about the murders all along. You, of all people, are the man on the inside, with all the knowledge about how we are conducting our investigation. You knew we were protecting all prospective clients. And here was one that no one knew about but you, *and you didn't tell us!* And now that man is dead."

I said nothing. But I felt, as I always seemed to when dealing with Sergeant Clark, both bad and angry. Yes, I should have told them, and I felt bad. Yes, I should have thought. I should have known. But, Jesus Christ, how the hell was I to know that the police didn't know about this one? I mean, they were in the office, monitoring the cases. How should I know they would have overlooked this one? Yeah, I could have figured it out, that with the appointment having been made three weeks ago, it wouldn't be coming in now, so there would be no phone call to monitor, and no new entry in the log. But could I really have been expected to have made that leap in logic? I didn't think so. So I felt justly angry.

But I felt bad, too. Even without that leap of logic, it

should have occurred to me that Sam's uncle was a potential victim. And that hadn't occurred to me at all. So Sergeant Clark's accusation, unjust as I felt it really was, had just enough elements of truth in it to make it hurt.

Which made me even angrier.

"So," Clark said. "At any rate, you told no one. And thus we find ourselves in this disgusting mess."

Richard came to my aid. "Bullshit!" he said. "The fact is, you guys blew it, and now you're trying to weasel out by blaming your own mistake on one of my investigators!"

Clark turned to Richard. "And now we come to you, Mr. Rosenberg."

Richard was startled. "Me! What do you mean, me? What, now you're suspecting me of these crimes?"

Clark smiled his frosty smile. "Not at all, Mr. Rosenberg. I was referring to what we are going to do with you. Or rather, what we are going to do with your firm."

The threat hung in the air. Richard shifted uncomfortably.

Clark kept quiet, prolonged the moment. I knew he was enjoying it.

Finally he spoke.

"The answer is, nothing. We shall maintain media silence. We shall proceed as we have been doing."

Richard blinked, but that was all. He was poker faced, giving nothing away. He kept quiet.

I jumped in. "Why?"

Clark ignored me. He replied to Richard, as if he were the one who had spoken. "Because, essentially, nothing has changed. This murder, if anything, has helped clarify the situation. I would expect a solution in the next few days."

Richard stared at him. "You're telling me you still believe the killer is a black man from Harlem?"

"I do."

"A client that I have wronged?"

"That's right."

Richard's only comment was a contemptuous snort.

"So," Clark said. "This is what I want. You will continue to run your business as usual, with Mr. Hastings and Mr. Gravston in the field. Now, Mr. Gravston will be tied up the rest of the day with the police investigation and matters pertaining to his uncle. But tomorrow, I want him back on the job. Now, that may not be easy. Right now he's had an emotional shock, but as soon as it wears off, he's going to realize that he probably stands to inherit money from his uncle and doesn't *need* this job. So it may take a personal appeal from you to keep him working." Clark looked evenly at Richard. "I want you to make that appeal. If necessary. If there is any question of Sam Gravston leaving work. Because I can't have anything altered. I must have all elements of the pattern remain the same, if we expect to clear this up. Do you understand?"

"I understand what you're asking, but—"

"Fine. Then do it. But the thing is, you can't let Mr. Gravston know *why* you're asking. I don't want him, or anyone else here, knowing what our plans are. That would ruin everything. That is why I stress a *personal* appeal. You are asking him to help *you*. You are willing to replace him, of course, but you are asking him to stay on the job just long enough for you to do so. You need help, that's the tack to take. Your business has been hurt, and you're desperate. Offer more money, if necessary."

Richard had opened his mouth to say something, but that suggestion left him speechless. He nearly gagged.

"And that's all, Mr. Rosenberg," Clark said. "If you can do that, and only that, you'll have nothing to worry about." Clark nodded in agreement with himself. "For I guarantee you, we are going to catch this killer."

35.

I wasn't convinced.

And neither was Richard. And, despite the fact that two new cases had come in and what with Sam Gravston out of the picture I was the only investigator left to sign them up, for once Richard let 'em hang. He kept me in the office a good two hours after Sergeant Clark finally left, and we painstakingly went over the fruits of my investigation.

I told him everything, and in minute detail. Except that I gave him a bowdlerized version of the account of my encounter with Wendy Millington's boyfriend. I'm not a tattletale, and I didn't feel such a juicy tidbit of gossip was fair game. It also made me feel sleazy, and put a taint on my whole investigation.

Of course, without it, the whole thing was rather dull. Dull and unprofitable. In the end, Richard was forced to admit we weren't any further advanced than we had been, despite what Sergeant Clark might think.

I finally got out of there, signed up the two clients and

one more that came in that day, all of whom were alive, and finally got home.

Where Alice put me through a similar interrogation. At least about the Gravston murder—she already knew all about my investigations.

But the Gravston murder was big news. After we got Tommie into bed, we batted it around for hours. And nothing helpful emerged. We both agreed that it was a terrible thing, but that was about it.

It was on the eleven o'clock news. Not the lead story—a fire in Brooklyn beat it out—but the one after that.

It was the first time one of the killings had made the TV news. That was for two reasons: 1), Sergeant Clark had the lid on, so no one knew the crimes were the work of a serial killer; and 2), Marvin Gravston was the first victim that had any money. "OILMAN MURDERED," was the heading in that rectangular box that's always projected on the screen behind the anchorman's head. The account wasn't much—just that Marvin Gravston had been brutally strangled, and that the police had no leads.

Rosenberg and Stone was not mentioned.

After that, I switched off the TV with the remote control and sat in bed, rubbing my head.

"It's not your fault," Alice said.

I looked at her. "I know that."

"I know you know that. But I think you need to hear it every now and then."

I smiled. "You're right. I do."

"And you're going to solve it."

I opened my mouth.

"No, you are," she said. "You're very good at stuff like that. Thinking things out. You just think you're not. But you are. You'll solve it."

"Sure," I said.

216

But I wasn't convinced.

We turned out the light shortly after that, but I couldn't sleep. I lay there in the dark, thinking about the case.

The case I was going to solve.

I thought about everything I knew. Everything I'd heard. Everything I'd seen.

I thought of the detective books I'd seen in Sam Gravston's loft. Particularly the Agatha Christies. And her famous protagonist, Hercule Poirot. Yeah, that was who I needed to be to solve this case. Hercule Poirot. Who could solve a crime by just thinking about it. By exercising the "little gray cells" of the brain.

Surely I had enough evidence now to solve the crime. It was just a question of sifting through it, discarding the irrelevant and latching on to the significant.

It could be done.

I thought about the suspects. Sam Gravston chief among them. Sam Gravston, who stood to inherit a pile of money now that his uncle was dead. An excellent motive for murder.

Of his uncle.

But not of a black man in Harlem.

Or even a white man in Queens.

I thought about Frank Burke. The failed investigator. The gutless wonder. Funny, I should be saying that. But suppose his cowardice, unlike mine, was merely feigned? Then he could have killed those people, even Marvin Gravston—the assignment was in the book and he could have seen it.

Was that it? Was it Frank Burke?

I didn't know.

I thought about Janet's boyfriend, Barry. And Wendy's boyfriend, David Cooper.

I suspected them both.

I had no idea why.

I thought about Sergeant Clark. I had twice suspected him of the killings, facetiously to be sure, but still he bore thinking about. His mimicry of Richard had been remarkable. And he certainly was privy to all the inside information. And wasn't his cold, reserved manner just the sort of facade that sometimes masked the violence within, the type of manner one associated with a form of insanity? And he had certainly showed a flagrant hostility toward Richard. And—

Richard.

Jesus.

The one person I'd never suspected. Never even thought of.

Richard.

Who else had all the information of Rosenberg and Stone at his fingertips? Who else had the brilliant mind necessary to plot and plan the whole incredible scheme. Who else—

Wait a minute. *What* incredible scheme? How the hell did bumping off his own clients benefit Richard?

I chuckled softly into my pillow. I'd just realized something. I'd been trying to think like Hercule Poirot, and I'd failed utterly. Instead, I'd been thinking like my namesake, Hercule Poirot's sidekick, Hastings, whose method of attempting to solve a crime was to indiscriminately suspect each person in turn.

I lay there, chuckling at my own folly, and thinking about Richard and Sam Gravston and Sergeant Clark and the Rosenberg and Stone murders and fictional detectives and neat and tidy solutions and murders and alibis and suspects, and the end result was I fell asleep and dreamed I was no longer the sidekick Hastings but Hercule Poirot himself and I was solving the case.

I awoke with a start and sat bolt upright in bed. My body

was tingling all over, and I discovered I was trembling. I was not surprised.

Because I knew who had committed the Rosenberg and Stone murders.

And why.

36.

"Agatha Christie."

MacAullif looked at me. "What?"

"Agatha Christie. The British novelist. She wrote murder mysteries. *The Murder of Roger Ackroyd* is considered a classic, one of the best murder mysteries of all time."

"I don't need a biography," MacAullif said. "I know who she is. What about her?"

"You ever read any of her books?"

"No."

"Sam Gravston has. He's got a whole shelf full of 'em."

MacAullif was looking at me narrowly. "Have you lost your marbles?"

"More than likely. Which is why I need your help."

"With what? What are you getting at?"

"*The A.B.C. Murders.*"

"What?"

"*The A.B.C. Murders,* by Agatha Christie. It's a murder mystery in which a man invents a serial killer in order to disguise his crime as part of a series."

MacAullif was still skeptical, but for the first time he showed interest. "You're saying there's a parallel?"

"There's more than a parallel. It's an exact duplicate."

"But that's absurd."

"Maybe." I opened my briefcase. "At any rate, I brought you a copy. You should read it."

MacAullif took the book gingerly, as if touching it might contaminate him with literature in some way. "So that's why you came here. To give me a book to read?"

"No. To tell you who committed the Rosenberg and Stone murders."

"Are you serious?"

"Absolutely."

"All right. Who?"

"Sam Gravston."

"What?"

"Sam Gravston did it. He needs money badly. He will inherit a bundle from his uncle. That's the motive."

"I see," MacAullif said.

I can't say he looked entirely convinced. I can say I know the look homicidal lunatics must have seen on his face before he had them locked in a padded cell.

"And what evidence do you have?" MacAullif asked.

I held up The A.B.C. Murders. "Sam Gravston has this book. I've been to his apartment. I've seen it on his bookshelf."

MacAullif blinked. "Oh?"

"He's read it. He has a whole shelf of Agatha Christies. They're well read. The guy's a mystery buff."

"That's very interesting," MacAullif said. I don't think he was attempting to impress me with his sincerity.

"It is," I said. "But the thing is, Sergeant Clark is off on his own tangent about some client Rosenberg wronged, and the son of a bitch is so sure of himself he's never going to listen to me."

"That could be annoying," MacAullif said. He looked uncharacteristically uncomfortable. I thought he might even begin to fidget.

"Don't worry," I told him. "I haven't really lost my marbles. I have the solution to the murders, but no one's gonna believe me. Which is why I've come to you."

"I see," MacAullif said cautiously. "And what is the solution to the murders?"

I pointed to the book. "It's in here. That's why I want you to read it. Sam Gravston read it, and he saw a neat way to cash in on his rich uncle's estate, so he just followed what it said in the book."

Sergeant MacAullif looked at me narrowly. "And just what makes you think Sam Gravston did that?"

I reached in my briefcase and pulled out another book. "This," I said.

Sergeant MacAullif blinked twice before he looked at me and said, "What is that?"

"*The Clocks*, by Agatha Christie."

I handed the book to MacAullif. He took it and looked at it as if it might have been booby trapped and somehow might explode.

"Oh?" he said. "What about it?"

"*The Clocks* is another book Sam Gravston owns and has read. In it, an efficient but unimaginative murderer, adapts the plot of a mystery novel in order to commit a totally baffling crime."

MacAullif stared at me. "You're saying Sam Gravston—"

"Yes, I am. It's all in there. That's why I want you to read the books. *The Clocks* gave him the idea. *The A.B.C. Murders* gave him the plot."

MacAullif shook his head. "I dunno."

"All right, look," I said. "Suppose the Rosenberg and Stone murders hadn't happened."

"What?"

"The murders. Suppose they hadn't happened. And then Sam Gravston's uncle got killed. Who would be the logical suspect?"

MacAullif shrugged. "Sam Gravston."

"Of course he would. He stands to benefit. He would not only be the logical suspect, he would be the *only* suspect."

MacAullif frowned. "That's hardly fair. His uncle was cutthroat businessman. He undoubtedly had a lot of enemies."

"Let's not quibble. Sam Gravston would be the main suspect. In which case, there would be a good chance the police could prove he did it."

"So?"

"But now there isn't. Because the murder isn't an *individual* crime. It's part of a *series* of crimes. It's the work of a *serial killer*. And now there's a good chance Sam Gravston will get away with it, because the police aren't looking for a motive for the murder of Sam's uncle, they're looking for a motive for a whole series of crimes, and the thing is, they aren't going to find it because there *isn't* one."

MacAullif took out a cigar and inspected it gravely. It gave him an excuse not to look at me.

"I see," he said.

I sighed. "No, you don't. But you should. Look, it all starts three weeks ago. Sam Gravston's uncle breaks his leg. Now, Richard pays a hundred-fifty dollar bonus to anyone who brings him a new client, so Sam sees a chance to make some money and tries to sign up his uncle. But the uncle's a pain in the ass type, he hasn't got time for Sam, he doesn't care, he's going to Texas as soon as he gets out of the hospital. But Sam persists because he really needs the money, and the long and the short of it is his uncle agrees to an appointment when he gets back from Texas three weeks later.

"So now Sam's got three weeks to sit around and stew about that. And think about what a tightass his uncle is, and how rich he is, and how he's never done shit for Sam. And slowly Sam comes to the realization of how great it would be if his uncle were to die.

"And he thinks about that some, and he starts playing with the idea, probably as a joke at first, and he starts figuring out how he could possibly do it.

"And eventually it come to him. His uncle's a client, just like all the other clients he calls on. Suppose a whole bunch of clients were to die, and his uncle just happened to be one of them? His motive would be hidden, he'd get away with it and he'd wind up rich."

MacAullif tapped the cigar into the palm of his hand. "That's quite a theory," he said. "Why bring it to me? Why not Sergeant Clark?"

"It would be a waste of time. Sergeant Clark has his own theory of the case. He's convinced the killer's some black man from Harlem that Richard's wronged. He wouldn't listen. He'd think I was out of my mind."

MacAullif looked at me. "Now why would he ever think that?"

I stood up. "All right. Fine," I said. "Don't believe me. I didn't really think you would. I didn't expect you to act on this. But I want you to do one thing for me. OK?"

MacAullif looked at me suspiciously. "What's that?"

"Read the books."

MacAullif squirmed uncomfortably. "Oh, now look—"

"Just read the damn books," I said irritably.

I turned and walked out.

37.

It was maddening. I had the solution—I was sure of it—but no one would believe me. I couldn't go to Sergeant Clark. As I'd told MacAullif, he'd have laughed in my face. I could tell Richard, but what good would that do? Richard was on Sergeant Clark's shitlist, too. Clark wouldn't listen to him any more than he would to me.

I thought about talking to Richard anyway. And I didn't want to do it. I know that seems strange. After all, Richard was the one who'd asked me to look into this thing in the first place. But I didn't want to go to him with something I couldn't prove. Not when it was an accusation against one of his employees. Somehow that didn't seem fair.

If that was the real reason. If it wasn't that this was my solution, and I didn't want to share it.

At least not until I could prove it.

That would be entirely different.

That would be just fine.

But how *could* I prove it? That was the thing. What the hell could I do?

I drove around that day on my appointed rounds, and thought about what to do. My first beep from Wendy/Janet supplied me with the information that Sam Gravston had indeed given in to Richard's entreaties, and was back on the job. So Sergeant Clark's plans, whatever they might be, were set in motion. But what about mine?

My first case was an old man out in Queens who had slipped in his bathtub and broken his hip. I drove out there, signed him up and shot pictures of the offending bathroom fixture. I was so preoccupied with thinking about Sam Gravston and the case that it wasn't until I was on my way out the door that I realized that it had never even occurred to me to wonder if the gentleman I was calling on would be alive.

Which started me thinking again. Were the murders over? I realized that without consciously considering it, I had assumed they were. Because I had picked Sam Gravston for the murderer and the murder of his uncle as the *real* murder, the one that completed the sequence.

But did it?

I realized, of course, that it didn't. It couldn't. Sam couldn't stop now. Because if he did, then the murder of his uncle would eventually stand out for what it was—the real murder. If there were no more murders, even the dumbest cop would soon realize that the murder of Sam's uncle had ended things. And it wouldn't take much thinking after that to arrive at the truth.

So there would have to be at least one more murder.

Sam Gravston would have to strike again.

And I would have to catch him at it.

I thought about that. I thought about that a lot. How the hell would I do it? Shadow him all the time? I couldn't do that. It might be days before he struck. And it might be by day, by night, any time at all. How the hell should I know? I couldn't stick with him. I'm no good at shadowing people, even if I had the resources and the time. So what the hell could I do?

It was excruciating. Sam could pick a victim, any victim. He could kill him, and then call in, using his jive black voice, and make an appointment. And that would be that.

He'd have won.

I couldn't let him win.

I had to get him.

But how?

Driving out to Brooklyn on my second assignment, it came to me.

A trap.

I needed to set a trap.

It was a nice idea. Not very original, I realized, but then I never was very original. And at this point, any idea at all was rather nice.

I drove on out to Bensonhurst, Brooklyn, and considered the dimensions of the trap.

By the time I had signed up the client—who was very much alive, and whose only problem happened to be fourteen stitches in her forehead she received when the taxicab she was riding in slammed into the back of a bus, catapulting her into the divider—I had my preliminary ideas all mapped out.

I refined them on the way back.

There was one major refinement.

The trap, primarily, was for Sam Gravston. He was my chief suspect. I was sure that he'd done it. To me, no other solution seemed possible.

But I felt it couldn't be only that. You see, I didn't want to make the same mistake Sergeant Clark was making. Sergeant Clark had his own idea of who had committed the murder, and his problem was that he was so pigheaded he wouldn't consider anything else. Now, certain as I was that I was right, it occurred to me that I should recognize and provide for the eventuality that I was wrong. To concede the possibility that Sergeant Clark could be right. I didn't believe it for a minute, but I was willing to concede the thought. Thus, I reasoned, the trap I designed would be one primarily to catch Sam Gravston, but it should also be designed to catch the killer, whomever he might be. In other words, specifically including the killer presumed by Sergeant Clark.

Thinking along those lines caused me to broaden my scheme, to lay out my grand design.

By the time I got beeped for my third assignment, which sent me back to Queens again, I had a pretty good idea of the specifics of the trap.

There was only one more thing I needed, and that was the one thing all traps need.

Bait.

38.

"I need a favor."

Leroy Stanhope Williams twirled the cognac around in his glass and looked at me inquiringly.

Leroy was one of Richard's clients. At least, one of Richard's former clients. And he was certainly not a disgruntled one. Leroy was someone I'd signed up way back in the first few months I'd worked for Richard. At the time he'd had a broken leg. Aside from Tessie the Tumbler, Leroy was the only client I'd ever called on more than once. Leroy had helped me out of a couple of jams in the past, and now I was hoping he could do it again.

We were sitting in the living room of Leroy's house out in Flushing. I was sitting on the couch, Leroy was in a chair. The chair was an antique, a period piece of some sort—I couldn't tell you what period, I'm no good at that—but it seemed medieval to me, and it resembled a throne. Or perhaps it was just Leroy that made it seem that way. Something about Leroy Stanhope Williams always struck me as regal.

Leroy was a black man somewhere in his mid-thirties, with chocolate brown skin, a high, sloping forehead that gave him an intellectual look and bemused eyes. His speech, cultured with a British hint, added to the impression of royalty.

As did his home. The room in which we were sitting was furnished with paintings, sculptures, hangings, tapestries, bric-a-brac and what have you, all of which, at one time or another, had adorned other people's homes.

You see, Leroy was a thief.

And not just an ordinary thief. He was an anachronism.

A gentleman jewel a thief.

"What kind of a favor?" Leroy asked.

"A big one," I said.

"I figured that," Leroy said.

"Oh? Why?"

"Last time you wanted a favor you called. This time you came."

"True," I said.

"So, what is it?"

"Well, for one thing," I said, "it may cost a little money. Money I don't happen to have."

"That's not necessarily a problem," Leroy said. "Unless you're talking millions."

"More like a few hundred."

"You have not deterred me so far," Leroy said. "Go on. What do you want me to do?"

"Do you have a good doctor?" I asked him.

"What kind?"

"The kind that will keep his mouth shut."

Leroy looked at me. "This is serious, isn't it?"

"Yes, it is. Do you have one? A general practitioner, I mean."

"I have one. What would he have to do?"

"He would have to dispense some treatment and then forget about it."

Leroy frowned. "Any drugs involved?"

"No."

"Then it shouldn't be a problem. What do you want him to do?"

"I want him to put a cast on your arm."

Leroy looked at me. "Are you serious?"

"Absolutely."

"Do you intend to tell me what this is all about?"

"I'm getting to it," I said. "Unless you'd like me to cut to the punch line."

Leroy held up his hand. "No, no. I'm enjoying the buildup. Go right ahead. So, the doctor puts a cast on my arm."

"That's right."

"Which arm?"

"I leave you your choice."

"Considerate of you. What then?"

"This is where the money comes in."

Leroy smiled. "I see. The doctor worked for free. So tell me about the money part."

"You have to rent an apartment."

"An apartment?"

"Yes."

"Where?"

"In Harlem."

Leroy smiled. "A black man in Harlem? I'll stand out like a sore thumb."

"You stand out anywhere," I told him. "That's another thing. You'll have to dress down for the part."

"Another expense," Leroy said. "How long must I rent this apartment for?"

"You'll only need it for a few days."

"That shouldn't be too bad. I still have connections in Harlem. I might not have to rent one at all."

"That's fine," I said. "But nobody can know about this."

"It's that bad?" Leroy said.

"It's worse," I told him.

"All right," Leroy said. "Let's say I am installed in this apartment in Harlem with a cast on my arm. Then what?"

"You take the name Duane Wilson."

"Hmm," Leroy said. "Sounds black."

"Probably is."

"Then what?"

"Then you call Rosenberg and Stone. You tell 'em your name's Duane Wilson, you give 'em the address of your apartment in Harlem, you tell 'em you want to see an investigator.

"But here's the thing. You're busy with doctors and what have you, you're in and out, and you don't want to see an investigator right away. So you make an appointment for two days later."

"Two days later?"

"Right. And make it for first thing in the morning. Say, nine A.M."

"OK."

"And one more thing. You have no phone. You tell 'em you want to fix the time of the appointment right then because they can't reach you because you have no phone."

Leroy shrugged. "So far it sounds incredibly easy. Then what?"

"Then you go hang out in a bar. Duke's Place, on Lenox Avenue."

"You've got to be kidding."

"I'm not."

"This does not sound like the type of establishment I would normally frequent."

"It isn't. In fact, it's the type of establishment where if you use words like 'regularly frequent' you're liable to find yourself thrown out on your educated ear."

"Sheee, no sweat, man, ah jus' jibe it up and blen' rite in."

I doubted that. Leroy's jive was passable at best. But it would have to do.

"That's fine," I told him.

"So what do I do then?" Leroy asked. He had reverted to his normal voice, for which I was grateful.

"You hang out in the bar, getting soused, telling everyone who will listen, and even those who won't, how you fell down and broke your arm, and how you're really pissed, and how you're gonna sue the city and make a shitload of money, and how you called Rosenberg and Stone and you got an appointment for nine in the morning."

"Jesus. How long do I have to do that?"

"For two days."

He looked at me. "Are you serious?"

"Yes, I am. Can you handle it?"

"Of course I can," Leroy said. "It's a bit of an inconvenience, but no problem. This doesn't seem to be that big of a favor."

"I'm not finished yet."

"I figured that. So what do I do then?"

"The night before your appointment, you hang out in the bar until midnight getting soused. Then you leave. When you do, you make a point of the fact you gotta go home because you gotta be up early in the morning to keep this appointment."

"Of course. Then what?"

"Then you go back to your apartment, and you wait."

"I see," Leroy said. "And what happens then?"

"Then," I told him, "someone will try to strangle you."

39.

It didn't take that long to set up. The whole charade must have appealed to Leroy's sense of adventure because he really threw himself into it. By the time I got home from my last assignment that evening at six-thirty, he had already left a message with Alice for me to call him. I did, and even though Leroy spoke in his usual reserved and refined manner, I could tell he was pretty pleased with himself.

I couldn't blame him. In the course of a few short hours, Leroy had managed to acquire himself an apartment in a brownstone on West 139th Street, not three blocks from Duke's Place. He had also managed to inveigle a doctor into encasing his left arm in a plaster cast that caused him only "a modicum of discomfort."

At any rate, Leroy was all set, and wanted to know if he should go ahead and call Rosenberg and Stone first thing in the morning.

I told him not to.

You see, since talking to Leroy I had had second

thoughts. Not about the trap itself—that was all right—just about certain aspects of it.

And one aspect in particular.

If Leroy called Rosenberg and Stone and asked for an appointment, then Sergeant Clark would know about it. And the thing was, I didn't know everything Sergeant Clark was doing. But I knew he was up to something. And it wasn't illogical to assume that he was thoroughly investigating every new client that came in. So if Leroy asked for an appointment two days in advance, that would give Sergeant Clark a lot of time to investigate. And the problem was, Duane Wilson's bonafides were not going to stand a lot of investigating. The minute the police began poking into Duane Wilson's background, they were going to realize something wasn't quite kosher.

That was one reason.

And I tried to tell myself it was the main reason, and maybe it was.

But there was another reason.

Because there was one thing I knew that Sergeant Clark was doing, and that was staking out the homes of all the clients that called in. And if the police staked out the apartment that Leroy had rented, even if they didn't realize it was bogus, even if they didn't realize the whole thing was a setup, they'd be there. And then if it worked, if everything went exactly as planned, then Sam Gravston would come walking into their trap and not mine.

And somehow that didn't seem fair.

So, for whichever reason you might choose, I didn't want Leroy calling Rosenberg and Stone.

And there was no reason that he should. I could work it perfectly well another way. Of course, by doing so, I'd be giving up the possibility of trapping any *other* employee of

Rosenberg and Stone, if indeed they were guilty and not Sam. But that didn't seem to me too great a loss. Having talked to all of them, and having investigated all the possibilities, I just couldn't imagine any of them being guilty. I had the answer, and the answer was Sam. It had to be. If this didn't work, well then I could backtrack and set up another trap for the rest of the office personnel. But I didn't think I'd have to.

It had to be Sam.

And if I needed any further reason for Leroy not calling Rosenberg and Stone, it was this: it was now Wednesday night. If Leroy called Thursday morning and asked for an appointment in two days, that would push it into the weekend and the appointment would be made for Monday.

And that was just too far off. It had to be soon. Actually, it had to be now. Right now. It had to be dangled in front of Sam's nose and made attractive enough that he would have to bite.

Before something better came along.

Before he killed someone else.

So I had decided to push the schedule up. The appointment would be made for Friday morning.

Which meant the dry run would be tonight.

That was no problem for Leroy. He was already installed in the apartment. He was actually calling from there. It was a furnished apartment that belonged to a friend of Leroy's, who had been happy to loan it to him for the purpose, which was one reason he'd been able to set it up so quickly. All it had entailed was sticking a strip of tape with the name Duane Wilson on it over the mail slot.

I got in my car and drove over there.

Leroy was waiting for me outside. He had dressed for the occasion in an old army jacket, blue jeans and a pair of sneakers with no laces.

Only one arm was through the sleeve of the army jacket. The left sleeve hung limply down from the shoulder, and the left arm that poked out from under the coat was encased in a white cast.

"Where'd you get the nifty threads?" I asked.

Leroy grinned. "Goodwill. Care to see my pad?"

"Don't mind if I do."

We went up the front steps and into the brownstone. Leroy pushed open the foyer door, which was unlocked.

"Security's not a big selling point here, I see," I said.

"It does leave a bit to be desired," Leroy said. "But the apartment's not bad."

It wasn't, either. The apartment was a fairly nice one-bedroom on the third floor. It was clean and tastefully, if modestly, furnished.

Which didn't really concern me. Oh sure, I wanted Leroy to be comfortable and all that, but I had more important considerations.

Specifically, the front door.

It had a police lock, one of the old-fashioned kind with a steel bar that sets in a metal plate on the floor and runs at an angle up to another metal plate on the door. I tested it, and it was sound. With the bar in place, there was no way anyone was going to get in the door.

I checked the windows. There were no fire escapes, bad in case the building should burn down, but great in that no one could get in through the window.

There was no service door. No other way in or out of the apartment.

So once Leroy was locked inside with the bar in place, he was presumably safe.

"OK," I said, after I had checked everything out. "Looks good."

"I thought so," Leroy said. "So, shall we begin?"

"I have to warn you. This could be dangerous."

I felt stupid saying that. It was so corny and dramatic.

It didn't help when Leroy laughed in my face. He smiled and shook his head. "But that's the whole point now, isn't it?" Leroy was really enjoying himself. He punched me in the arm playfully, which was totally out of character for him. "Come on," he said. "Let's go."

We went.

I left my car where it was and walked with Leroy over to Lenox Avenue. We split up there, as I didn't want to be seen with him, and he walked on up Lenox Avenue to Duke's Place. I tailed along, across the street and about a half a block behind. I stopped in the shadows and watched as Leroy pushed open the door and went into Duke's Place.

The bar was not the type of place that made a selling point of putting its patrons on display. The front windows were blacked out. The front door had two narrow panes of clear glass in it, so I could see light within, but that was about it.

I walked on up Lenox Avenue, crossed the street and started back down again. I slowed down as I passed the bar and snuck a look in door. It was just a glance, but it was enough for me to get a glimpse of Leroy Stanhope Williams standing at the bar. He had shrugged the army coat off his shoulders, and he was gesticulating with his cast-encased left arm, while in his right hand he held a shot glass of what I am sure he considered to be particularly foul spirits.

I kept on going. I couldn't risk stopping, and there was no need. Nothing was going to happen in the bar. And, after all, this was just the dry run.

I walked back to the apartment. My car was parked right out front, where I'd left it. That, I realized, was something I couldn't do tomorrow. Sam Gravston knew my car. It would be a dead giveaway.

I hadn't thought of that until now.

It occurred to me it was a good thing I'd had a dry run.

No, I couldn't be waiting in my car. But I had to have somewhere to wait. I wasn't going to stake out the bar. There was no point. That was just my back-up plan, anyway, my tip of the hat to Sergeant Clark. But Sam Gravston didn't know about the bar. All he would have would be Duane Wilson's address. I had to stake out the apartment.

I looked around for a spot. Across the street would be best. I looked for an alcove, and soon found one. It was one building further down the street, away from Lenox Avenue, so I'd be looking diagonally across the street, but that was fine by me. It was steps down to a cellar door and a row of garbage cans. I went down. It was pitch dark. No chance of being seen. It was perfect.

But I didn't have to stay there tonight. Not for a dry run. It was only nine-thirty by then. I went out and walked around.

And thought about the case. The whole setup. The whole plan.

And I liked it. I mean, I hated the whole thing: the fact that Sam was guilty, the fact that I had to trap him and the whole bit. But, given the circumstances, I liked the plan.

By the time midnight rolled around, and from my alcove I watched a rather unsteady Leroy Stanhope Williams come down the street, push open his foyer door and go up the steps to his apartment. I was convinced of one thing.

It was going to work.

40.

D-Day.

I called Sam Gravston at seven-thirty in the morning and fed him the bullshit spiel: I'd been given a signup for Friday morning, but I'd forgotten that Tommie had a doctor's appointment I had to take him to, and the client had no phone so I couldn't call and change it, and could he cover for me?

What could he say? After all the cases I'd covered for him in the last week, the only thing he could say was yes, and that's what he said.

So the trap was set. It was as easy as that. Sam Gravston now thought that he had a genuine signup for Friday morning at nine. There'd be no reason for him to check back with Rosenberg and Stone to make sure it was legitimate. Why should he doubt it?

But it wasn't a real signup, and it wasn't on the books of Rosenberg and Stone, and there was no way Sergeant Clark and the police could know anything about it.

It was perfect.

After that, the day dragged. I did three signups, and I sure hope I got the information right, because, I must confess, my mind was elsewhere.

I got home by six. Alice had dinner waiting for me, but I was too nervous to eat. I kept choking on my food. Alice seemed nervous, too, and dinner was a strain. The only one who was relaxed at all was Tommie, and even he was bolting his food so he could get back into the living room to watch "The Monkees."

When he finally fled, Alice turned to me and said, "Nervous?"

"Yeah."

"Me, too."

"I'll be all right."

She smiled. "I know you will. It's just—"

"What?"

"Well . . ." She looked down at her plate. "I hope you're wrong."

"What?"

She looked up at me. "I hope it isn't Sam."

"Oh."

That bothered me. That was, of course, the bottom line for Alice. She hoped it wasn't Sam. She didn't want that nice young man to be guilty of murder.

And I didn't either. I didn't want it to be Sam. But it was, and I'd figured it out and solved the case. And while I didn't want it to be Sam, I didn't want it not to be Sam, if you know what I mean.

And that bothered me.

We finished up dinner, and I called Leroy Stanhope Williams. At his home in Queens, not at the apartment in Harlem. I hadn't wanted Leroy hanging out there during the day. In the first place, there was no need—Sam wouldn't strike during the day and so far in advance. And in the

second place, if Sam did, if he tried it, I wouldn't be there
to stop him. So Leroy had spent the day at home.

Leroy was all set and raring to go. You'd have thought he
liked the idea of being strangled.

"OK, I'm leaving now," I told him.

"Me, too."

"Be sure you give me time to get in place."

"Don't worry. I have to come all the way from Queens."

"Yeah. I know."

"So don't worry."

I worried. I worried driving over there that I'd get stuck
in traffic, that I'd have a flat tire, and that I wouldn't find a
parking place.

I didn't. Everything was smooth as silk. I parked three
blocks over and two blocks down, so there'd be no chance
of Sam spotting my car, and walked over to Leroy's address.

To Duane Wilson's address.

It was seven-fifteen when I got there. It was dark, which
was good, because I needed to hide, and bad because I
needed to see. Because I didn't know what Sam Gravston
was doing. He could be watching the building now. He
could be in the building now.

I took up my position on the cellar steps and waited.

It was close to eight when Leroy showed. We'd agreed
that he'd take a taxi into town and get off several blocks
away, just in case anyone was watching. So when he
showed up, it was on foot. He came walking down the
street from the direction of Lenox Avenue.

There was no one around. I was sure of it. I'd been keeping careful watch. So when Leroy reached the front of the
building, I stepped out from my hiding place.

"All clear," I said.

"As expected."

"You see anyone taking any interest in you?"

"No. Why should there be?"

"There shouldn't. I'm just edgy."

Leroy smiled. "Relax. After all, it's my neck."

"Yeah," I said. "Well, let's go."

We went up the steps and in the door. This was all according to plan. Because, with the foyer door unlocked, it was *possible* that Sam Gravston was already waiting inside.

He wasn't. The hallways were clear. I checked them all, right up to the fourth floor. There was no access to the roof, either—I checked that, too.

Leroy unlocked the door and let us into the apartment. He locked it behind us, went over and sat down on the couch. He sighed, and rubbed his head.

"You OK?" I said. "Having second thoughts?"

Leroy waved it away. "No," he said. He grinned. "It's this damned cheap booze they serve."

I smiled. "A little out of your league, huh?"

"It tastes like kerosene, but it has quite a kick. And the thing is, you wake up feeling like having another."

"We'd better solve this thing fast, before you're ready for detox."

"A valid point." Leroy got up. "OK, I'm ready."

"Fine. Give me ten minutes to get in place."

Leroy let me out the door. I went outside and checked up and down the street. No one was in sight. I crossed the street and took up my position on the cellar stairs.

Leroy was out ten minutes later. He didn't look around for me, or wave, or wink or do anything cute. He was playing his part. He just walked off down the street.

Leaving me to wait.

See, I wasn't going to stake out the bar. In the first place,

there was no point. Sam didn't know about the bar. The bar
thing was just my personal insecurity, my nod to Sergeant
Clark. But it wasn't important.

But the apartment was. Sam couldn't know whether or
not Duane Wilson was home. Sam could come at any time.
So I had to wait.

It was a long wait. You ever sit on a cellar steps in Harlem for four hours? I wouldn't recommend it. It's uncomfortable. It's boring. It's dull.

And it's scary.

People pass by. You have to see them, but you don't want
them to see you. If they did see you, what would they
think? What would they do?

Time passes quickly when you're having fun.

Time crawled.

By the time I thought I'd reached the end of my endur-
ance, it was nine o'clock.

Jesus.

Three hours to go.

And that was just until Leroy got back. Which really
meant nothing in terms of the trap. Because Sam didn't
know about the bar, and didn't know who Leroy was, and
didn't know whether he was in or out. So midnight meant
nothing. In all probability Sam wouldn't strike until three
or four in the morning.

If he struck at all. That was the thing. And as I sat there
watching and waiting, the doubts came thick and fast. I
mean, the plan had seemed so good in theory, but was it?
Well, on the plus side was the fact that I had given Sam the
case. That was a big lure. Because, in Sam's mind, that
would make it fit the pattern. All the clients that had been
killed had been ones that I had in some way been involved
with. Making me a suspect. And if Sam wanted to shift

suspicion from himself, what could be better than another crime where I had the victim's name and address? Where I could have done it.

Yeah, that was the plus side. That and the fact that Sam didn't know what the police were doing. He didn't know that they were staking out the addresses of each case that came in.

But on the minus side, he could guess. I mean, Christ, it was such an obvious move, wasn't it? So Sam should know. Right? Wrong. He didn't know, otherwise he would never have killed his uncle. If he'd thought the police were staking out the houses, then that would presumably have been walking into a trap. But he'd done it. So he couldn't know. Right? But if he did suspect, then he'd be sure to kill the night before, wouldn't he? That was the beauty of the trap, wasn't it? That was why it would work. Right?

I was driving myself crazy.

And the hours dragged by.

By eleven I was sure the trap would never work.

By eleven-thirty I wasn't sure I even cared.

Midnight.

There came the sound of footsteps from the other side of the street.

I tensed up. Watched.

A man came walking from the direction of Lenox Avenue. He was a black man, wearing a dark coat and a knit cap. I couldn't see well enough to make out his features, just well enough to tell that it wasn't Leroy.

He went up the steps and into the building.

Not a totally unexpected occurrence, but still it caught me flat-footed. No one had been in and out of the building all night, so it hadn't occurred to me. But Leroy hadn't rented the whole building. People lived there. And by midnight, it was not unreasonable to assume they might want to go home.

More footsteps. I looked, but once again, it wasn't Leroy. Another black man. He went into the building, too.

Christ, what was it, Grand Central Station?

More footsteps. Third time's the charm. Yes, this time it was Leroy. Stepping along. Staggering a little. I wondered if the stagger was feigned. I thought not. I figured Leroy wasn't going to have a good time in the morning.

Leroy turned and started up the steps.

That's when I saw him.

He was in the shadows, behind a parked car. His head came up slightly, and I caught the movement. Then I saw the silhouette. A man, that's all I could tell. A man. I knew instinctively who it was, but I couldn't see him. Just his shadow.

Leroy went in the front door and it banged shut.

The man moved.

He crept out from behind the car and darted toward the steps. He was crouched over with his head down. All I could see was that he was also wearing a dark jacket and knit cap.

But there was no doubt who he was.

He was not some resident of the building returning to his apartment.

He was the murderer.

The murderer reached out his hand for the stair rail.

Shock.

The hand was black!

The murderer was not Sam Gravston.

The murderer was black.

A black man from Harlem.

Jesus.

STRANGLER

The murderer started up the front steps. As he reached the top step, light from the upstairs window fell on his face.

I gasped.

The murderer was Detective Thomas Walker.

41.

Some things are too hard to comprehend. You see them or hear them, but you don't believe them. The mind leaps up and says, "That can't be true."

That happened now. I saw Detective Thomas Walker, and I realized he was the murderer, but I couldn't make myself believe it. I mean, I'd spent time with the man. I'd ridden around in my car with him for two days. He was a responsible police officer. He had a wife and kids, for Christ's sake. It *couldn't* be.

But it was. And in a flash, I realized that that day when Clarence White had turned out to have been killed the night before, so it hadn't cleared me, it hadn't cleared Detective Thomas Walker either. He also had no alibi.

And now I knew why.

I watched in horror as Detective Thomas Walker pushed his way in the front door.

My mind leapt to Sergeant Clark. A black man. All right, a black man. But not from Harlem. And not poor. And not uneducated. So did this really bear out his theory?

A crash from within brought me to my senses.

Schmuck!

It doesn't matter who's right or who's wrong. Or what motive could drive a seemingly normal cop to turn to crime. Your friend, Leroy Stanhope Williams, is about to be strangled, and you're just standing there off on an ego trip!

I vaulted out of my hiding place and ran across the street. I took the front steps two at a time. I jerked open the front door.

I could hear the sound of a struggle up above. Christ, don't let me be too late.

I raced up the stairs, turned the corner. Ahead of me was the other stairs. But it was dark. There'd been a hall light on the third floor, but it was out now.

A thud and a grunt.

A grunt!

He's still alive!

I tore up the stairs.

I grabbed the top of the banister, vaulted around the corner into the hallway.

And tripped over them.

I couldn't see them, of course, but I felt them. And I felt myself going down. I flung out my hands, barely got them out in time, protected my face. And then I was on the floor, bracing myself, cushioning the blow, rolling over, and coming into position to get to my feet.

Something hit me hard in the side, thrust me back down, landed on top of me. It was as if I were a running-back being tackled short of first down. As I hit the floor I felt my arms being grabbed and wrestled behind me, and then I felt something cold and hard on my wrist. Seconds later I was jerked to my feet.

The light clicked on.

The first thing I saw was Leroy Stanhope Williams. He

was sitting on the floor of the hallway with his back propped up against the wall. He must have had a good few at Duke's Place, because I swear in spite of everything that had just happened, there was a bemused expression on his face.

The next thing I saw was the man holding me. He was a black man, and he had his hand on the pair of handcuffs that he had just clapped on my wrists.

Then I saw the other two men.

One was Detective Thomas Walker. He was breathing heavily, and holding onto the man behind him. Walker's back was to me, and he was blocking my view of the man.

Walker straightened up and jerked on the handcuffs the man was wearing.

The man swung around and I saw his face.

He was Tessie the Tumbler's boyfriend, Charlie.

42.

Recipe: take one medium crow, skin, season with pepper and thyme, fry till golden brown.

Sergeant Clark, Detective Thomas Walker, Richard Rosenberg and I were in Richard's office.

Sergeant Clark was explaining about the murders.

I was eating crow.

"As I have said," Sergeant Clark began, "it was early in the game that we deduced that the murders were the work of an uneducated black man from Harlem. Everything pointed to it. Even the apparent contradictions were not contradictions. The answer, as it usually is in these situations, was obvious. As long as we ignored any distractions and concentrated on the obvious, a solution was inevitable.

"Again, as I said, the answer was in the files. And, without making any excuses, I must state that the only reason the case was not solved before now was owing to the fact that the files were in such disarray."

Richard stirred restlessly and seemed about to say something. I hoped he wouldn't. I hoped he'd shut up and let

Clark get on with it. Nothing Richard could say would help, and I didn't want to prolong the moment.

"So," Clark said, "I'll tell you briefly how things progressed. To begin with, the obvious suspect was Mr. Hastings here. When I say 'obvious suspect,' don't be confused with 'obvious solution.' Hastings was the obvious suspect, but I never seriously considered that he had committed the crimes. He was one of those distractions I mentioned, one I wanted to dispense with as quickly as possible. I did so by assigning Walker to ride with him. And while this didn't provide the optimum result, an unimpeachable alibi, it did the next best thing. It gave me Walker's confirmed opinion that Mr. Hastings had not, indeed, committed the crimes.

"Which was enough for me. I pulled Walker off Hastings, not because Hastings was conclusively cleared, but because, as I said, I had better things for him to do."

Sergeant Clark walked over to the window and looked out. We all sat, watching him. No one said anything. We waited. Clark turned back.

"The Clarence White killing went a long way toward clearing things up. The killer phoned in, giving the name George Webb. He had the right address, but the wrong name. This told us that, one, the killer didn't know Clarence White, two, Clarence White was not a real client, and three, the killer had gone to great pains to make it appear that Clarence White was a client. This confirmed without question the fact that the killer had no animosity against Richard Rosenberg's clients, but against Richard Rosenberg himself, and that the whole point of the series of crimes was to discredit Mr. Rosenberg.

"And then there was the phone call itself. There were a lot of possibilities—the killer could have had an accomplice, the killer could have paid someone to make the call, the killer could have been a white man disguising his voice. But, once again, the obvious solution was the best—the phone call was from the killer himself, an uneducated black man living in Harlem.

"This allowed us to narrow the field. We were looking for a black client in Harlem. Now, I admit that was not as much help as it seems. The files, as I've said, were barely adequate. They are certainly not cross-filed by location. About fifty percent of all clients were black, and of those, a large number lived in Harlem. Still, the field had narrowed down from several thousand to several hundred cases.

"The other thing, of course, was we were looking for a man. At the risk of being labeled a sexist, I must state that I concluded that a woman could not have strangled those people. And the phone call was, almost definitely, a male voice. This narrowed the field further—or so we thought."

Clark pulled a pen from his pocket and tapped it into his palm.

"Now we come to the murder of Marvin Gravston. And this was the key. This was the dead giveaway.

"Marvin Gravston was a genuine client. The case had been on the books for three weeks. So this could not be a case of the killer murdering the victim and then calling in. This was a bonafide client.

"This required specific knowledge."

Clark looked at Richard, then at me. "You will recall, when Sam Gravston was in here I questioned him about when his uncle was admitted to the hospital with relation to when he saw him there and persuaded him to make the call to Rosenberg and Stone. He said he saw his uncle the day after he was admitted.

"A check with the hospital records gave us the date when Marvin Gravston was admitted. The call to Rosenberg and Stone was presumably the following day."

Clark snapped his fingers. "And that was the key. That

was the day the information about Marvin Gravston came in and was entered into the log. That was the only day the log would have been turned to that page. So, for a client to have had that information, they would have to have been in the office on that particular day.

"We went straight to the books. And there, at least, the records were helpful. Richard Rosenberg's appointments are logged. On the day in question, only one client came to the office to keep an appointment with Mr. Rosenberg. And that client was Shirley Woll."

I started. Tessie the Tumbler. My déjà vu.

Clark saw me. "Yes, Mr. Hastings. Shirley Woll. And that did throw us for a while because we knew the killer was a man. But one of the secretaries happened to recall—which is remarkable, knowing them—that Shirley Woll had brought a boyfriend with her. He didn't accompany her into Mr. Rosenberg's office—not being the husband, just the boyfriend, that was not allowed. So he had to wait in the outer office by the switchboards. This boyfriend, one Charles Banks, was a rather hostile, aggressive type. I rather think that's why Miss Millington remembered him. He made her nervous. At any rate, he was out there for the whole meeting.

"Which is when the phone call from Marvin Gravston would have come in. And been entered into the log, three weeks in advance, on an otherwise blank page."

Clark paused for emphasis. "Another key. An otherwise blank page. One lone name on an empty page. Charles Banks would look at it, and all he would see would be one name and address. And the name Gravston would be unusual enough to stick in the memory. He would look at it, first think it said Gravestone, look again, and maybe think, "That cat got some weird name.""

Another of my extraneous questions answered. Sergeant Clark could do jive black.

"So he would know. He would have the information, and at the proper moment, he could act."

I could contain myself no longer. "But why?" I said. "Why would he do that? You've been talking about a disgruntled client, someone Richard wronged. She was a *happy* client. She got thirty thousand dollars, for Christ's sake."

Sergeant Clark favored me with the cold, thin-lipped smile. "Mr. Hastings," he said. "Do you understand your job?"

I stared at him. "What?"

"Your job. What you do. Do you know what it's all about?"

"Of course I do."

"Fine. Tell me."

"What?"

"Tell me. Tell me what you do."

"I don't understand."

"Well, as I understand it, you were the one who originally signed up Shirley Woll as a client. Is that right?"

"Yes."

"Fine. Tell me what you did."

I blinked. I felt totally stupid. Because I didn't know what he wanted or what he was getting at. Recite what I did? It was like a job interview. And I hate job interviews.

"Well," I said. "I called on her, took down the information about the accident and signed her up."

Sergeant Clark raised a finger. "Ah. You signed her up. And how did you do that?"

"I beg your pardon?"

"What did you have her sign?"

"A retainer, of course."

Clark nodded. "Yes. A retainer. And are you familiar with the provisions of that retainer?"

I stared at him. "It's a standard form. There is nothing sinister about the retainer."

"I never said there was. I just asked if you were familiar with the provisions. If you know what you are asking people to sign."

"Yes, I do," I said, irritably.

"Fine. And what are they?"

I sighed. "It is a standard form. The client employs Richard Rosenberg to act on his behalf on a contingency basis. There is no charge to the client except in the event of a settlement, in which case Mr. Rosenberg retains one third of the settlement as his fee."

Clark nodded. "Yes, but that's not exactly right. He retains one third of the settlement *after* recouping his expenses off the top."

My jaw dropped open. "Are you accusing Richard Rosenberg of padding his expenses?"

Clark shook his head. "Not at all. Don't be so quick to jump to conclusions and fly off the handle. I am merely stating facts. Your statement of how the settlement is split was slightly inaccurate, that's all. But leave it for a moment. Going back to the retainer. Isn't there a paragraph in their stating that any liens against the client shall be settled from the clients share of the settlement, and shall in no way reduce the amount of Mr. Rosenberg's fee?"

"Yes. Of course. If the client has outstanding debts, they're responsible, not Richard."

"Exactly," Clark said. "Which is totally fair and as it should be. But which is a fact."

"What's the point?" I said.

256

Clark didn't answer. "What about the other papers you have the client sign?"

"What about them?"

"Tell me what they are."

I took a breath and blew it out again. "There's a Request For Aided Accident form to get the police report. There's hospital release forms to get the patients medical records. There's two sets of them, actually, one set for us, and one set for the attorneys of the defendant. There's an assignment to the hospital, assuring them of payment in the case of a settlement."

"Ah, yes," Clark said, "an assignment to the hospital. What is the purpose of that form?"

I shrugged. "Basically, it's to enable us to get the client's medical records. When we ask the hospital for the records we give 'em that form. That tells them the case isn't a medical malpractice against them, and that they have something to gain by cooperating, and then they release the records to us."

Sergeant Clark nodded. "Yes. That's what you use it for. That's what it means to you. But what it is, actually, is just what it says—an assignment. It allows the hospital to attach the client's settlement to cover any outstanding bills."

I sat up in my chair. "Are you saying—"

"I am," Clark said. "Here's what happened in the case of Shirley Woll. Richard Rosenberg got her a settlement of thirty thousand dollars. His expenses, in round numbers, were about fifteen hundred dollars." He held up his hands. "Perfectly reasonable. No argument there. Fifteen hundred. We take that off the top. Leaves twenty eight thousand, five hundred. Rosenberg takes a third of that as his fee, that's nine thousand five hundred. Leaves nineteen thousand.

"Now here's the thing. Shirley Woll was not on Medicare.

257

She had no medical insurance of any kind. And her injury was somewhat complicated. She had to have a pin put in her ankle. Two operations. Several weeks in the hospital. At any rate, her bills came to sixteen thousand, five hundred dollars. At the time of the settlement, those bills were unpaid."

Sergeant Clark held out his hands wide. "And there you are. Due to the assignment papers you had Shirley Woll sign, Harlem Hospital was able to take the entire amount out of her share of the settlement."

Richard Rosenberg was on his feet. "Now just a minute. You're talking as if I've done something wrong here. As if I've slighted my client. I'll have you know everything you've just said is entirely legal, ethical and standard practice for an attorney at law."

Sergeant Clark held up his hand. "Absolutely, Mr. Rosenberg. I never said it wasn't. You do your job, you get your fee. The hospital is owed, and the hospital must be paid."

"Exactly. Shirley Woll wasn't ripped off. Shirley Woll got her hospital bills paid, and a cash bonus to boot."

"I understand," Clark said. "I have no problem with that. There is no question of any impropriety on your part. And as I understand it, Shirley Woll was perfectly satisfied."

Sergeant Clark held up his hand. "But," he said, "Charles Banks wasn't. Now, Charles Banks, from what we've been able to gather, is a crack addict. As such, he was desperate for money. So what happens? His girl friend gets a call from her lawyer that she had gotten a settlement in her case. And how much is the settlement? Thirty thousand dollars."

Sergeant Clark smiled the thin smile. "Well, Charles Banks hears that and he thinks he's died and gone to heaven. Thirty thousand dollars. Maybe he even tells some crack dealers about it, gets them to advance him some merchandise on the strength of his windfall. After all, he's about to be a wealthy man. Now, he knows the lawyer gets a third, but still, that leaves twenty thousand dollars he's got coming.

"Or so he thinks.

"So what happens? He goes with his girl friend down to the lawyer's to sign the release form and pick up the check. And he waits outside in the outer office for her to come out. And when she does he looks at the check, and is it for twenty thousand dollars? No. It's for twenty five *hundred* dollars. And he's furious. The lawyer ripped him off!"

"No such thing," Richard put in hotly.

"Yes, yes, Mr. Rosenberg, no such thing." Clark said, waving his hands. "I am getting a little weary of these self-serving interruptions. No such thing. I am referring to what this man thought.

"Now, if I might resume. Charles Banks is furious. He's been taken. He's been ripped off.

"On the other hand. Shirley Woll is perfectly happy. She'd gotten her hospital bills paid, and she's got a little money besides. She's quite content. Because she is, to all intents and purposes, a perfectly sound and reasonable person. Except, of course, in her choice of boyfriends.

"So what happens? The ultimate irony. That weekend. Shirley Woll falls and breaks her ankle again. And, because she's perfectly happy with the settlement that she got, she immediately calls Rosenberg and Stone.

"When Charles Banks hear this he's furious, he's out of his mind. He tries to talk her out of it, but she won't listen. He storms out of the place. He goes out and gets drunk.

"And that would have been the end of it. Except for one thing. Who should he meet in the bar but a man with a broken arm who's telling everyone how he's gonna make a lot of money calling Rosenberg and Stone.

"And Charles Banks snaps. Not if he can help it. He'll

beat Richard Rosenberg out of that fee, and give him a nice kick in the teeth, too.

"So he follows the man home and finds out where he lives. And he knows what time the guys gonna call Rosenberg and Stone. So the next morning he goes there, right after the phone call, knocks on the guys door, says, 'Rosenberg and Stone,' walks in, verifies the fact that the guy did indeed make the call—if he hadn't, Banks would have called for him—and then strangles him."

Sergeant Clark spread his hands. "A totally sick, pointless and ineffective type of revenge. But we have known from the first that we were not dealing with a sane man.

"So, what happens next?" Clark pointed to me. "Mr. Hastings calls on Shirley Woll to sign up her newly fractured ankle. Charles Banks is there. He makes one last attempt to talk her out of it. He fails. He is consigned to the bedroom, where he broods.

"Then Mr. Hastings gets beeped. He calls his office, and is given the Gerald Finklestein case.

"Charles Banks listens in on the bedroom extension. He gets Gerald Finklestein's name and address. Hastings is beeped again and directed to go see me. Banks listens in on that call, so he knows Mr. Hastings will be delayed in getting to Mr. Finklestein. So he dashes out to Queens and kills him."

Sergeant Clark paused, took a breath, blew it out again. "The thing about a serial killer is, the more they get away with it, the more of an obsession it becomes.

"The next murder is simple. Charles Banks sees a man with a broken arm in the bar. The man has no intention of calling Rosenberg and Stone, but by now Banks has realized that this doesn't matter. He follows the man home, strangles him, and the following day he calls Rosenberg and Stone, asking for an appointment.

"All well and good. But now, we have to get inside the mind of the killer for a moment. So far, everything is going according to plan. Except for one thing. Publicity. There is a reference to Rosenberg and Stone after the first murder, but nothing after that. Charles Banks can't understand it, but he doesn't like it. He wants his crimes to be known. More important, he wants the name Rosenberg and Stone to be known. This isn't happening. He wonders why."

It occurred to me that this might be a good time for Sergeant Clark to throw a nod in my direction that the withholding of publicity had been my idea, but he didn't do so.

"So," Clark continued, "he figures maybe the people he killed weren't prominent enough. Maybe he needs a more affluent victim.

"And that's when he remembers Marvin Gravston. The client with the strange name he had seen on the blank sheet of paper dated weeks in advance. Now, it's probably too much to assume he remembers the exact address, but he might have noted it at the time. Noted that here was a man with a fashionable East Side address. So he looks it up in the phone book. Marvin Gravston is listed, and there is only one in the book. So now he has the address, and he remembers the date of the appointment, and he goes there that morning and kills him.

"Well and good. The murder of Marvin Gravston rates a good deal of publicity, but once again, there is no mention of Rosenberg and Stone. Frustrating, no doubt.

"But by now the killing is a compulsion. Charles Banks will strike again.

"Which brings us to last night."

Sergeant Clark now favored me with a totally condescending look. "Mr. Hastings here, with his typical layman's contempt for the abilities of the police, decides to take things into his own hands. He devises a trap." Sergeant Clark paused, then continued with withering sarcasm. "A wholly original idea. Our decoy injured man sat in the bar, Duke's Place, for four straight nights before we decided to abandon the idea and use him elsewhere. But, as it turned out, that idea had been right to begin with. It was just that, for whatever reasons he might have had, Charles Banks had been hanging out elsewhere.

"However, Mr. Hastings employs his decoy, one Leroy Stanhope Williams, to sit in the bar. And two nights ago he begins.

"Now, by this time, we, the bungling, inefficient police, have run down the appointment that was made in advance. We have checked on who was in the office the day the call came in, and come up with the one client, Shirley Woll. We know her boyfriend was with her, and we have traced him and ID'd him as Charles Banks, a known crack addict with a history of drug arrests. Through discrete inquiries of Shirley Woll, who could not possibly have known what we were after, we have ascertained that Charles Banks was indeed present when Mr. Hastings called at her apartment, and thus could have overheard the telephone conversation and gotten Gerald Finklestein's address.

"So we have our murderer. The only thing is, we have no proof. But this is no real problem because we know that Charles Banks will strike again.

"So, Detective Walker here is assigned to follow him. And what happens? He goes straight back to Duke's place. That was two nights ago. Wednesday night. And who should be sitting in the bar but a black man with a cast on his arm, who just happens to be telling everybody that he's calling Rosenberg and Stone. Now, Charles Banks may not be very bright, but Detective Walker is, and he immediately smells a big fat fish. But that's all right because Charles Banks is too dumb to catch on, and what's more, he seems to be taking some interest. So Detective Walker just sits back and watches the show.

"Midnight comes, and the man with the broken arm leaves the bar. Surprise, surprise, Charles Banks seems to be leaving, too. Walker, of course, tags along. There is no real danger at this point, because the man with the cast has taken careful pains to tell everyone that his appointment if for Friday morning. Since it's only Wednesday night, it's too soon for Banks to strike.

"Sure enough, Banks merely tails the man home to learn his address. After that, he goes home.

"We also learn the address. And the next day we investigate. A check of the log at Rosenberg and Stone reveals that no such appointment exists. A check of the bonafides of the man listed as Duane Wilson at the address in question reveals that no such gentleman exists. As far as we are concerned, this confirms the fact that what we have stumbled on is an attempt at amateur detective work. While this doesn't please us, we're not proud. Since it's working, we'll ride along.

"Which brings us to last night. Once again, the man with the cast is in the bar. Also in the bar are Charles Banks, Detective Walker and Detective Henderson, called in for backup. Once again, the man with the cast proclaims his intentions. Once again, he prepares to leave the bar at midnight.

"This time, Charles Banks leaves first. He knows where the man's going, so he'll beat him home and lie in wait for him. So he leaves, with Henderson following. Banks goes to the address, and, as the front door is unlocked, he goes in. Henderson goes in after him.

"Minutes later, the decoy with the cast comes down the street and enters the building, followed by Detective Walker."

Sergeant Clark paused and spread his arms. "The rest you know. Banks attempts to kill the decoy. Mr. Hastings here, who has been staking out the apartment, bumbles in just in time to witness the arrest. We have Charles Banks dead to rights on attempted murder. Right now the gentleman isn't talking, but as soon as he gets an attorney, he's going to find out we have enough circumstantial evidence to nail him on at least one or two of the other murders. At that point, he's going to attempt to make a deal. And by that time. I doubt if the D.A. will be much inclined to listen."

Sergeant Clark clapped his hands together like a teacher finishing a lecture.

"And that, gentlemen, is that."

43.

It was a tough day.

What made it tough was that after Sergeant Clark had finished his triumphant dissertation, I still had to go out and sign up my cases. My heart wasn't in it. Neither was my mind. I can't recall anyone I called on that afternoon, or any of their cases, or even where they lived. I did the job because I had to, but that was all. The best I can say was I got through it.

Then I went home.

Where Alice was delighted. She was delighted because the murders had been solved, and she was delighted because Sam Gravston wasn't guilty.

I was glad Sam wasn't guilty, too. I really was. Even though it made me wrong. Even though it made Sergeant Clark right. I was happy for him.

But I still felt like shit.

Alice knew. She always knows. And she managed to temper her glee and be supportive and sympathetic.

Which just made me feel worse. Why should I rain on

her parade? Why couldn't we just be happy it was over?

Why indeed?

I lay awake in bed for a long time that night, thinking about the case. I tried to think of other things, but nothing could crowd it from my mind.

Damn.

I have a digital clock on my bureau, and you can read the damn thing in the dark.

As I lay there, it clicked over to two-thirty.

And sleep would not come.

Thoughts kept flitting through my head. Details. Flashes. Glimpses. Snippets of conversation.

It seemed to me there was something very important in all of it, if I could just put my finger on it.

But I couldn't. Because I was a fool and an idiot who'd been tilting at windmills and fighting paper dragons. Agatha Christie, for Christ's sake! Yeah, what a great deduction that was.

But the thoughts kept coming. The conversations kept replaying in my head.

Particularly the conversation from today—Sergeant Clark's summation of the case in Richard's office. Of course, that would be the one that stood out. Where every comment was like a whiplash. A whiplash aimed at me.

I thought back to the first meeting with Sergeant Clark in Richard's office. Way back in the beginning. After the Gerald Finklestein case. How different everything had seemed then.

I tried to think back over the conversation. It seemed to me there was something significant there—something I should have picked up on. I tried to remember, but it was so hard. So much had happened that time. Wendy had been in there, and Janet, and there'd been the question of who took which phone call and the whole bit. Such confusion.

No wonder I couldn't remember whatever it was I couldn't remember. If there was anything to remember to begin with. If it wasn't just my sense of uselessness driving me to think that there was.

Which had to be it. Because, what was the point? Sergeant Clark had the murderer. And the murderer had committed the crimes. All except Darryl Jackson—thank god Sergeant Clark wasn't still pushing that.

So what was the point?

What did it matter?

I didn't know.

But still I couldn't sleep.

I kept coming back to that first meeting with Sergeant Clark in Richard's office. It was important. Somehow, it was important. Something that was done or said. And if I just thought long enough, I'd think of it.

I didn't.

I fell asleep.

44.

MacAullif's voice was drugged with sleep. "Hello."

"Hello. MacAullif?"

"Yeah. Who's this?"

"Stanley Hastings."

"Who?"

"Hastings. Stanley Hastings."

"Stanley? . . ."

"Hastings."

"Stanley Hastings? Shit. What the hell time is it?"

"Six o'clock."

"Six in the morning?"

"Yes."

"Jesus. What the hell you calling me now for?"

"The Rosenberg and Stone murders."

"What?"

"The Rosenberg and Stone murders."

"What, are you nuts? The case is solved."

"No, it isn't. Sergeant Clark fucked up."

"What?"

"Sergeant Clark blew it. And he's too pigheaded to admit it. But we're going to set him straight."

"Oh, we are, are we?"

"Yes, we are."

"Well, I'm glad you think so. I, for one, am going back to sleep."

"No, you're not. You're meeting me at the corner of Houston and Varrick in one hour."

"That's what you think."

"That's what I know. Listen. You owe me a favor, and I'm calling it in. Houston and Varrick. Seven o'clock. You be there."

I slammed down the phone.

45.

MacAullif was there. He was tired, disheveled and pissed as hell, but he was there.

He was even there ahead of me, remarkable, seeing as how he had to come from Bay Ridge. He was sitting on the hood of his car, holding a paper cup of coffee when I drove up. I parked my car, got out and walked over to him.

"This better be good," he said.

"It is."

"So whaddya want?"

"Let's take a little ride," I said.

I walked around his car to the passenger door.

MacAullif looked at me, totally exasperated. He slid down off the hood of his car, opened his door and got in. He leaned over and unlocked the door for me. I got in the front seat. MacAullif started the engine.

"OK," he said. "Where to?"

I gave him the address.

MacAullif didn't pull out. He just sat there looking at me.

"And why are we going there?"

"Got your badge with you?" I asked.

MacAullif looked ready to strangle me. "Yeah. Why?"

"You're going to make an arrest."

"Oh yeah? And just who am I going to arrest?"

"Sam Gravston."

MacAullif blinked. "Sam Gravston. And why am I going to arrest Sam Gravston?"

"For the murder of his uncle."

MacAullif just stared at me for a few seconds. Then he reached over and switched off the engine.

"Come on, let's go," I said impatiently.

MacAullif shook his head. "You've gotta be kidding."

"I'm not," I said. "Look. Just listen to me a minute. This whole thing's been driving me crazy. I couldn't sleep last night. Something was bothering me and I didn't know what it was. You know how it is when you know you've heard something that's important but you can't put your finger on it?"

MacAullif glared at me. "Get to the point," he growled.

"OK, OK," I said. "The thing is, the solution I gave you— what I told you in your office—it just had to be right. But it wasn't. So nothing made sense. But I kept thinking and thinking about it, and something kept nagging at me, but I didn't know what it was, but it seemed to me it had something to do with Sergeant Clark. And then last night—this morning, really—I realized what it was."

"What?"

"Copycat crime."

"What?"

"Copycat crime. That's what I talked about with Sergeant Clark, way back at the beginning. At the time it was bullshit, just something I came up with to try to take the heat off me and Rosenberg and Stone. But that's the answer. Copycat crime."

271

MacAullif glared at me. "I have not finished my coffee yet. Would you mind putting this in plain English?"

"Sure. Copycat crime. Sam Gravston didn't commit the Rosenberg and Stone murders. But he did kill his uncle. It explains everything. See, everything I told you about the books, and the crime disguised to look like part of a series —it was too perfect. It simply had to be. But it wasn't. Charles Banks was the killer. A blatant contradiction. An impossibility. It simply couldn't be.

"And it wasn't. Sam Gravston killed his uncle, just as I said. And he did it because of the books. Because of the identical pattern. The only thing was, he didn't *plan* the pattern. That just happened. But after it happened, he *recognized* the pattern. He saw the similarity to what he'd read, and he suddenly realized if he killed his uncle he could get away with it because it would seem to be just another part of the series."

I paused. Shrugged my shoulders.

"So he did."

MacAullif took a breath and blew it out. "Jesus Christ."

"All right, look," I said irritably. "Sam's basically a nice guy. This has to be eating away at him. It's not going to take much to cave him in. You don't have to do anything. I'll do all the talking. You just sit there. When he breaks down, read him his rights and take him in."

MacAullif stared at me for a long time. Then he sighed, reached down and started the car.

We pulled up in front of Sam's building five minutes later. I got out and started for the door. MacAullif trailed reluctantly behind. I pushed the front door open and went up the steps. MacAullif came clumping up behind me.

I banged on Sam's door. We waited. There was no answer. I banged louder.

Nothing.

"Shit," I said under my breath.

"He's sleeping," MacAullif said.

"No, he's not," I said.

I banged as hard as I could.

Nothing.

I felt as if the bottom had dropped out of my stomach. I wheeled on MacAullif.

"Break it down!"

MacAullif was startled. "What?"

"Damnit," I said. "I told you, he's basically a nice guy. He can't handle this. He may have taken pills, or anything. We gotta break it down."

"That's a steel door," MacAullif said.

"Damnit, I know that," I said.

I turned and banged furiously on the door.

"Sam!" I shouted. "Sam!"

The door behind us opened.

Standing there was an old woman with long, stringy hair. She was obviously an artist. She was dressed in a night-gown, but the robe she had thrown over it was actually a painter's smock.

"What's all the racket?" she said.

"Listen," I said urgently. "Who's got a key to this door?"

"You looking for Sam?"

"Yes. We gotta get in."

She shook her head. "Sam's gone."

My heart sank. "What?"

She nodded. "Yup," she said. "The police were here. Took Sam away."

"No," I said. "When?"

She shrugged. "A half hour ago. They woke me up, too."

I rubbed my head. God, it couldn't be true. I had to ask, but I already knew the answer.

"Why?" I said. "Why did they take him?"

She shook her head, but her eyes were bright, and I could tell she was thrilled at what she was about to say.

"Terrible thing," she said. She nodded agreement with herself. "Terrible." She looked up at us and shook her head again. "Killed his uncle."

46.

They can't all be winners.

Sergeant MacAullif and I were sitting in a small diner on the Bowery drinking coffee.

"Cheer up," he said.

"Can you give me one good reason why I should?" I said.

"Yes, I can," MacAullif said.

"What's that?"

"You're learning."

"Thanks a lot."

"No, I mean it. You're learning."

"That's bullshit," I said. "That's not the problem."

"What's the problem?"

"Sergeant Clark."

"What about him?"

"I misjudged him."

"Yeah. I told you you did."

"I didn't listen."

"I know."

"I didn't want to hear it."

"Nobody wants to hear free advice. That's the rule. You know what they call a person who gives free advice?"

"What is this, twenty questions? All right, I'll bite. What do they call him?"

"Oh, an asshole, a shithead, a scumbag. Whatever comes to mind."

"What?"

"Yeah. That's what they call him."

"I thought this was a joke."

"What made you think that?"

"Jesus."

"Hey," MacAullif said. "Nobody likes to lose. It's the way we're brought up. The World Series. The Super Bowl. Win, win, win. And then you see it every night on the TV. The super detective who always wins. The thing is, if you start believing that shit—I mean, if I thought like that, I'd be a lousy cop. You do the best you can, and pull down your percentage. If you're doin' good, your percentage goes up. If you're doin' bad, it goes down. It's like having a fucking batting average, you know? Ted Williams. Last man to hit four hundred. By now nearly fifty years ago. Incredible feat. What does it mean? Means he fucked up sixty percent of the time and failed to do his job."

Ted Williams. Jesus Christ. MacAullif was throwing Ted Williams at me.

"Look, MacAullif," I said. "I know you mean well, but I could do without your cracker-barrel philosophy. Ted Williams, for Christ's sake."

"Some fucking hitter, though," MacAullif said.

"Never saw him play."

"Me neither. But it's legend, you know. Like him not sittin' down the last day of the season when three-hundred-ninety-nine-point-whatever would have been rounded up to four hundred if he had. He came to play."

I was getting pissed. "Look, MacAullif. I'm not in a great mood. I am really getting sick of Ted fucking Williams."

"I know. I know you are," MacAullif said. "But here's the thing. You're not a cop. You're not even really a detective. You're an ambulance chaser. What you are is a gifted amateur. As such, you got a lot to learn. You do have a bit of a flair. In this particular case, you were one step behind Sergeant Clark. And that's what's eating you up. That's what's tearing away at you. Which is stupid. So stupid."

MacAullif took a sip of coffee. "George Brett hit three-ninety," he said. "What does that make him? An asshole? A loser? When the name George Brett comes up, the first thing you think of is, 'Ah, terrible hitter,' right?" MacAullif shook his head. "One step behind Sergeant Clark. I can think of a lot of cops who would like to be able to say that."

"You're telling me Sergeant Clark is Ted Williams?"

"He's good. He's damn good. Too straight-laced, too by-the-book for my taste, but the man is damn good."

"I thought he was a moron."

"I know."

"That doesn't say much for my judgment."

"Well, your judgment's never been too hot anyway. Look, I'd like to feel sorry for you and all that," MacAullif said. "But if that's all that's bugging you, a lot of people should have your problems."

"That's not all," I said.

"Oh? What else?"

"Enrico Hernandez."

"Who?"

I told MacAullif the whole thing. The story of Enrico Hernandez's arrest. The subsequent suit against officers

Morris and Beame. Sergeant Clark coming across it in the files. And how he made me feel about it.

"That's stupid," MacAullif said. "You did your job to the best of your ability. It's out of your hands now. It's got nothing to do with you."

"Those guys are probably innocent."

"Then the courts will probably find them so."

"If not, they've been fucked, and I'm the guy who fucked them."

"You can't see it that way," MacAullif said. "Look. I have a horror of arresting an innocent man. And I try not to. But I'm sure occasionally I do. If I do, the court should set him free. And if it doesn't, who fucked him, me or the court? I don't know. But I can't spend all my time thinking about it, 'cause if I did, I'd never get anything done. I have my job to do, and I do it the best I can. And that's all I can do."

"This is different."

"Why?"

"I took pictures of the handcuffs. I tried to slant the case in the client's favor."

"That's your job. You think cops don't try to slant the facts in the prosecutions favor? What are you, out for fucking sainthood or something?"

"Oh, go on."

"No, you go on. You hear what I'm sayin' to you?"

"I hear what you're sayin'. I know what you mean. It just doesn't do any good."

I took another sip of my coffee.

MacAullif took another sip of his. Thought for a moment.

"All right," MacAullif said. "I owe you a favor, so I'm gonna tell you something. The thing is, what I'm gonna tell you shouldn't make any difference. But you're such a schmuck, it probably will. But here's the thing. I told you, cops are partisan. They look out for each other. Cops don't talk about other cops. I wouldn't talk about other cops.

"But I owe you a favor, so I'm gonna tell you this for what it's worth.

"This Officer Morris you're talkin' about. I happen to know about him. He has a reputation on the force. He has a history of leaning on suspects, particularly suspects who might be resisting arrest. There've been cases of prisoners who came in roughed up when he was part of the arresting team."

I'd put my coffee cup down and I was staring at MacAullif, my eyes wide.

"Yeah, sure," MacAullif said. "Look at me like that. The thing is, it shouldn't matter. It don't mean Morris is guilty. Maybe he is, maybe he isn't. Either way, it shouldn't matter." MacAullif shook his head. "You think Sergeant Clark doesn't know that? About Morris's history, I mean? He comes in there and lays a whole thing on you and Rosenberg about filin' suit against Morris. You think he lets on? Hell, no. He sticks up for him, because Morris is a cop and he's a cop, and that's his job. You think Sergeant Clark goes home at night and his conscience bothers him cause he stuck up for Morris and laid a trip on you and Rosenberg? Hell, no. He goes home at night, knowin' he's done his job. 'Cause cops stick up for cops. And damn it, I'm a cop, and I wouldn't be tellin' you this if I didn't owe you a favor. Telling you this feels bad to me.

"The thing is, damn it, it shouldn't matter. You knowin' this or not. You have these stupid, romantic ideas about right and wrong and good and bad. If you're the good guy, then Sergeant Clark has to be the bad guy, and is Morris the good guy or the bad guy, and what's your client? That's bullshit, man."

MacAullif stood up, pushed back his coffee cup, slid a dollar bill on the counter.

"So," he said, "any time you'd like to stop thinking of yourself as some fucking storybook detective and join the human race again, give me a call."

He turned and walked out.

41.

I had a bad week. In my head, anyway. Otherwise, as far as weeks went, it was just about average. Despite the killings, Richard Rosenberg's business hadn't seemed to suffer any. And I realized it wouldn't. Of course, if Sam Gravston had been guilty of all the murders it would have been different. Then it would have been the case of one of Richard Rosenberg's investigators going around bumping off his clients, and that would have been enough to scare people away. But it wasn't. It wasn't even the case of an investigator killing one client. It was the case of a nephew bumping off his uncle to get his money, and that made all the difference in the world.

So it was business as usual at Rosenberg and Stone. I even had an above-average week, seeing as how Richard was short one investigator, and I was shouldering the whole load while he tried to find a replacement. Meanwhile, Richard Rosenberg's ad for an investigator was running, and two guys about Sam's age were training, and I was making book they wouldn't last a week between 'em, and everything was more or less back to normal.

Except in my head, where I was still sorting things out. I seemed to have a lot of that to do.

I felt bad about Sam Gravston. I felt bad for him, and I felt bad for me. The thing is, I felt guilty. The guilt I felt was the guilt you feel when you hear someone has an incurable disease. That's because you can't help the momentary feeling of exultation, "Thank god it isn't me." And then you feel guilty for having felt that, 'cause "Thank god it isn't me" implies "Thank god it's him," which means you felt good it happened to him, so you feel guilty as hell.

And in this case it was worse. 'Cause I'd felt jealous of Sam, I could admit that now. Being so young and so successful and so outgoing and so sure of himself—so everything I'm not. Yeah. I'd felt jealous of Sam, and of his potential success. Which gave even more of a kick to the "Thank god it's him" feeling. I had reason to believe I actually did feel good when I found out it was Sam. So I tortured myself with that a lot.

But I was sad about Sam. Really sad. And his agent supplied the final ironic kick, calling up the same morning he'd been arrested and leaving a message on his answering machine, saying he'd finally gotten the part after all.

Yeah, I felt sad and all of that, and I felt sorry for Sam. But when I finally worked it out in my head, the thing I couldn't get away from was, I don't like murder. Which I realize is a comical understatement, but there you are. And whatever the provocation might have been, and however desperate Sam might have felt, what he did to his uncle was an unforgivable thing, and however bad I might feel, or sympathetic I might feel, or guilty I might feel, Sam had done that, and there was no reason for me to like him anymore.

And that's how it had to be.

And as far as the whole Hernandez thing went, it was as Sergeant MacAullif had said. It shouldn't bother me. And what he told me about Officer Morris shouldn't have made any difference. But I knew damn well it did. And it helped. I spent a lot of time thinking about that.

And then there was Sergeant Clark. It was galling to think he'd been right. He'd been right for all the wrong reasons. First, getting involved because of the Darryl Jackson case, which actually had nothing to do with anything. And then cracking the case on a sheer coincidence—yes, Charles Banks had been in the office the day the Marvin Gravston call had come in, but he hadn't seen the signup in the book and then killed him. And yet, that was the peg on which Sergeant Clark had hung his solution to the case.

It wasn't fair, somehow.

It took a while for me to realize it didn't have to be fair. And that, even without that coincidence, Sergeant Clark would have cracked the case. Because the method he was using was basically sound. And eventually it would have paid off.

Yeah, as far as Sergeant Clark went, I realized I'd made a big mistake there. A terrible mistake. And it bothered me. Not so much losing to him. I could accept that pretty well after a while. No, what bothered me was having misjudged him. Having made a snap decision about him, and having been too pigheaded to realize it. Despite what everyone told me. Despite having it staring me right in the face.

Yeah, that's what really bothered me.

And finally I realized I had to do something about it.

48.

"I owe you an apology."

Sergeant Clark was seated at his desk. He was playing with a rubber band with one hand and holding a newspaper with the other. He was wearing reading glasses, which he probably considered another shortcoming on his part for which he had to compensate. He took them off and looked up at me.

"What for?"

I considered my answer. There were so many ways to phrase it. I could be tactful. I could be humble. I could put myself in a better light. I could put him in a better light.

But I figured after all we'd been through, and after everything that had happened, and after the way it had all turned out, Sergeant Clark deserved to hear the simple truth. And somehow I needed to say it, too.

"For thinking you were an asshole," I said.

Sergeant Clark considered that. For a second, I could have sworn I saw a twinkle in his eye. But it quickly passed. He nodded judiciously.

"Your apology is noted," he said.

And he slipped on his glasses and went back to his paper.

I went out and walked down the hall to MacAullif's office. He was at his desk.

"What brings you here?" MacAullif asked.

"I apologized to Sergeant Clark," I said.

"What for?"

"For misjudging him."

"You realize that wasn't necessary?"

"I know. It was just something I had to do."

MacAullif nodded. He opened his desk drawer and pulled out the two paperbacks.

"Here's your books back," he said.

"Oh. Did you read them?"

"Oh, sure," MacAullif said. "You know, they're damn good. I liked 'em. I didn't think I would. But the characters, you know, are really good. Particularly the detective. That Hercule Poirot."

I couldn't even begin to reproduce MacAullif's pronunciation of Agatha Christie's Belgian protagonist. But I didn't attempt to correct him.

"You liked him, huh?" I said.

"Yeah, I did," MacAullif said. "Say, tell me. This Agatha Christie. Did she write any more books about him?"

"You're in luck," I told him.

"Oh?" MacAullif said. "How's that?"

I smiled. And I felt good. I hadn't thought I'd be smiling again so soon.

"It's a series."